VALLEY OF PRETENDERS

Borgo Press Books by JOHN RUSSELL FEARN

*1,000-Year Voyage: A Science Fiction Novel * Anjani the Mighty: A Lost Race Novel* (Anjani #2) * *Black Maria, M.A.: A Classic Crime Novel* (Black Maria #1) * *A Case for Brutus Lloyd * The Crimson Rambler: A Crime Novel * Death in Silhouette* (Black Maria #5) * *Don't Touch Me: A Crime Novel * Dynasty of the Small: Classic Science Fiction Stories * The Empty Coffins: A Mystery of Horror * The Fourth Door: A Mystery Novel * From Afar: A Science Fiction Mystery * Fugitive of Time: A Classic Science Fiction Novel * The G-Bomb: A Science Fiction Novel * The Genial Dinosaur* (Herbert the Dinosaur #2) * *The Gold of Akada: A Jungle Adventure Novel* (Anjani #1) * *Here and Now: A Science Fiction Novel * Into the Unknown: A Science Fiction Tale * Last Conflict: Classic Science Fiction Stories * Legacy from Sirius: A Classic Science Fiction Novel * The Man from Hell: Classic Science Fiction Stories * The Man Who Was Not: A Crime Novel * Manton's World: A Classic Science Fiction Novel * Moon Magic: A Novel of Romance* (as Elizabeth Rutland) * *The Murdered Schoolgirl: A Classic Crime Novel* (Black Maria #2) * *One Remained Seated: A Classic Crime Novel* (Black Maria #3) * *One Way Out: A Crime Novel* (with Philip Harbottle) * *Pattern of Murder: A Classic Crime Novel * Reflected Glory: A Dr. Castle Classic Crime Novel * Robbery Without Violence: Two Science Fiction Crime Stories * Rule of the Brains: Classic Science Fiction Stories * Shattering Glass: A Crime Novel * The Silvered Cage: A Scientific Murder Mystery * Slaves of Ijax: A Science Fiction Novel * Something from Mercury: Classic Science Fiction Stories * The Space Warp: A Science Fiction Novel * A Thing of the Past* (Herbert the Dinosaur #1) * *Thy Arm Alone: A Classic Crime Novel* (Black Maria #4) * *The Time Trap: A Science Fiction Novel * Vision Sinister: A Scientific Detective Thriller * Voice of the Conqueror: A Classic Science Fiction Novel * What Happened to Hammond? A Scientific Mystery * Within That Room!: A Classic Crime Novel * World Without Chance*

THE GOLDEN AMAZON SAGA

1. *World Beneath Ice* * 2. *Lord of Atlantis* * 3. *Triangle of Power* * 4. *The Amethyst City* * 5. *Daughter of the Amazon* * 6. *Quorne Returns* * 7. *The Central Intelligence* * 8. *The Cosmic Crusaders* * 9. *Parasite Planet* * 10. *World Out of Step* * 11. *The Shadow People* * 12. *Kingpin Planet* * 13. *World in Reverse* * 14. *Dwellers in Darkness* * 15. *World in Duplicate* * 16. *Lords of Creation* * 17. *Duel with Colossus* * 18. *Standstill Planet* * 19. *Ghost World* * 20. *Earth Divided* * 21. *Chameleon Planet* (with Philip Harbottle)

VALLEY OF PRETENDERS

CLASSIC PULP SCIENCE FICTION STORIES IN THE VEIN OF STANLEY G. WEINBAUM

JOHN RUSSELL FEARN

Edited by Philip Harbottle

THE BORGO PRESS
MMXIII

VALLEY OF PRETENDERS

FIRST EDITION

Published by Wildside Press LLC

www.wildsidebooks.com

DEDICATION

For Geoffrey H. Medley

CONTENTS

INTRODUCTION

by Philip Harbottle

The two best-known early science fiction magazine pseudonyms of English writer John Russell Fearn were 'Thornton Ayre' and 'Polton Cross'. The perceived wisdom amongst SF commentators is that both pseudonyms were conceived by Fearn more or less simultaneously in 1937 in order to increase his chances of selling to the American pulp magazines. And further, that initially stories under these names were written in an imitation of the style of the late Stanley G. Weinbaum. Then, when the 'fad' for Weinbaum imitations began to die out in the magazines—led by John W. Campbell at *Astounding*—Fearn changed his style and thereafter wrote under both pseudonyms in his own original style (or rather, two styles.)

Whilst such a summation is broadly correct, it is actually grossly simplified, and barely hints at the full, quite complicated background story. The full story of Fearn's Weinbaum imitations is rather fascinating, and has never been fully documented. The present two-volume Borgo Press original set, *World Without Chance* and *Valley of Pretenders*, which collects these stories for the first time, is the result of many years of research. It uses primary sources that, collectively, are simply unavailable to other commentators. Most valuably, I been able to draw on information contained in Fearn's personal prewar and early wartime letters to British SF magazine editor Walter Gillings, and to his friend and fellow author William F. Temple. Additionally, I have complete runs of the early magazines during the period Fearn contributed to them, and I myself have conducted further correspondence with Fearn's agent at the time, the late Julius Schwartz, and with Geoffrey H. Medley. Medley, who lived near Fearn in Blackpool, was one of Fearn's closest prewar friends. In his letters to magazine editors, Fearn had claimed that 'Thornton Ayre' was actually one Frank Jones, who was initially resident in the same house as Medley!

In October 1952, some five years after the last Thornton Ayre story had appeared, Fearn gave a speech as Guest of Honour at a Manchester SF Convention. He was then questioned about his pseudonyms and asked directly as to whether he was 'Polton Cross' and 'Thornton Ayre'. He readily confirmed he was Cross, but had apparently replied that he was *not* Ayre, and that the name belonged to a friend of his, Frank Jones! His talk was reported in a couple of UK fanzines, the most detailed account appearing in *Camber* No. 1 (1953), written by attendee H. P. 'Sandy' Sanderson. Speaking about the Ayre byline, Sanderson wrote:

> "Reverting back to pen names, he does insist that Thornton Ayre is not one of his. Apparently it belongs to a friend of his, Frank Jones. Mr. Jones does a lot of travelling, and he leaves his MSS with JRF. Publisher's sending cheques to JRF's house must have assumed he was Thornton Ayre."

We can't know if Sanderson's account was entirely accurate, but the salient fact was certainly confirmed in a concurrent report in another fanzine by the Liverpool fan Group that stated: "Polton Cross is one of his pseudos, but Thornton Ayre, it seems, is not."

But if Fearn's remarks *were* correctly reported, it seems clear that he was speaking with his tongue very firmly in his cheek, and was just pulling the legs of his audience, for he most assuredly *was* Thornton Ayre! It would seem that Fearn could never quite get over the fact that his secret authorship could have been exposed when the Thornton Ayre byline *had* in fact been invented and used by someone else!

But who *was* this Frank Jones? Did he really exist? Hitherto, no SF historian or commentator has ever troubled to find out. The assumption has been that he did not exist.

In point of fact, Temple's correspondence in the late 1930s contained many letters actually signed 'Frank Jones', and claiming to be that separate person, By then Jones was no longer living at the same house as Geoff Medley, and the letters to Temple gave his address as that of Fearn—Jones was now allegedly *lodging at Fearn's home*!

Recalling these letters from Thornton Ayre (which he generously allowed me to copy), Temple told me: "…Jack kept trying to kid me he was really another person. I didn't believe it…but I played along with him for the fun of it."

In his first letter to Fearn's alter ego Frank Jones (Thornton Ayre) in December of 1939, Temple touched briefly on the personal side:

> "Re you being Jack—Jack has told me you are not, and I'm quite willing to believe him. In fact, I'm sure that Thornton Ayre and JRF are too different personalities. I do not pursue inquiries as to whether Jack is schizophrenic or not; his business is his business and not mine, or anyone's. All I know is that he is a decent chap himself, generous and helpful to those who cannot be helpful to him; and an unfairly maligned author. I hope you won't think it is flattery if I say that your letter shows traces of this same unasked-for generosity too. To continue this psycho-analysis, I'd say that this generosity is not a weak point because you both have hard business heads (which I definitely have not) and have it well under control."

And to add to the mystery, Walter Gillings' earlier 1936-1938 editorial correspondence details separate story submissions from a Frank Jones, sent from a different address than Fearn's!

So how to reconcile the above with the fact that all of the published Thornton Ayre stories were all quite definitely written entirely by Fearn? My own careful analysis of the style of the Ayre stories—and much more significantly, the fact that years later Fearn would "mine" many of these stories and incorporate them, in adapted form, into his own novels, not to mention his reprinting several of them in the *British Science Fiction Magazine* in 1954-55, after he became its editor, have established Fearn's sole authorship beyond all reasonable doubt. And the only story actually published under the name Frank Jones ("Arctic God", *Amazing Stories*, May 1942) was also definitely 100% by Fearn. So…was there really anyone called Frank Jones? And what was his connection with 'Thornton Ayre'? I have now uncovered the answer to that question.…

Around 1935, Fearn had become a member of the Blackpool Writers' Circle, one of the many regional writers' club support groups which flourished in England, and who were the target audience for Hutchinson's national monthly magazine *The Writer*, which gave them publicity and regularly printed the addresses of their Secretaries. The first Secretary and founder of the Blackpool group was Miss Margaret Dulling, who was later to become a very successful romantic novelist, writing as Margaret St. John Bathe. Two young sisters, Doris and Muriel Howe, also became prolific romantic novelists. Yet another successful romantic novelist to emerge from the Circle was Iris Weigh. Iris became a particularly close friend of Fearn's, and when he founded a rival Circle, the Fylde Writing Society, after the war, she moved to join him there.

Because of his rapid success in the American pulps, Fearn soon became a leading light in the Blackpool Circle, and he would have been friendly with one Frank Jones, who took over the Circle's Secretarial duties in January 1937. The evidence for this can be found in the contemporaneous issues of the magazine *The Writer*, which announced that Frank Jones was now the Secretary, and gave his address as 51 Cheltenham Road, Blackpool—totally separate from Fearn's address at 164 Abbey Road, Blackpool. So Frank Jones *was* a real person, *and* a writer.

On 7th September 1936 Gillings had informed Fearn that he had been secretly given the go-ahead by the World's Work publishers to prepare a trial issue of a new British science fiction magazine, *Tales of Wonder*. Secretly, because a rival publisher, Newnes, was also preparing a new SF magazine, *Fantasy*. Jones had then been encouraged by Fearn to try his hand at writing science fiction short stories, with Fearn subbing and revising his mss.

Frank Jones' first story was submitted to Gillings on 18th September 1936 on his behalf by Fearn. His covering letter to Gillings read:

> "Herewith is Frank Jones' 'Mr. Podmore Does It,' written under the name of 'Briggs Mendel'. I've read it through and made one or two minor pen corrections. Personally I don't think it half bad. If you can give him a break any way it will encourage him a lot. He has other Podmore stories, which he intends to work on. I feel, and maybe you will too after you've read it, that a series of this quaint little gentleman will interest British readers quite a lot. Enclosed also is one of mine which I came across. 'Planet X,' refused recently by *Thrilling Wonder Stories* as not quite convincing enough, but would, I feel make a good English one."

Gillings was told to reply to Jones direct concerning his story. Gillings, however, had very rigid editorial criteria—he was reluctant to use anything that was too imaginative or took SF tropes for granted, in the style of the US pulps, He rejected and returned Jones' first story.

On 27th January 1937, Fearn sent the following 'Flash' to Gillings:

"*Thrilling Wonder Stories* have accepted my 'Lords of 9016.' Frank Jones, whom you met in London, is writing science fiction under the name of 'Thornton Ayre' (and this name *only* must be used in publications, *not* his own.) Julie [Schwartz] thinks he has promise. He tells me that he's just done 'Little God', after his first, 'Composite Man', failed. Oddly enough, Julie believes he might click. Will send you his address when he gets it fixed. Like me he is in removal at the moment."

On 22nd February 1937, Fearn again told Gillings:

"Now here's something else. I spent Saturday evening with Frank Jones—or, as he calls himself for fiction—Thornton Ayre. So his name won't leak out and perhaps queer his pension for an accident of long ago, I suspect. Anyway, I do believe I had that guy all wrong! He *can* write SF! His latest story, 'Dark World', is in my opinion a corker with real thought-variant slants. Can it be that a rival grows on my own doorstep? Anyway, I've suggested that he write to you so perhaps he did so over the weekend. In any case—confidentially—though he seems a bit odd on the surface, he certainly knows how to slap words together. I'm very surprised to find he really knows his stuff. Unless I'm mistaken he will click before long."

On 4th March 1937 Gillings told Fearn that Frank Jones had indeed contacted him direct, and he was intending to give him a write-up in the next edition of his printed fanzine *Scientifiction*. Sure enough, there was an announcement in the magazine's second, April 1937 issue:

"Another newcomer to fantasy field is Thornton Ayre, Blackpool protégé of John Russell Fearn, who predicts he will burst into print shortly with thought variant, 'Dark World', following inevitable rejections of first efforts."

On 24th April 1937, Fearn told Gillings in another letter:

> "Here's another secret—for you ALONE and not for any publication. Schwartz has suggested, in view of my turning out work so fast as Fearn, that I become somebody else with a totally different style, different typewriter, different paper and what not. So I have become Polton Cross (a village two miles out of Blackpool) and have turned out two yarns on the Weinbaum style, namely 'World Without Chance' (10,000 words) and 'Outpost' (6,000). If these yarns do click, I defy you to tell it's me, so totally new is the arrangement of the ideas. The idea being, of course, that Fearn and Cross can click simultaneously and double my chances all round.
>
> "I've only told Frank Jones about World's Work— and your secret is safe with him. He wants to know if you'd like to see some of his work? Carbons, I suppose. Maybe he'll write you himself, but if not perhaps you'll tell me and I'll relay it. He's rather a dilatory letter writer. He's down in the mouth too because he hasn't clicked over the ocean so far."

In the ensuing months, from time to time, Jones tried Gillings again, but without success. In order to try and help his friend, Fearn's revisions to his mss. became more and more extensive, so much so that Gillings actually doubted whether Frank Jones actually existed; he suspected that the prolific Fearn (who was himself submitting stories unsuccessfully to Gillings under his own name) was using a pseudonym to increase his chances of success.

In this Gillings was initially quite mistaken. Frank Jones

was a member of the Blackpool Writers Circle. But the overly-suspicious Gillings remained intractable. He remained equally so when Fearn began to submit mss. by his other friends in the Blackpool Circle, Edgar Spencer and Geoffrey Medley.

On 26th May 1937 Fearn wrote Gillings again:

> "You'll find an MS herewith from Geoff Medley. He lives at the same house as Frank Jones, and, to my mind, has turned out a fairly decent English or *Amazing* type sf yarn. I suggested he might try you before *Amazing* and see if you could find room anywhere in a future edition of *Tales of Wonder* for him. I've enclosed a stamped envelope for him. Please write to him direct. Don't be too hard on the guy. He spent all his Whit Weekend typing on this machine (which he borrowed) in order to complete the yarn. If you think anything of it, OK. No business of mine."

But Gillings would reject this story, plus Medley's follow-up effort, "Carcinoma Menace".

On June 10th 1937 Fearn reported to Gillings:

> "Julie thinks that 'World Without Chance,' Cross' first effort, is a first class effort and remarkably like Weinbaum. Same applies to 'Chameleon Planet,' which I've just completed. If Cross should prove more of a hit than Fearn I'll be tickled to death!"

Fearn wrote to Gillings again on 19th June 1937:

> "I saw Frank Jones the other day and so far his yarns haven't clicked in the US, because they're too simple. I've read them through and I think they're pretty good for England. I'm attaching their synopses also. If you think them worthy I'll get him to send them on."

I managed to trace and contact Geoffrey Medley a number of years ago, and he told me how he had come to know Fearn:

> "Fresh from school at the age of fourteen, I reported to 15, Birley Street, Blackpool, to take up the duties of junior office boy to the pompous Mr. John W. Roberts, Solicitor, Town Councillor and drunkard...."

Geoff went on to identify the other staff members, including the senior office boy, the common law clerk, the secretary and cashier. He continued:

> "...During my five years at Birley Street (we moved from No.15 to No.16, across the road) other junior office boys came and went.... It was some time before I came to know the part-time typist. Full-time there was Marjorie Nixon, plus another girl whose name I forget. But this man was of another world. He showed no knowledge of law, no interest in the clients at the practice, and he seldom spoke to anybody. At irregular intervals he just was there, hawk-nosed, smouldering-eyed, apparently unaware of his surroundings. Usually a cigarette dangled from one corner of his mouth, and one eye was half-closed against its rising smoke, as two fingers of each hand pounded the keys of the big, brief-carriage typewriter, churning out abstracts of Title—long, rambling documents—faster than the girls could type with five fingers, and faster than I have ever heard a man type.
>
> "This was John Francis Russell Fearn.
>
> "Gradually I came to know that he did our typing jobs just to eke out, and that his main occupation was writing magazine stories. This was exciting news to a boy who had always been top of his classes in English and who vaguely felt that his own best hope of success was to be a writer. And when Jack learned this

he was more than helpful. I came to know *Amazing Stories* and *Astounding Stories*, and his contributions to them....

"I went to his house and used his typewriter to rattle out my own attempts at science fiction stories, which he read through and said were in his opinion worthy of publication. The magazine editors never agreed. In retrospect I think the yarns were too juvenile. The only one I remember now *['Carcinoma Menace'—editor]* was about a cancer sufferer in whom the malignant cells, treated with radiation in an effort to kill them, re-acted rather unexpectedly. The radiation triggered off mutations in the cells, and the chap finished up with an intelligent being—malignant, of course—inside him, and taking over. The science was suitably blinding, but the fiction, I fear, was rather lame." *[In point of fact, this plot seems to be an uncanny anticipation of one used by John Kippax (John Hynam) in his powerful short story "It" a full twenty years later in* Nebula, *November 1958 issue!—editor]*

"Sometimes we took a break from writing, largely at Jack's mother's instigation, and we all three played Bezique, watched by 'Benjie,' their wire-haired ter-rier."

By then Medley had joined the Blackpool Writers Circle, where he would also do a stint as Secretary later in 1938 (taking over from Fearn, who had succeeded the now departed Jones). Geoff recalled these days thusly:

"Coming back to the period when I was typing my MSS at the Fearn house, I recall that Jack was work-ing on a 'straight' novel in the intervals between writ-ing his science fiction potboilers. It was called *Little Winter*, and dealt with Blackpool seen from the resi-dent's viewpoint. I don't remember his completing it."

{Fearn did in fact complete this during the war, and entrusted it to a literary agency. Unfortunately it never sold, and the MSS was inadvertently destroyed following the death of his widow in 1982—editor}.

"Jack and I were members of the Blackpool Writers' Circle, which met on one evening each week in Jenkinson's café, in Talbot Square. Jack was then the only full-time writer in the membership."

Other members whom Geoff recalled included Edgar Spencer and Arthur Waterhouse Painter ("whose legs were paralyzed". *[Painter became a particular friend of Fearn and his mother, and was a very successful writer of juvenile fiction after the war; he also appeared in the* Vargo Statten/British SF Magazine—*editor.]* Geoff continued his reminiscences:

"The Misses Howe were our most regular attendees. One sister, innocent of make-up, wrote for publications like *The Methodist Recorder*. The other, more smartly dressed and colourfully powdered, wrote for more romantic women's magazines.

"We all discussed and criticized the MS. of the evening, giving quite well-reasoned analyses, and being ever mindful of the criteria which the books on writing laid down. All except Jack. He listened gravely, but his own contributions to the criticism were not particularly well argued or explained. All Jack could do, really, was write—and make money by it. The rest of us seldom sold anything.

"I lost touch with Jack during the War, and I outgrew my boyhood interest in science fiction. The brown Bombardier who produced and acted in plays in the Orkney Islands was a different person from the wide-eyed youth who had concocted 'Carcinoma Menace'. Or nearly. Just once my old science fiction familiarity surfaced. It was on Salisbury Plain. One of our sergeants came back from the mess bubbling over with good news. 'You know them bombs, Geoff, that they used to bust them dams in Germany—they were over a ton apiece. Well, it's on the wireless over in the mess, we've got a bomb over a hundred times more powerful than them, and do yon know how big it is?'

"I froze. His lead-up could only be to an impressively *smaller* bomb.

"'Christ!' I said. 'Don't tell me they've already got some form of atomic power....'

"'That's what they said—atomic or something....'

"'Now,' I said, 'we're really in trouble.'

"'You don't understand, Geoff. We've got it—not them.'

"It took a science fiction man, then, to realize what trouble we were in."

In a letter dated 5th July 1937, the suspicious Gillings told Fearn:

"I'm afraid, as far as my anticipations go, 'Thornton Ayre' doesn't get much of a look in; nor, so far, does your friend Geoff Medley, whose 'Death From the Star' is much too advanced. Incidentally, these two write surprisingly complex stuff for amateurs at SF don't they? Particularly Frank Jones, whose style and ideas are remarkably reminiscent of your own. So much so that in 'Dark World' he gives almost word for word the same account of the destruction of Atlantis as you do in your 'Born of Atlantis' (which would be okay for England if it was more leisurely-written and more convincing in spots, by the way), and even chooses the same name—Izma—for the arch-villain scientist, also making the same acknowledgement to Manly P. Hall! Can you explain this, to satisfy my curiosity?

"I still don't realize who Frank Jones is. You say I met him in London. I recall meeting two of your friends; the tall one, who said little, and the other one who spoke so quietly, and who seemed to have invented such a lot of useful things. Is he the latter? I believe it was he who wrote the Podmore story you sent me before Sprigg closed down; if so, he's improved mightily since then.... How was it his yarns didn't click in the U.S.? They seem just cut out for *Thrilling Wonder* to me. Medley, however, wants a little more practice, though he certainly has ideas."

Fearn replied on 7th July 1937:

"Haven't seen Geoff or Frank, but I guess they'll both be a trifle cut up. No matter—the editor's decision is final. Jones is the tall one who spoke little; the other is Ed. Spencer. With regard to Jones' stories, probably the similarity of style is accounted for by the fact that I did piles of correction to his MSS to try and help him, and my own flavouring has crept in. I noticed it myself. The destruction of Atlantis accounts being similar is easily explained since they're both lifted piecemeal from the quotations of Manly P. Hall, hence the acknowledgement in both cases. Afraid I can't figure out how we both got Izma. Unless with his reading my 'Born of Atlantis' he unconsciously clicked on the same name. I didn't remember the name again when I read his, which shows my rotten memory for the things I write.

"Frank Jones' yarns didn't click for *Thrilling Wonder* because they were too tame and too unconvincing, I understand. Ah me!"

Fearn, meantime, had learned from Schwartz that "World Without Chance" by Polton Cross had been accepted by

Thrilling Wonder Stories in July 1937, but that publication was likely to be delayed for some little time, because the magazine was overstocked. At this point, it would appear that Frank Jones more or less gave up any hope of making it as a SF writer. Fearn may have told him that since he was now writing stories as Fearn *and* Cross, he was unable to extensively rewrite his mss. as he had been doing. It is not known what became of Jones, but it is possible that the clinching reason why he gave up SF writing was that he may have left Blackpool altogether. Fearn had stated that his regular profession was that of a commercial traveller.

However, Frank Jones would have been grateful to Fearn for the help he had given him, and so, whilst dropping out of writing himself, he must have agreed that Fearn could appropriate his— as yet unpublished—pseudonym 'Thornton Ayre', And Geoff Medley agreed to let Fearn continue to use his (Medley's) home address on his 'Thornton Ayre' mss.

For the astute Fearn had scented a golden opportunity, and hatched a cunning scheme. Whilst his agent Schwartz knew that Fearn was Polton Cross, and would keep this a secret for commercial purposes, Schwartz also believed that 'Thornton Ayre' was another person entirely—Frank Jones. As indeed he then actually was! But what if *Fearn* was to now begin secretly writing stories *himself* as Thornton Ayre, also in the Weinbaum style? With Schwartz believing he was still Frank Jones (the Weinbaum imitation technique would effectively disguise the fact that Fearn and not Jones was now writing the stories), Fearn reasoned that his chances of regular sales under all three names, Fearn, Cross, and Ayre, would be immeasurably increased.

How right Fearn was would soon be proved when the January 1938 *Astounding Stories* would carry stories under *all three* names—"Red Heritage" by Fearn, "Whispering Satellite" by Ayre, and "The Mental Ultimate" by Cross! (He would repeat the same trick in the May 1942 *Amazing Stories*, even adding a *fourth* story—as by Frank Jones!)

When I wrote to Julius Schwartz in 1983 (after I had discovered in *The Writer* that Frank Jones had been a real person), and asked him if he had known Fearn was Thornton Ayre when he began selling his stories, he confessed:

> "I didn't deduce that Thornton Ayre was Polton Cross till *much* later! Same goes for the SF Editors!"

John W. Campbell was certainly one of the editors to be fooled. The January 1938 issue of Gillings' fanzine *Scientifiction* ran a real scoop article, "Campbell's Plans for *Astounding*", quoting from a postal interview with Campbell himself.:

> "Included in the January (1938) issue will be stories by Warner Van Lorne, Clifton B. Kruse, John Russell Fearn, Thornton Ayre (the English Author, whom Campbell describes as 'one of the best of the newer writers'), and Don A. Stuart, otherwise Campbell himself."

On November 25th 1937 Fearn had told Gillings:

> "Frank seems to be doing all right for himself. I understand that Julie highly praised his recently sold 'Whispering Satellite' as one of the best things he'd read. I did think it was tops myself, though confidentially how he ever manages to have such a swell slant on the Weinbaum angle will be an eternal mystery to me. His latest efforts, 'The Minitors' and 'Sanctuary', are both real pips. Certainly he no longer needs me to help him!"

Thereafter, all of Fearn's Thornton Ayre stories would be first directed to America, and all of them would eventually sell there.

So there we have it. Frank Jones had indeed been a real person, and, coached by Fearn, he had tried writing SF in 1936 (as Briggs Mendel) and continued into 1937 (as Thornton Ayre). Then he had given up and handed his Thornton Ayre pseudonym to Fearn, who had already created his own pseudonym of Polton Cross, initially writing in the style of Weinbaum. And when Fearn began writing *Ayre* stories, even more blatantly in the style of Weinbaum, he was initially very successful, selling his first two stories to *Astounding Stories*. For his 'Cross' efforts, Fearn abandoned the Weinbaum slant, and instead developed a third quite distinct style of "scientific nemesis" stories, beginning with "The Mental Ultimate" (*Astounding Stories*, January 1938).

What happened next is best illustrated in an article Fearn wrote (as Thornton Ayre) that was published in the March 1939 first issue of Ted Carnell's fanzine *New Worlds*, entitled "Concerning Webwork":

> "Some little time ago a much esteemed mutual friend Julius Schwartz paid me the compliment of calling me a webwork writer. Since then the words have stuck in my mind—and since English readers will be as much in the dark as I was I might as well explain that 'webwork' means a complicated mystery wherein all the strands are drawn together in the last chapter to form the complete whole. By accident I stumbled upon this mystic formula in 'Locked City' and repeated it in 'The Secret of the Ring' (originally called 'The Circle of Life.')
>
> "Now all of this brings me to something. If webwork mystery is a new slant to science fiction—and presumably it is—what a colossal field it opens up for other writers as well. I don't mean in webwork (I stick to that now as my personal angle) but in other slants. Consider a moment—what has SF been like up to now? I am virtually new to the game but I've read tons of it since being a boy.

"Here's my reaction. It's all been *adventure*. The pages of past SF reek with curly headed heroes and smooth hipped heroines. Villains have been monstrosities of other worlds. Rarely if ever was the formula altered, save for a few gems from Campbell, Smith, Keller or Taine. Yet even they—though their characters were life-like—pandered to the eternal hackwork *adventure* formula.

"Yes, and even Weinbaum. What are all his stories but adventure? True, they are magnificent adventure with living people—but they remain the same.

"For myself, I copied his style in my yarns 'Penal World' and 'Whispering Satellite' because, in the words of the old song, 'It seemed the right and proper thing to do.' Then it occurred to me, after a series of rejections, that something had gone wrong. I needed a new technique—I tried a complicated mystery ingredient *added* to adventure. It worked!"

These sidelights on Fearn's writing as Ayre were further clarified when Fearn wrote an "About the Author" article to accompany his Thornton Ayre story "Face in the Sky" in the September 1939 *Amazing Stories*:

"…It all started about two years ago when I was getting pretty fed up with poor returns from occasional articles and short straight yarns in England. You see, the trouble over here is they don't like anything sensational, or off the beaten track. At least, they didn't *then*! But times are changed.

"As I was saying, I was getting fed up when my closest friend, the redoubtable dynamo known as Fearn, slanted my ideas towards science fiction. I'd read several odd tons of the stuff and I must confess it had appealed to me quite a lot. I thought there was nothing to lose by having a shot at it—but oh! Those first efforts were pretty awful, My brains, what there are of them, revolved around queer asteroids, men down in the sea, talking protoplasm, and other things usually associated with over-indulgence in opium or heavy cheese late at night.

"About that time Stanley G. Weinbaum was at his peak. Everybody was nuts about his particular slant and so, being a trier, I imitated his style and produced Jo, the ammonia man of the planet Jupiter. This was in the yarn 'Penal World' published in *Astounding*, in 1937. Shortly afterwards I followed it up with a similar type of yarn called 'Whispering Satellite,' also in *Astounding*. On that point my activities with *Astounding* terminated because everybody was going like Weinbaum and the Editor was plenty sick. Campbell wrote me an explanatory letter and suggested changes of style.

"I chewed things over. The science fiction business was getting a hold on me, and imitation would not do any longer. Why not try the other extreme and find out what had *not* been done? I felt I had got something there. Well, what hadn't been done? *Mystery!*

"Mystery! Of course! So far as I could figure out all the yarns were more or less straight experiments, adventures, theories—or, very rarely—a detective sort of problem. But what about a real juicy mystery woven round with science? Something to explain Mars, for instance, as it had never been explained before?

"So I launched on a style which, I have since found, was unique. I unwittingly brought webwork plots into science fiction with my initial yarn in a new style— 'Locked City.' The praise for that one made me all of a benevolent glow and produced 'Secret of the Ring' (which I shall always privately regard as the best yarn I've written so far)."

Fearn's initial stratagem to write stories as Polton Cross in imitation of Weinbaum (who had died in December 1935) would almost certainly have been suggested to him by his U.S. agent, Julius Schwartz. So when shortly thereafter 'Thornton Ayre' followed suit, Schwartz would have been quite happy about it.

Schwartz, in fact, had been Weinbaum's agent, and in 1937 he was also representing many of the most prolific and successful American authors. It was surely no coincidence that many of those in his stable all began to write Weinbaum imitations at about the same time.

In his introduction, "The Wonder of Weinbaum" in the landmark Weinbaum collection, *A Martian Odyssey* (Lancer, 1962) the leading SF historian Sam Moskowitz outlined just how celebrated and influential Weinbaum's short career (1934-35, with posthumous stories in the next few years) had been:

> "Many devotees of science fiction sincerely believe that the true beginning of modern science fiction with it emphasis on polished writing, otherworldly psychology, philosophy and stronger characterization began with Stanley G. Weinbaum. Certainly few authors in this branch of literature have exercised a more obvious and persuasive influence on the attitudes of his contemporaries and through them on the states of the readers....
>
> "...what cannot be argued away are the strong influences of Weinbaum to be found in the work of authors as outstanding in science fiction as Henry Kuttner, Eric Frank Russell, Philip Jose Farmer and Clifford D. Simak specifically."

The full roll call of other authors following in his footsteps is even longer, including, amongst others, Arthur K. Barnes, Eando Binder, Moskowitz himself, and not least John Russell Fearn.

Their borrowings involved not just the stories themselves, but Weinbaum's astronomical backcloth to his stories. This useful framework was astutely identified by Isaac Asimov in his brilliant introduction to *The Best of Stanley G. Weinbaum* (Del Rey, 1974):

> "Weinbaum had a consistent picture of the solar system (his stories never went beyond Pluto) that was astronomically correct in terms of the knowledge of the mid-1930s. He could not be wiser than his time, however, so he gave Venus a day-side and a night-side, and Mars an only moderately thin atmosphere and canals. He also took the chance (though the theory was already pretty well knocked out at the time) of making the outer planets hot rather than cold so that the satellites of Jupiter and Saturn could be habitable.
>
> "On each of the worlds he deals with, then, he allows for the astronomic difference and creates a world of life adapted to the circumstances of that world."

These two new Fearn collections present all of the Weinbaum pastiches that Fearn published—a dozen in total. And, as a bonus, the second volume also contains a thirteenth story, "Locked City" by Thornton Ayre, his first story marking the radical new direction Fearn was to take when he *abandoned* the Weinbaum slant. Each story is annotated with further sidelights, setting the stories in the context of the science fiction magazine scene in the late 1930s and early 1940s, one of its most interesting and dynamic periods.

I hope you will enjoy reading these stories as much as I did compiling them...and that they may intrigue you enough to want to seek out Weinbaum's own stories if you have not already encountered them.

—Philip Harbottle,
Wallsend, England, July 2012

VALLEY OF PRETENDERS
BY DENNIS CLIVE

FROM *SCIENCE FICTION*, MARCH 1939

Commenting on the magazine's first issue in a letter in the June 1939 issue of *Science Fiction*, reader Garfield Hoffman lauded "Valley of Pretenders" by Dennis Clive as a "brilliantly outstanding tale among ten splendid yarns," with "a dash of humanness, of realism that imparts to [its] bizarre setting a convincing smack of the authentic...."

An editorial note in the magazine's next issue revealed that "Valley of the Pretenders" had been adjudged the most popular story by the readers' response. Something that no doubt prompted its choice to lead off the publisher's booklet reprint series of *Science Fiction Classics* in 1941. Fearn's later 'Clive' novelette, "The Voice Commands"(*Science Fiction* January 1940), a non-Weinbaim story, was also included in this six-booklet reprint series. Both are now valuable collectors' items and, technically, Fearn's first 'book' editions. *[Note for trivia fiends! The booklet has a printer's error, transposing a paragraph from Chapter III to Chapter IV. This reprinting, taken from the magazine version, corrects the booklet's error.]*

A good deal of this story was later incorporated—revised—in one of Fearn's "fix-up" Vargo Statten novels, *The Eclipse Express* (Scion, 1952). The novel also incorporated a revision of another story from around this same period, "Eclipse Bears Witness" (*Science Fiction*, March 1940, as by Ephriam Winiki.)

VALLEY OF PRETENDERS

Great is the dismay of Mart and Eda when they find themselves trapped on a cruel moon-world—how can they hope for rescue now that the giant spaceship has risen into the void?

Those four wandering Earth people soon regret leaving the vicinity of the spaceship—for they find themselves the captives of the strangest race of creatures ever to inhabit a world of the Solar System!

CHAPTER I

"Hell, that's darned funny!" Mart Latham sat up in his comfortably sprung seat and stared in surprise through the huge window. "Look, we're turning towards Rhea.... Rhea of all places!" he whistled blankly.

He was not the only one who had noticed the fact. A general chatter of surprised conversation rose from the passengers in the immense, comfortable lounge. Faces angled towards windows in complete amazement.

"Nothing to worry about, folks. Just keep your seats, please."

A trim, white-coated steward of the giant Earth-Europa space liner suddenly appeared at the main door. He was smiling apologetically.

"We've developed a jet fault," he explained. "It's too risky to attempt the complete run to Earth without having it fixed— so we're making a temporary landing on Rhea. We'll be there about four hours—"

He was cut short by a chorus of protest. Some had appointments, some had wives, some hoped to have wives, others were darn glad they hadn't—and so forth. The steward met the onslaught with his best 'customer is always right' smile.

"I am so sorry, ladies and gentlemen, but the Interplanetary Corporation reserves the right to land in an emergency.....

Thank you." He departed as silently as he had come.

Mart Latham looked disgustedly out the window again.

"Well, what do you know about that?" he grunted. "Ditched for four hours on the fifth satellite from Saturn with nothing to look at but jungle, and rocks—and things," he finished vaguely.

The girl by his side looked up from a half-doze and revealed a freshly youthful face framed in corn-colored hair.

"Never mind, darling," she consoled him. "It'll give you time to realize how beautiful I am."

"I don't feel like being gallant," Mart growled. "Besides, a guy doesn't tell his wife how beautiful she is after being married to her for five years.... Or does he?" he mused.

Eda Latham elevated her tip-tilted nose disdainfully.

"Noted chemist on holiday from Europa trade satellite makes analysis of matrimony," she sniffed. "O.K., be high hat if you want to!"

"Rhea," Mart murmured, hardly listening to her, his gray eyes fixed on the 1,500-mile diameter moon of Saturn as the vast space liner curved around towards it. "Y'know, I've often wondered what Rhea has on it. Titan's pretty well known, of course, but the other smaller moons, Rhea among them, hasn't had much to say for itself. Inhabitants of sorts, I understand; even an atmosphere. But devilish hot."

"Naturally, being near Saturn," Eda said, regarding him with level blue eyes. "Let me think now.... Rhea is 337,000 miles from the primary. Right?"

"Right!" Mart agreed laconically. "Revolves in relation to the Sun at the speed of 4 days, 12 hours, and 25 minutes. Gravitation somewhat less than that of Earth's moon. Atmosphere breathable, but only to a height of 1,500 feet. Satisfied?—or shall I get you a guide book?"

The girl didn't answer. She was watching the little moon rising up to meet the ship. Exhaust sparks, prevented from igniting the vegetation below by reason of subsidiary foam nozzles, spouted from the under-jets. Saturn, vast and magnificent with its planetoidial rings, dominated all space. A partly molten, partly solid, but at all times rather grim, world.

Further in the distance beyond the rings moved the trading moon of Titan, and at varied intervals the but little explored other moons of Hyperion, Japetus, and Phoebe....

Eda started to speak as the ship began to settle down carefully over a waste of sprawling green jungle; then she stopped and turned a little as a voice cut above hers. It was a slow voice, sonorously British, steeped in the toneless impartiality of the law courts.

"...but, m'lud, I would bring to your learned notice the case of Simmons-v-Simmons in 2415, exactly five years ago There, the plaintiff alleged—"

"I am not interested, Sir Basil! Not interested in the least."

Sir Basil Emmot, world and space renowned interplanetary Counsel of British law, mopped a bald head and blinked protruding, bovine eyes. Next to him, Judge Asa Walbrook— thin and wizened as a disinterred corpse, and about as attractive—looked at him sourly. Nobody spoke. Nobody dared to. Judge Walbrook had captured and condemned more criminals in his career than any other man alive; even now he was heading earthwards to preside over the trial of Nick Andrews, long evasive spatial filibuster.

"Cheery looking old dear, isn't he?" Eda murmured, turning back to Mart. "That face of his would make any lemon jealous."

She stopped again as the ship suddenly jolted slightly and became still. The throbbing of the tremendous rocket engines ceased; the vessel lay in the half-shade of towering trees that stretched upwards to surprising heights against the slight gravity. The multiple lights of Saturn and the moons filled the outside jungle with a curiously ghostly white tinge, not unlike indirect floodlighting.

The steward appeared again. "If you wish to take exercise, ladies and gentlemen, you are at liberty to do so. But you are warned not to move more than two hundred yards from the ship. We are by no means sure of what this moon contains. If you go any further, you do so at your own risk. Kindly leave your names with the purser as you go out, so a complete check of passengers may be made before we start again. We have four hours' wait."

He disappeared actively, and Mart got to his feet. Languidly he zipped up his shoes. They were special shoes, worn by every space traveler—steel-soled to hold firmly to the attractive gravity-compensator plates in the floor. Nor were they any too comfortable....

"Guess we might as well have a look at Rhea," he murmured. "How about you, Eda?"

"Naturally!" She fixed her own shoes and patted her hair. Behind her, Judge Walbrook rose up with a face of vinegar, Emmot beside him.

"I have always felt, Sir Basil, that your learned talents are better exercised in unconfined surroundings," Walbrook observed, chopping his words with vicious economy. "We can continue this discussion on Simpson-v-Simpson outside."

"Simmons-v-Simmons, I assure you," the Counsel corrected hotly, tugging out his pipe and filling it.

"Don't be impudent! And kindly refrain from lighting that archaic incinerator in here, too! Come!"

Mart stared after them, grinning. "That Simmons-v-Simmons case must be a honey," he said seriously. "Be glad you married a chemist and not a judge...."

He took the girl's arm and headed from the lounge into the main hall. Men and women were queued up before the purser's desk. Then in a few minutes Mart found himself outside the airlock on Rhea's soft, vegetation-smothered surface. Immediately a sense of amazing lightness buoyed him up. Years on Europa, however, with its slight attraction, had made him— and Eda too—practiced in the art of counterbalancing themselves.

"Pretty dry here," Eda remarked, stirring the tindery stuff at her feet. "The other satellites are wet by comparison."

"Less humidity here," Mart observed.

For a moment or two they both stood, accustoming themselves, breathing the somewhat dry but tolerable atmosphere, conscious too of sweltering, burning warmth.

The people broke up into parties, wandered around the giant liner, peered into the corners of the clearing. The sound of the ship's mechanics began to echo vigorously—but above them came a fading, occasional didactic reference to "Simmons-v-Simmons" as Walbrook and Emmot wandered off to the far side of the clearing, oblivious to all warnings to stay near the ship.

"Well, what now?" Eda asked, dabbing her face languidly. "Do we stick around, or look around?"

Mart answered her by strolling towards the wall of jungle. Through the trees, the remarkably near horizon was visible, giving the odd effect of the jungle suddenly sloping away almost in sheerness.

"Mart, what exactly is that?" asked the girl suddenly, when they reached the jungle's first trees, and she pointed to a quivering rim of pale fire just visible over the near horizon. In some strange way it resembled a pale edition of the Earthly Northern Lights.

Mart shrugged. "No idea—and we can't risk going too far to find out. Pity! You know, I'd like to come here someday and—" He broke off, sniffing hard. "Smell something?" he asked sharply.

Eda elevated her nose, then looked surprised. "I believe I do! Burning wood.... Maybe old Lemon Pan and the Counsel have built themselves a fire, seeing it's only one hundred and thirty in the shade—"

"Look!" Mart interrupted her, pointing, and she gave a startled gasp at a vision of sooty smoke rising into the air perhaps a quarter of a mile distant.

"It's a fire all right," Mart went on tensely. "And if this stuff gets ablaze—Holy Smoke! We've got to warn them back at the ship...."

But there was no need for that. The officers of the vessel, conducting the mechanics' operations, had already seen the smoke and were issuing quick orders to the crew to fetch the powerful fire extinguishers.

"Inside, everybody!" roared the chief steward, through his wrist-microphone. "We can't afford to take chances."

"He's right there," Mart muttered, catching the girl's arm. "We'd better—"

"Help!"

It wasn't a very audible call; in fact, it would probably have missed being heard altogether had not Mart and Eda been at that particular part of the clearing. They turned sharply, startled and even as they did so it came again.

"It's coming from somewhere near that smoke column!" Eda cried.

Mart glanced back towards the ship. Nobody else seemed to have heard the cry: they were all too busy dashing for the ship in case the fire developed into a genuine conflagration.

"We've got to help," he stated briefly. "You go back to the ship and—"

"Rats!" Eda cut in tersely. "I married you until death do us part. This may be the break I'm waiting for...."

Without waiting, she turned and headed into the jungle with Mart immediately behind her. With the lesser gravity to aid them, they progressed in immense leaps, floating across considerable distances, coughing as the smoke grew denser and surged into their lungs.

"Hey! Where are you?" Mart yelled, pausing a moment.

"Here! Here! Quick—!"

"It's Lemon Pan all right," Eda gasped, then she jumped back as the foliage of a nearby tree began to sizzle and wither in a blighting shaft of flame shooting up its length. All the groundwork of a forest fire was laid.

The smoke was a fog now, but the two blundered forward again, to come suddenly on Judge Walbrook and Emmot standing in the middle of a little clearing, tugging oddly enough at their own legs, while around them the flames of burning vegetation were spurting dangerously close.

"Keep away!" Emmot cried, as Mart prepared to leap

forward. "You'll be as bad as we are if you come here. We're stuck!" he wailed dismally.

"But—but you can't be!" Mart yelled. "You're not in a bog; you're on solid ground. What sort of a game is this? Come on!"

Ignoring the warning, he jumped forward, Eda beside him, but the moment they landed they felt themselves gripped by something of viselike power. They couldn't move one foot beyond the other.

"You see?" Walbrook bleated, more crinkled than ever now he was alarmed. "This is the fault of my learned friend. I told him not to scatter his pipe ashes in the vegetation—" He broke off with a yelp as a crackling runner of fire spat towards him.

Mart coughed violently and tugged at his feet. It was useless; he was rooted. Then he started suddenly as Eda came to his side in her stockinged feet. Her shoes lay behind her, zipped wide open.

"Take your shoes off, smart guys!" she suggested tartly. "This stuff's magnetized, or something—holds the steel soles of our shoes. You two do the same." She gazed witheringly at the best brains in British law, then helped to rip open the zippers.

"But this is perfectly preposterous!" Sir Basil cried, stumbling free of the danger area. "I cannot reconcile the fact that—"

"Never mind reconciling facts," the girl said practically. "We've got to head back to the ship before we're cut off. If we can!" she finished in dismay. "Look, Mart!"

She jabbed an arm at the pouring flood of choking smoke, the crackling advance of flames. The way back was ruthlessly cut off by a solid, raging wall.

But Mart wasn't looking. He was on his knees staring at the sticky substance whereon the four pairs of shoes were still immovably riveted.

"Say, this stuff is magnetite!" he exclaimed in astonishment, glancing up. "Natural lodestone—like the Swedish deposits on Earth. Magnetic oxide of iron."

"So what?" demanded Eda impatiently. "Take a look at the fire."

He sprang up from his futile efforts to dislodge the shoes, stumbled backwards, and cursed as a sharp bramble stabbed his besocked feet. In dismay he stared at the beating, torrid wall of flame moving inwards.

"Come on—we've got to travel," he panted. "That way...."

Stumbling helplessly, he led the way to the opposite side of the clearing with Eda and the legal men picking their way behind him.

CHAPTER II

Only when the holocaust was some two hundred yards behind them did they stop.

"Now what?" Eda demanded, wiping her smutty, greasy face. "How do we get back to the ship? We're heading away from it all the time. Besides, this jungle is no place to hike around without shoes."

"What do you suggest?—that we walk through the fire like a collection of Hindu fakirs?" Mart asked tartly. "We've got to keep moving until it dies down, or the ship's crew extinguishes it. Come on—it's catching up again."

He began to resume the advance, but Walbrook caught his arm.

"Listen to me, young man!" he panted. "Back on the Earth I have to preside over the case of Andrews-v-Interplanetary, and it is quite unthinkable that my learned colleague and I—"

"Forget your briefs and follow me," Mart snapped out. "That fire's gaining...."

Onrushing flame made further argument impossible. Floundering wildly in the slight gravity, stabbed by barbs and vicious thorned roots, the quartet blundered on, they knew not where, all sense of direction hopelessly at sea, the smoke of the forest fire formed into a dense, impenetrable fog behind them.

They became aware of other things too—the bellowing of enigmatic beasts, the shriek of unknown birds, all stampeded by the conflagration. Here and there through the rifts were glimpses of incredible objects plunging and plowing through the undergrowth.

"Looks like we loosed some kind of zoo around here," Eda said breathlessly, rubbing her gashed feet painfully. "And if you, my learned friend," she went on bitterly, glaring at Sir Basil, "had taken care where you parked your pipe ash, this wouldn't have happened. Of all the darned crazy things to do! Here!"

The Counsel's veiny brown eyes protruded nauseatingly.

"But, my dear young lady—"

"Don't 'dear young lady' me! You ought to start a Nicotine Abolition Act with that profound brain of yours— Gosh, Mart, what's that?" Eda finished with a scream, and the others looked up in time to see a vast pair of saucer eyes staring at them malevolently from a hundred-foot high body.

"Some sort of dinosaur," Mart panted. "Can't try conclusions with that brute. This way—"

He swung off to the right, clutching the girl's arm. Together they vaulted the nearest five-foot high row of bushes, but they did not strike solid ground beyond. Instead they found themselves in the midst of warm, fast-moving water, struggling desperately amidst a jammed, screaming mass of animals, none of which resembled anything Earthly.

Two splashes from the rear announced that Judge and Counsel had also landed. Walbrook rose up screaming words not entirely legal and finally choked out that he couldn't swim.

"But I can, m'lud," Emmot gaspingly assured him. "Leave everything to me."

He clutched the older man tightly and struck out towards Mart and Eda. His bald head looked like an emerald bladder with scum draped round it.

"Most belittling," he groaned, as he came level. "The dignity of the law, upheld by—"

"Watch yourself!" Mart interrupted him, gaze darting around him at the fighting creatures. "A flick from one of those supertails and it'll be curtains. Take it easy; the flow'll carry us along."

"Curtains?" wheezed Walbrook, smothered in mud, scum, and fury. "Curtains? Confound you, sir, how are window adornments applicable to our present position?"

Emmot ejected a mouthful of filthy water. "Americanism, m'lud," he gurgled to explain, "implying, as I understand it, a rather sudden cessation of life—symbolical, to wit, with the descent of a curtain upon a stage act, m'lud, whereby—"

"Oh, shut up!" yelled Mart. "This is no law court— Look out there!"

He ducked suddenly, forced Eda down, too. A mighty object, mad with fright and twice the size of a crocodile, breathed its last as its abdomen was transfixed by a vicious spire of dead tree stump projecting from the water. With bursting lungs the quartet emerged from the froth and foam of the death struggle.

"This is all most irregular—" Walbrook began to bleat, but Mart yelled above him:

"Say, that carcass wouldn't make a bad raft! The lesser gravity will help it to float, too. Give me a hand with it. I don't think these other creatures will attack us; they're too concerned for their own safety."

He struck out vigorously and clutched the object's scaly body with both hands. It rolled over in a tumult of water. With some effort, which somehow reminded him of riding a bladder-horse in a swimming pool, Mart scrambled onto the broad back. Wedging himself as well as possible, he held down his hand, dragged the girl up with ease against the lesser gravity. Floundering crazily, Walbrook and Emmot followed suit.

"And now?" the Judge panted, very wet and monkeylike, as they began to drift downstream amidst the bubble and smother of stampeded animals.

Mart shrugged his shoulders. "I'm no fortune teller, judge. All we can do is go where this takes us. We're safe enough from fire here, anyway. The space liner crew will douse it with their high-power apparatus, anyway.... At the moment our lives are still our own."

"But for how long?" groaned Sir Basil, wiping his taut, scummy head. "Oh, woe is me! An unknown world, an unknown river—drifting further and further away from the ship.… And did you notice the water was quite warm?" he finished with sudden brightness.

"Naturally, on a world so near to Saturn," panted Walbrook. "Where are your finer powers of perception, Sir Basil?"

"Rhea's nearness to Saturn doesn't altogether explain such warm water," Mart murmured. "I'm inclined to suspect volcanic forces."

"That's right; be cheerful!" snapped Eda, tossing back her damp hair. "Next thing you'll be telling us is that we're drifting into a boiling whirlpool or something. If so, I'm heading for the bank. I never did like lobster."

Mart didn't answer her, and for a moment the party was silent. Then a bend in the river brought into view that strange aurora display the girl had pointed out a little while before— a quivering band of white, but augmented now by streaks of amber and lilac arcing across the purplish-blue sky.

"Wish I could figure out what that is," Mart mused. "Seems to be centered over Rhea's North Magnetic pole. High electrical energy of some kind—maybe connected somehow with that natural lodestone area we found.…"

He stared up at titanic Saturn flooding his warmth and light down on this fantastic little satellite, then suddenly he looked ahead again as there came to his ears the unmistakable sound of a dim, booming roar.

For the first time he noticed that the animals in the river were battling aside, struggling towards the silent, weird masses of the jungle on either bank. There was no danger of fire here; the danger area was far behind.

"Mart, what is that noise?" Eda demanded suddenly, seizing his arm. "It's funny, but—but I remember that—Niagara sounded like that from a distance. Remember? Our honeymoon?"

"It's a waterfall!" cried Walbrook hoarsely, clutching his

skimpy gray hair. "It's a waterfall, I tell you!" He danced perilously on the carcass. "Do something! Don't you realize that my life is valuable? My—"

"Oh, shut up!" Mart growled. "You're no more valuable than we are...." He broke off, studying the accelerated speed of the water. "If it is a waterfall, we're going right over it," he breathed. "We couldn't swim to the bank against this current in any case. The animals knew what was ahead; they got free in time. River's clear of 'em.... Looks like we're going places."

Sir Basil gave a groan of despair. "And me with the case of Andrews-v-Interplanetary on hand! My brief—everything—for nothing!" His pop-eyes stared down the river, much as a cow regards a cloudbank.

The others stared with him, nor was it very long before another bend of the river brought into sight the filmy mist that hangs eternally over plunging waters. Backed by the rainbow hues of the distant aurora, the effect was both beautiful and extraordinary.

The carcass quickened speed. Mart turned to the legal men, clutching Eda to him.

"It's a waterfall, all right—tidy size too, if the din and mist is any guide. The only thing that can save us is the lesser gravitation. As we go over, jump outward—outward for your lives.... You'll miss the main water impact that way."

He tensed himself as he spoke, keeping his balance with difficulty as the carcass bobbed up and down with ever increasing speed.

"This is most disturbing," moaned Walbrook; then he turned a ripely jaundiced eye on Emmot. "Sir Basil, I shall look to you for assistance."

"Willingly, m'lud—but I would bring to your learned notice that I am not proficient in the art of acrobatics."

"Mart, suppose—" whispered Eda hopelessly; but he only tightened his hold.

"Take it easy, Eda. We've taken the hurdles so far and we'll take this one—somehow.... Uh-uh! We're off now—"

The carcass suddenly jolted forward, so violently that the four were nearly pitched off. As they rocked and swayed they felt it hurtle towards the creaming cataract ahead. Beyond, they had a transient glimpse of the river's continuation through a deeply-wooded valley, to the left of which was a blunted, sullenly smoking volcano.

"Jump for your life!" Mart screamed suddenly, and simultaneously hurled himself outwards into space with all his power.

The effort of his jump dislodged Eda from him; in the lesser gravity she went soaring absurdly away from him, turning slow somersaults. To the rear Emmot and Walbrook rose up, looking curiously like effigies on Independence Day.

Twirling through the air Mart got a brief glimpse of the waterfall. It was at least 200 feet high.... He began to drop towards the river below with ever-increasing speed—automatically straightening his body for a dive. Eda was falling too, yards away.... He struck water—but struck something else as well that burst the universe into soundless white fire....

CHAPTER III

Mart struggled back to consciousness, to the awareness of a throbbing head and murmuring voices. He opened his eyes to the full-bodied glare of Saturn streaming down upon him with its feverish warmth. The ground underneath him was stony and warm; several feet away the river raced past.

"Mart—! Oh, Mart, thank Heaven!" It was Eda suddenly beside him, her clothes nearly dry now in the blighting heat, her hands holding his head thankfully.

"O.K., don't strangle me," he mumbled, emerging from the clinch. "I'm all right now.... But say, what happened?"

"You caught yourself a glancing blow on a submerged rock. No damage done, thank goodness. We managed to pull you out."

"Oh...." Mart turned and caught sight of Emmot and Walbrook sitting a little distance off, looking behind them in blank astonishment. Mart turned again and winced as his head swam.

"Say, what—what the—?" he began blankly, and Eda cut in quickly:

"They've been waiting for you to recover, she explained anxiously. "They talk—talk English!"

"Th-the devil they do!" he stammered back, and stared in amazement at a group of twenty men and women, all of them but scantily attired, practically Earthly in general development save that the lesser gravity had given them shorter stature and more highly efficient biceps. All the men were white-bearded.

Their faces were strikingly childlike and docile, differing but little from good-tempered Earth boys and girls of some ten years of age. The only oddity lay in the slit, catlike pupils of their innocent misty blue eyes—pupils which visibly dilated and contracted under the changing lights of Saturn and the various moons.

Beyond them stood a rather makeshift city of dried mud; yet remarkably enough it looked as though it was meant to resemble modern New York—a miniature version of it in mud flung here amidst the wilds of Rhea. There were recognizable edifices, even streets, but there was a complete lack of unity and careful planning.

Behind it was again the evidence of that enigmatic, multi-colored aurora, while to the right, lifting to a height of some 800 feet, and smoking sullenly, stood a squat but nonetheless deadly volcano....

Mart scrambled to his feet at last with his eyes on the men's beards.

"So this is where Santa Claus hails from," he muttered. "Methinks this is where we have plenty palaver, eh, squaw?" He grinned at Eda, then with upraised hand went slowly forward.

"Here's looking at you!" he cried, halting before the foremost man.

"Mud in your eye," responded the four-foot leader gravely, and bowed profoundly so that his beard eclipsed his narrow waistline. Then, straightening up and looking Mart full in the eye, he asked politely, "Did you brush your teeth this morning?"

"Huh?" Mart blinked in astonishment, was hardly aware that Eda, Walbrook, and Emmot had come silently up behind him.

"I speak to you by courtesy of the people of Malinjah," the man went on. "We, the Malinjahs, offer you a free sample of our excellent hospitality. Come at once, or write at once, as you will...."

Mart shook himself, thumped his forehead. "No doubt about it," he muttered. "That slug on the head has made me daffy. Why, this guy talks like a radio television announcer handing out blah.... There ain't no such animal! Who'd you say you are?" he asked abruptly, looking up again.

"The Malinjahs. I am Ansid Rawl, leader of my people's network, complete with hookups."

"We'll skip the hookups. How'd you come to be here? How did you learn English?"

For answer Rawl turned and pointed towards the aurora. "Knowledge is cheap when it is free," he said poetically. "Write now for my prospectus. Send no money."

Eda started to snicker at the astounded expression on Mart's face. Even Walbrook's withered mouth creased painfully at the corners. Emmot's eyes had nearly parted company with his face.

"Don't you get it, Mart?" the girl gasped at last, holding her sides. "Some—somehow these people have a means of hooking onto Earthly television broadcasts; the radio part at any rate. Very probably American broadcasts, since they're the most widely distributed and work on the strongest power. That's where they've picked up the language and they use advertisement slogans and bits and pieces out of plays, sketches, and political blurbs to talk with. Gosh, who'd have thought it!"

"I don't believe it," Mart stated stubbornly. "There's no signs of radio aerials in that city of theirs...." He stopped, trying to collect his thoughts, and the quaint people looked gravely at him with their big, slumbrous blue eyes and cat-like pupils.

"We're from the Earth—third planet out from the $un," he

hesitated. "We're—er— We're trapped. Want food. We are friends."

"You believe in democracy?" Rawl asked surprisingly.

"Eh? Yeah, sure we do.... But what's that to do with it?"

"If you did not, we would declare a state of war. Democracy for the democrats. Non-party; unilateral. That's us."

"War? With whom?"

"Anybody," Rawl said complacently. "So long as we are right."

Mart began to gesticulate, finally blurted out, "Be damned to the politics! What about a bite to eat?"

"Eat with pleasure—fear of pain afterwards positively banished! This way...."

Turning suddenly, Rawl led the way up the shingle towards the Saturn-lit city. Rubbing his bruised head Mart began to follow, Eda at his side.

"Tell me, young man, what do you imagine is the matter with these people?" asked Walbrook, coming level. "In a way, I am—ah, reminded of the case of Munro-v-Munro, wherein the plaintiff complained that her husband developed a mania for writing for advertised samples.... Very similar, eh, Sir Basil?"

"Very similar, m'lud. Clearly these people are strongly influenced by the advertisements of the time.... You're a chemist, Mr. Latham. Can you account for it?"

"You've got me there—up to now," Mart confessed. "They strike me as being really quite childlike, with little initiative of their own. Take this city we're coming to. It's not built by their own ingenuity; it's taken from descriptions they've heard over innumerable radio broadcasts. Note the lack of unity, showing minds that are only half-developed in the matter of self-government and control. Rawl said that the aurora caused him to know English—" Mart broke off and stared at the strange display. "North magnetic Polar Lights all right," he breathed. "I just wonder how—"

"Gosh, what a smell!" Eda interrupted him, pinching her tilted nose. "Who's opened the sewers around here?"

"Like—like rotten eggs," Sir Basil observed, and seemed ashamed of his brief lapse from dignity.

"There's the source of it," Mart remarked, nodding towards the volcano. "H_2S gas—better known as sulphretted hydrogen—Say, that gives me an idea!"

"Wad?" Eda asked nasally, still clutching her nose. "How der dooce do dese folks live arou'd here wid dat udhody odor blowi'g arou'd?"

"That's just it. Maybe they don't smell it."

"Boy, dey'd wad sub code in de dose dot to smell dat!"

"No, I mean maybe some other sense is developed instead. It might be. For instance, animals have sense of smell developed above sense of eyesight. With humans, sight comes first, hearing second, and smell last. Some even have no sense of smell."

"So whad?"

"I dunno; 'cept that perhaps these folks have a sense we don't know about which compensates them for lack of smell."

"I'd give all I've godt to loose my sedse of smell right dow—"

Eda broke off and released her nose as Rawl pointed to the nearest building of the mud city. With a beaming smile and a good deal of ceremony, surrounded by his silent people, he led the way into it. To the deepening amazement of the Earthlings, it was furnished in a style that was crudely terrestrial, There were chairs and tables in the center of a vast room that filled the entire length of the building. There were no other floors: the ceiling went up to an amazing height.

"More evidences of lack of brains," Mart commented. "They don't seem to realize that Earthly buildings have several floors and not only one ground floor.... Guess they're just playing at being civilized, like kids play at shop. They're just—well, just Pretenders."

Inside this room, lighted by naturally ignited volcanic gas spouting from crudely designed jets on the stone walls, the odor of sulphretted hydrogen had diminished considerably. The light of Saturn cast silver oblongs on the floor....

Rawl motioned to the chairs. "If you want food, we have it—

and then some," he said affably.

Turning aside he clapped his hands sharply, spoke for the first time in an unknown language. It was the signal for his childish, passive followers to spring into action. They vanished into unknown recesses of the slipshod building and returned bearing armfuls of fruit, presumably jungle products.

"Are we expected to eat these—these overgrown bananas?" demanded Walbrook, as they were laid on the table.

"Most irregular, m'lud, but without alternative," Emmot murmured, then he looked at Mart questioningly.

"O.K.," Mart announced, sampling one. "They're safe enough. Overgrown plantains, or something. Not poisonous to our constitution, anyhow."

Rawl watched in blasé contentment as the four began to appease their hunger, sharpened by their experiences. One of the women slipped outside and returned shortly afterwards with four garlands of livid-hued flowers. With a little cry of girlish delight, she placed one around Sir Basil's perfectly bald head.

"Really, young woman, I protest!" he shouted, looking up. "And at my age—!"

"Irrelevant and immaterial," grinned. Mart, looking at him critically. "But you'd better not take it off. These folks have evidently got you down as a sort of god, or something— Hey, what the—" He broke off in dismay as soft white arms passed against his ears and he found himself similarly adorned.

Eda looked remarkably pretty with hers—but Judge Walbrook looked about as attractive as a pig with a lemon between its teeth.

"Most irregular!" he fumed, crinkling with passion. "I refuse to wear it!"

"You'd better," Mart counselled quickly, glancing up. "Our friend Aniseed Ball has his eye on you.… Keep your shirt on."

"I assure you," Walbrook said, with measured acidity, "that I have no intention of taking my shirt off."

"Oh, skip it," Mart groaned. "Why don't you learn English?"

Rawl came forward from the ranks of his smiling, highly

delighted people.

"I bring you a message," he stated, waving his small arm. "We wait for the appointed ones: they who will show us peace. You are the appointed ones."

"Oh, but we're not," Mart protested, jumping up. "You're talking about things religious, Rawl; things you've heard over the radio. Some religious denominations wait for the appointed ones, yes—but that's not us. We've got to leave here. We have a ship waiting for us."

Rawl shook his head steadily and smiled. "We have waited long. We shall honor and cherish so long as you all shall live."

"So long as—" Mart gulped, stared, then sat down with a thud. He spread his hands helplessly. "That's the marriage service you're mangling!" he yelled. "And it's time this sort of foolery came to an end. We can't stop here."

"You are here…on a journey which knows no returning," Rawl observed calmly.

"That's—that's Shakespeare," Eda said quickly. "An' maybe he means it, Mart. There is no way back over that waterfall.…"

"Hell!" Mart said helplessly, and all sat looking at each other, too concerned to notice how absurd they all looked with their garlands—all save Eda. Emmot was looking at her with a pop-eyed expression that might have either been fascinated appreciation or incipient cardiac.

CHAPTER IV

After a time Rawl and his people began to hum, in not unmusical voices, watching the four intently as they did so. At first it did not occur to Mart what they were chanting, then he suddenly leaped up.

"Listen to 'em!" he shouted. "That song is 'I'll Buy Me a Robot'—the latest American craze song! They can only have contacted that by direct radio.…" He swung around to Rawl. "Look here, where is your radio receiver?" he demanded.

Rawl shrugged, tapped his head. "Why travel far when it comes to your door?" he asked, then pointed again towards the far end of the room. It was obvious he meant the aurora, hidden from sight now, of course.

Mart stared, perplexedly, then suddenly Eda cried, "Listen, Mart, is it possible that these folks are natural radio receivers? They haven't the brains to build apparatus; they're only like kids."

"Say, I believe you've got something there, Eda. Their lack of a sense of smell, for instance, might be compensated for by another unknown sense. Here's to trying, anyhow.... Rawl, can you hear radio waves?"

"All-wave receiver given free," he said in gratification, thudding his white-haired head again.

"It is inside his brain!" Eda cried. "What there is of his brain, that is."

"But how—?" Mart kicked his chair back and began to pace the room, thinking. "Short-wave radio waves do penetrate this far, of course, especially the ones linked with television. They travel as far from Earth as Pluto. But—Good Lord!" he broke off with a gasp. "I begin to get it now—the connection between the aurora and this radio reception. This planet is naturally highly magnetic; we know that by discovering that lodestone area back in the forest. There may be thousands of 'em knocking around different parts of Rhea, particularly at the poles."

"Well?" Eda questioned, and the people themselves moved closer to hear Mart's halting, thoughtful exposition.

"Is there any reason," he deliberated, "why the free electrons of short radio waves cannot be caught by Rhea's lines of magnetic force spiraling around its magnetic poles? It's a highly magnetized satellite for one thing; it doesn't spin too fast, of course, but quite fast enough to form itself into a planetary dynamo and collect radio waves and redistribute them— Gosh, yes! That would account for the weird electrical display at the pole. Probably the same thing happens at the other pole, too. Not only trapped radio wave electrons, but electric radiations of various sorts have full play. This planet has such a high magne-tization it captures them pretty freely, both from outer space and Saturn's own emanations."

"That may be right," Eda admitted, thinking, "but how do you account for these folks being able to hear them?"

"Just a minute," Mart said, and turning to the table he picked up the skin of one of the plantain fruits. Gently he folded it and rubbed it together.

"Rawl, what does that sound like to you?" he asked quickly.

"Visit Niagara Falls for your honeymoon," Rawl smiled back—and Mart gave a yelp, slammed the peel emphatically back on the table.

"There you are! To us that sounded like a faint, slippy sort of noise. To him it sounds like the din of Niagara. You get it? The hearing perception of these people is way ahead of ours. Human ear limit is 10-12 watt power, and that's mighty low. Animals a bit higher. These people are above our audible frequency."

"Maybe," Eda mused, "but how does that connect up with them hearing radio waves—electronic waves? Those aren't audible anyway; they're electrical."

"I know that, sweetheart! Point is, their brains are adapted differently than ours. If they can hear inaudible sounds, and magnify them as much as they do, it logically indicates that they can also receive electrical waves and interpret them."

"But how?"

"How the devil should I know?" Mart snorted exasperatedly. "Give me some cooperation, can't you? When a stream of elec-trons changes its course in, say, the Sun, it produces the sensa-tion of light in our brains, via our eyes. Well, what happens inside our brains to transform electron agitation into light? We don't know; nobody does. It's a thought mutation; a cellular response as impossible to describe as explaining a color to a blind man."

Eda looked about her at the child-like faces and shrugged her slim shoulders.

"Can you beat it?" she asked at last, "Kids with radio-receiver minds in a mud city on a cock-eyed moon! And I thought I knew all the answers about space and its contents."

"Personally," said Walbrook sadly, fingering his garland, "I am not in the least interested in space or vulgar radio.... I really must insist we find our way back to the ship. I have a case to judge."

"You've said something there," Mart assented grimly. "We have got to take a chance...." He swung around on the smiling Rawl.

"Listen, Rawl, there must be another way through the jungle without climbing two hundred feet of sheer cliff," he insisted. "A pass, or something. What about it?"

Rawl shrugged; his people giggled among themselves, as amused as children at the Earthlings' anxiety. It was perfectly plain that their strange minds saw no seriousness in the situation.

"Happy the man, whatever his lot, is he who's content with whatever he's got," Rawl observed with a certain fatalism, and folded his arms to verify his belief.

Mart groaned and clutched his hair. "Listen to him!" he muttered bitterly. "That statement's plain enough—there is no way, or if there is these walking radio receivers don't know about it.... Come to think of it, they're probably right," he went on gloomily, thinking. "There are no animals down in this valley. The cliff and waterfall stops them. They'd be down here and wipe these folks out like a shot otherwise."

"We might try walking round Rhea," Eda ruminated.

"Sorry, Bright Eyes, I don't feel up to walking a couple of thousand miles without shoes on...." Mart glanced at his watch. "The ship's due to leave in about ten minutes," he groaned. "Once that happens we're here for keeps probably—"

"There's that smell again," Eda whistled, clamping down on her nose. "Seems like the wind's off the gas-works this morning."

"Do you think if we shouted—?" Emmot began, eyes glistening with unexpected discovery—but Mart waved a hand at him.

"What do you think we are—yodelers?"

He stalked impatiently to the door of the place and stared moodily out over the little clearing towards the river, across at the sullenly smoking volcano. The odor was disgustingly strong.... Eda came quietly to his side.

"I'm sorry, Mart," she murmured, and without turning, he grunted absently:

"Sorry? What about?"

"Well, I seemed kind of silly making cracks when this situation's so desperate. I—" She stopped suddenly and twisted her head sharply. Mart glanced at her and she raised a quick finger for silence.

"Listen!" she breathed. "Our funeral guns!"

He caught her meaning immediately. On the odorous wind came the distinct roaring boom of rocket blasts—the rockets of the distant liner as it lifted from Rhea into the void. Right on time, too.

"Well," Mart growled, "they aren't losing any sleep over us, that's evident." He stared forlornly at the purplish sky. "Just the same, you'd think since we left our names with the purser that they'd—"

"Mart, the sound's coming nearer!" Eda shouted suddenly, in quick delight.

"Listen! It isn't fading away into space— There!" she screamed, jabbing out her arm. "There, near the waterfall! The ship! They're looking for us!"

She was right. Not a thousand feet above the waterfall and jungle swept the titanic bulk of the space liner, under-jets and foam nozzles working vigorously. Here and there dull red ashy deposit missed the foam nozzles and sizzled in the river.

Then the ship began to circle as slowly as its huge, ponderous bulk would permit. There were dimly visible figures standing in the airlock, gazing down.

Mart came to himself abruptly and raced wildly into the center of the clearing in huge, stumbling leaps. Eda joined him in frantic arm-waving. Emmot and Walbrook came out of the building too, and began an insane war dance in the lesser gravity, a dance entirely inappropriate to their station.

After a while, Rawl and his people came as well and copied the Earthlings' example because it amused them. Linking hands they danced around like a circle of elves and fairies, chanting that damnable craze song, "I'll Buy Me a Robot...."

"Hey!" screamed Mart frantically, as the ship moved towards the smoking volcano. "Hey! Come back here! Can't you see us? Hey!" He cupped his hands and bawled his lungs hoarse.

A stream of red, glowing deposits crawled up the volcano side as the liner swept over it. Something was wrong somewhere; that foam nozzle wasn't dead true—then suddenly it seemed that the entire crazy moon went out in a flash of blindingly brilliant light and sound.

Mart and Eda found themselves flung backwards by the force of a terrific explosion, flung clean on top of the wildly struggling Emmot and Walbrook. Every one of the Rheans fell to the ground, holding they ears in anguish, their higher hearing power wrenched and hammered by the frightful concussion.

"Look!" Eda screamed, scrambling up. "An—an eruption!"

"It can't be—" Mart began, clutching hold of her; then he broke off in astounded horror at the vision of the giant liner reeling violently as it recovered from the shock of that explosion.

It was heading swiftly away now from a sudden newly born rift in the volcano side through which was spouting a hellish fury of cinders, pumice, poisonous fumes, and bubbling lava.

"I get it!" Mart cried. "That sulphuric gas must have been ignited somewhere by that under-jet deposit. The nozzle's wrong; must be the one they've repaired. The sparks blew out a blind cone or blister when the gas ignited, started an uprush of matter...."

He stopped, gasping, staring through the swirling, darkening smoke clouds at the lurching space liner. It could not land in the clearing in any case; it was far too huge.

"Ahoy!" he bawled, and an amplified voice thundered out over the din of escaping volcanic steam.

"You have been seen. Prepare for rope ladder escape."

"Make it snappy!" Mart howled, jumping back as a lump of hot lava spattered onto his hand and stung viciously.

"This—this is all most disturbing," panted Walbrook, coming up through the smoke. "What do we do with the rope ladder? Hang onto it?"

"Or else fry," Mart answered him briefly. He swung round, struck with a sudden thought, stared in pitying amazement at the Rheans. Every one of them was lying on the already smouldering vegetation, gasping desperately, twisting and turning.

"Rawl, what's the matter?" he panted, lifting the head of the queer, bearded little ruler.

The strange creature tried to smile, choked over his words.

"Pa—parting is such sweet s-sorrow...," he whispered. "Undertaking estimates g-given. Write for—for my prospectus." That was all he said, quivered and smiled over it, then relaxed.

"Dead," Mart said very quietly.

"Poor, strange people," Eda whispered her eyes moist. "The noise?"

"Must have been," Mart muttered. "It nearly deafened us. To these creatures it must have been brain-destroying. Perhaps it's as well. What with the volcano and that faulty under-jet on the ship, the whole darned moon will be ablaze in an hour...." He stared around pityingly, through the smoke, on the sprawled, child-like figures. Then he looked up at a yell from Emmot.

"The rope ladder! Come on!"

He tore towards it in frantic leaps as it hung like a runged snake from the twilit gloom. Then he was pulled up short as Mart seized him savagely by the shoulder.

"Lay off, can't you? Eda first! Up you get...."

He swung the girl upwards. She gripped the rungs and began to climb. Emmot followed, and after him came the panting and thoroughly frightened judge.

Mart came last, felt the ladder swinging him away from that

fated clearing towards the clearer air. He could not take his eyes from that group of silent beings near their doomed, toy city.

"Pretenders, playing at life," he muttered, "only to meet death through the damnable blunderings of Earthlings. God, it's like mowing down children with ray guns—"

"Hey!" came Eda's voice from above him, and he looked up to see she'd reached the airlock.

"Better come up," she called, "You might find it cold out there when we head off into space...."

The smoke of the eruption hid the dead Pretenders from sight as Mart began to climb....

OUTLAW OF SATURN
BY JOHN COTTON

FROM *SCIENCE FICTION*, MARCH 1939
& *BRITISH SCIENCE FICTION MAGAZINE*, #7, 1954

First published in the debut issue of *Science Fiction* under the pseudonym of John Cotton (which became a publisher house name, used only this one time on a Fearn story), "Outlaw of Saturn" (originally entitled "The Minitors") received positive reader acclaim. In a letter in the June 1939 issue Garfield Hoffman referred to the story as "outstanding…John Cotton's George is an appealing feathered character, introducing agreeable touches of humor so naturally that our minds do not balk at his ponderous bulk and subhuman intelligence."

"Outlaw of Saturn" was very closely modelled on Weinbaum's story, "The Mad Moon," which opened with the hero in his hut in an alien jungle, berating the local natives and exhorting them to gather medicinal plant leaves, which he needed to treat his fever. His pet alien animal, the parcat, has the ability to parrot his words in an amusing fashion.

This opening is almost identical with that of "Outlaw of Saturn," and the parroting of human speech is echoed with the ostrich-like character of 'George'. However, as the story progresses, it rapidly diverges from Weinbaum's, and there are enough clever twists and original touches to assuage the literary theft involved

Interested magazine collectors might like to check out Eando

Binder's story "Moon of Intoxication" in the June 1939 *Thrilling Wonder Stories.* This was also a Weinbaum imitation (of which Binder did quite a few), and was also blatantly based on "The Mad Moon." In my opinion it is totally inferior to Fearn's effort!

Should anyone have doubted Fearn's authorship of "Outlaw of Saturn," all doubt was removed when Fearn became editor of the *British Science Fiction Magazine* in September 1954, taking over as editor from Alistair Paterson.

Previous to this, Fearn had been contributing stories to Paterson on a freelance basis, whilst he was contracted to write two novels a month for the magazine's publisher, Scion Ltd. Scion had gone into liquidation, and their former printers, Dragon Press, took over Scion's assets, including the magazine and Fearn's two-novels-a-month contract (which still had more than a year to run). To economise on their expenses, Dragon sacked Paterson and appointed Fearn as editor. Fearn had agreed to the renegotiation of his contract, committing him to now provide *one* novel and one issue of the magazine each month. As editor, Fearn was severely handicapped by his rapacious publisher: he was paid a flat fee for the novel and magazine issue alike, Obviously, it was to Fearn's advantage to write as much of the contents of the magazine as he could, but in fact, he contented himself with having just two stories in each issue, one of them as Vargo Statten. For the second story, he decided to reprint some of his old American magazine stories under new titles and pseudonyms. His publishers were quite unaware of this, and so, apparently were the readers and the SF community at large. It was not until many years later that my own researches identified all of the reprinted stories, and I published my findings—most prominently in a booklet published by the National Fantasy Fan Federation in 1965, *Science Fiction Title Changes*, compiled by Michael Viggiano and Donald Franson.

Fearn's first reprinted story was "Outlaw of Saturn," which he retitled as "Saturnian Odyssey," as by 'Francis Rose'. Francis was one of Fearn's rarely-used Christian names, and Rose was the middle name of his Mother, Florence Rose Fearn.

What was especially interesting with this story is that Fearn did not use the original magazine version. It transpired that this had been slightly abridged by editor Horning in packing ten stories into the first issue of *Science Fiction*. For the reprint, Fearn worked from his carbon copy ms. of the original story. Thus, "Saturnian Odyssey" is slightly longer (and better) than the original! For this first book edition, I am here reprinting Fearn's original, uncut version.

OUTLAW OF SATURN

He was little concerned about his fate at the hands of the law—for Outlaw Bruce Lanning finds himself faced with the far more hideous vengeance of the Minitors!

It was Lena's job to bring Bruce Lanning to justice—but the accursed world of the Minitors had planned a worse fate for him than the avenging arm of the law!

The heavy log floor, fast rotting in the eternal damp of Saturn, creaked protestingly as Bruce Lanning strode back and forth across it. Being a good natural fifteen stone, and gaining one pound in five on the ringed planet due to its gravitational pull, he certainly gave the hut's underpinnings plenty of work to do.

"It won't do!" he shouted at last, swinging round and jabbing an accusing finger. "You've got to get these plantations cleaned up before the mud-tides start, else you'll find yourselves without sugar! Understand? If you weren't such a damned shiftless lot, you'd have cleaned the seeds up long ago!"

The creature facing Bruce Lanning stood only two feet high—an almost perfect miniature of an Earthian, save that his eyes, wide and innocent, were pink and his skin deep amber. The Minitors of Saturn—'Minitor' being a corruption of 'Miniature'—were vest-pocket Terranians, childlike, amazingly passive and exasperatingly lazy. And, underneath it all, vindictive. In their eyes this tough Earthman was a dynamo, a destroyer of their lotus-eating existence.

Lifican, the Minitor, waved a thin arm timidly. His voice sounded like a badly played flute.

"Mister Lanning, please sir, plenty work is difficult. Opius seeds damn hard to collect. Beg for lots of time, please."

"You'll beg for nothing!" Lanning retorted. "You've been lazing your time like the rest of your no-account pals. You're the boss of them, so it's up to you. Now get out of here before I beat the daylights out of you!"

Lanning strode forward menacingly. Instantly the little creature twisted and flew outside with a yelp, accustomed by his small size to the heavy going of the giant, steamy planet. Lanning watched him go and then pushed a powerful hand through his damp hair.

"Rip Van Winkles!" he grunted. "They'll never get the stuff away in time at this rate—then I'll be in a grand spot trying to explain to Davis.… Huh! I just wonder what's the use of it all, anyway?"

He knew the use of it well enough. The common necessity of making a living had driven him into this business of racketeering, this illicit trading in opius seeds. Once the seeds reached Earth, various methods were utilized for their disposal. The wealthy were willing to pay any price for a few hours of glorious dreams, surcease from the boredom of 22nd-Century perfection.

Dreams produced by opius, unlike its deadly cousin opium, left no ill effects on the constitution. More, it produced a kind of sublime anesthesia and detached the mind from the body. Just the same, the business was still illegal, despite sundry efforts on the part of John Davis, chief of the enterprise, to make it a lawful business. Not that Bruce Lanning minded: the salary was worth it. The only drawback was the climate.

Yes, the ghastly climate of Saturn—that was the thing that

got him, particularly here on the North Equatorial Belt where the opius plants flourished. It wasn't so bad over at Green City, the civilized Saturnian quarter, but here...! He was becoming wearied with the myriads of childish Minitor workers on the plantation; the seasonal mud-flows from Saturn's fifty-mile-distant volcanic area; the senseless drivellings of the mimical birds; the alternating lights of the arcing rings of Saturn; the wild glimpses ever and again of the ten moons through heavens that were almost eternally wreathed in green clouds.

In the higher levels the air was unfit to breathe, but down here a preponderance of breathable oxygen remained. Unlike the penal world of Jupiter, where the vast pressure had crushed out all the oxygen, Saturn still possessed some—at any rate in a percentage high enough to support Earth-type life.

And the heat! All internal. An almost unvarying temperature of 115° Fahrenheit.... Lanning grunted with discomfiture and mopped his streaming face and neck. Then, arousing himself from his musings, he went outside to the short ladder propped against the doorway. His hut was on stilts to raise it above the periodic mud-flows.

Steadily he descended the ladder and sank the accustomed two inches into the spongy loam of the clearing. He nodded in satisfaction as he beheld the Minitors at work again, dwarfed by the weird, fern-like plants whose seeds they collected. They worked with a certain sullen persistence, reminding him of children who have received a severe scolding.

"Rip Van Winkles!" he repeated again, and yet could not help smiling a little. "Just the same, I'd rather be back on Earth. No Minitors, no jungle, no cockeyed trees that are both organic and inorganic, no mud...."

His blue eyes traveled over the packed mass of the flesh-eating and normal trees rearing to the green heavens. He listened in silence to the eternal chattering of Saturn's jungle life—then his attention was suddenly caught by his own pet mimical bird, George, as his clumsy but skilful bulk came like a bullet from the upper air.

Far larger than an Earthly ostrich, resembling a parakeet about the beak and face, his main qualities were a sublime gift of mimicry, sub-human intelligence, and magnificent plumage. He landed in the muddy ground with a thud, folded his wings, then scanned Lanning as he raised a lazy hand in acknowledgement.

"Hello there, George! I wondered where you'd got to."

"Seed thief!" George retorted, in a voice unmistakably that of a girl's. "Seed thief. Go wash your neck!"

Lanning straightened in surprise. "Hey, wait a minute! Where'd you pick up that girl's voice?"

"Hellish hot! Seed thief! Racketeer!"

"Racketeeer, eh?" Lanning scowled. "Sounds like you've been places where you shouldn't. Don't tell me you flew as far as Green City! Here! Come here!"

George wasn't having any. He stood on one leg and contemplated Lanning impassively. The Earthman sighed.

"Maybe it was the Minitors," he remarked. "They're not half so darned innocent as they look, the lazy—"

"They'd probably be all right if you didn't have to act like Simon Legree!"

Lanning twirled, his jaw sagging. His surprise was absolute as he beheld a slim girl attired in conventional shorts and the silk blouse of the North Equatorial Belt advancing towards him. Apparently she had come from the side of the clearing facing the plantation. She lifted her broad-welted boots with the air of a mud-trekking expert.

Lanning said nothing as the girl presently reached him. She had smoke-grey eyes, and corn-coloured hair peeped from under a soiled white hat. Lanning's gaze dropped to the gun in the belt of her shorts.

"You Bruce Lanning?" she asked abruptly.

"That's right— Who the devil are you, anyway? Don't you know that nobody in their right senses is allowed beyond the two-mile zone limit of Green City? That's twenty miles north of here."

"I'm aware of it: I came from there." The girl's voice was level and uncompromising. "Also, I'm going back there almost at once, and you're coming with me."

Lanning raised his eyebrows. He noted the small, efficient pack on the girl's back.

"Maybe we'd better go inside my place and talk things over?"

"Wash your necks!" agreed George, waddling forward as the girl turned to the ladder....

"I suppose," Lanning said, as they entered the little living-room, "that it was you who called me a seed-thief and racketeer in George's hearing?"

The girl glanced towards the bird and then said bluntly:

"Well, aren't you?" She took the cup of restorative Lanning held out to her and continued slowly, "Yes, I did call you that. I was annoyed at the time. I'd lost my way and I called you names because I considered you responsible. I didn't see this bird though. Maybe he was above me somewhere."

"Maybe." Lanning looked at her pensively. "Maybe I'm dense, but I don't understand why you came. Why you trekked across mud and jungle to get here. You've no right here anyway!"

"No?" The girl smiled contemptuously. "You're afraid how much I'll find out, I suppose? You need be, because that's what I'm here for.... I'm Lena Tavistock."

"Doesn't mean a thing. I'm Bruce Lanning, as you already know."

"More precisely," the girl explained, "I am Number Sixteen of the Outer Planets Service. You are trading in illicit drugs and I'm here to stop it and run you in. You're under arrest, Mr. Lanning!"

Before Lanning could recover from his surprise the girl had jumped to her feet with her gun deftly levelled.

"Apparently you have the advantage, madam," Lanning murmured dryly, raising his hands.

"You can put your hands down, but don't try anything. And we've got to get moving! You're coming back to Green City with me to answer a few questions. You know you have no right to use the Minitors as workers. By interplanetary law they're the natural inhabitants of this world and not under the dictates of outlaw Earthmen like yourself."

Lanning shrugged. "It isn't my doing, believe me. I take orders from my chief. He put the Minitors to work and I just look after them. They're congenitally lazy, but they'll work their heads off for a bag of sugar."

"Your chief, eh?" the girl repeated. "Where can we find him?"

"Green City. Looks as though you might as well have saved yourself the trouble of chasing after me, eh?"

"You're wrong there, Lanning. I'll run both you and your chief in. Come on; let's move. You don't need to pack. I've plenty of tabloid provisions."

"Hellish hot again!" George whistled, hopping about wildly.

"You're telling me," Lanning growled, turning to the doorway. Then as he reached it, with the girl inexorably behind him, he paused, tensed.

"Well?" Lena Tavistock demanded. "What's the matter?"

"Quiet! Listen!" Lanning cocked his head. "There! Hear it?"

The girl stood motionless, presently frowning as she caught the sound of distant rumblings. And they seemed to be coming slowly nearer.

"That's nothing," she snapped. "Only a volcanic area blowing itself up. They're common enough, aren't they?"

"To me it sounds like mud on the move," Lanning answered her.

Just the same, he did not argue any further but descended the ladder to the ground. As the girl dropped beside him, a group of Minitor men and women came speeding up, chattering at the top of their voices. They clutched at Lanning and the girl with their tiny hands, nearly deflecting Lena's steady pointing of her gun.

"Can't you call these creatures off?" she demanded irritably. "I don't like being pawed all over—"

"Then you should have stopped away!" Lanning retorted. He

swung to the nearest Minitor. "What's wrong?"

"Mister Lanning, sir, seeds we no longer get. Mud flow coming this way! Plenty danger...."

Lanning looked up sharply. The Minitors were now fleeing pell-mell from the plantation, more active than they had ever been in their lazy lives. The jungle trees' vegetation was shifting in the advance winds produced by the superheated blasts of air from the distant mud tidal wave.

As Lanning well knew the stuff often wiped out everything in its path—hence the stilts on his hut. Saturn, with its ten-moon gravitations, together with a swift, ten-hour rotation and consequent equatorial bulge, suffered from mud tides of vast height and power.

Lena too looked anxiously about her as the wind blew hot and odorous in her face. Then she turned suddenly as Lanning clutched her arm.

"Put that toy of yours away and be yourself," he ordered briskly. "We've got to step on it!"

She tried to pull free but he was too strong for her. Shaking clear of the whimpering Minitors, they raced swiftly across the clearing and plunged into the jungle. A little way inside it Lanning stopped and surveyed a towering, notched tree stabbing up into the misty, uncertain moonlight.

"Up you get!" he commanded, and Lena stared, appalled.

"Up there? But why? I—"

"It's my safety tree. I use it when there's an extra heavy mud flow like the one coming up. It's notched, and there's a platform at the top. Either that or drown."

"But I—" Lena broke off in bewildered surprise as Lanning grabbed her and shot her to the first branch. She looked down at his grim face below her.

"Climb—and quick!" he ordered.

She stared up at the lofty height and then began to climb notch by notch. Lanning came slowly behind her. Little by little the whole clearing and neighbouring plantation became visible to them. By the time they had reached the little platform at the top, they could descry the mud sea rolling inwards from the north, ploughing down weaker trees and undergrowth, frothing in great steamy globules of dirty ochre.

Lena looked apprehensive as Lanning came level.

"You're—you're sure we're safe?" All her former coldness and authority had gone now. She was very much a woman, and a good deal frightened, but she'd rather have cut out her tongue than admit the fact.

"No, I'm not sure we're safe," Lanning answered her, watching the mud intently. "This tree of mine has stood mud tides before and it should do so again. If it doesn't— Well, you won't need to run me in to Green City, or yourself either for that matter."

Lena did not answer him and he looked at her strangely.

"You know something?" he went on. "You're much too nice a girl to run around arresting people. I'll hand it to you that you've got plenty of nerve, though—coming through the jungle from Green City, I mean."

She shrugged, her eyes on the mud. "It didn't take nerve. I knew where you were and I hired some guides to help me. After all, I'm used to Saturn. I was born here. My father lives in Green City."

"And does he approve of this Secret Service stuff?"

"He doesn't know. It's four years since I saw him—"

Lena paused as George suddenly came whirring through the air and alighted heavily. The little platform swayed.

"Hellish hot!" George commented affably, folding his wings.

"It's going to get a good deal hotter," Lanning told him moodily. "This is about the biggest flood tide I ever saw."

He stared over the fast approaching morass. It was only a matter of yards from his hut. He and Lena watched it intently, catching their breath as the whole hut and plantation vanished in the smother. The surging, rolling mass bubbled swiftly beneath them, but since the tree afforded little resistance they experienced little beyond a fierce swaying, which quickly subsided. But all about them the lower trees of the jungle swayed and collapsed.

"Funny, isn't it," Lanning mused. "Saturn's surface, around here anyhow, is nothing but successive layers of mud from each succeeding drift. The tops of the trees and plants get snapped off, yet the roots remain to push through the hardening mud when the flow stops. Damned queer place."

"Where do the Minitors go at times likes these?" the girl asked.

Lanning pointed to a rocky cliff bounding the southern end of the clearing.

"They live just beyond there in a sort of valley. There's a cleft they go through. The mud never reaches high enough to get down there."

Lena nodded slowly. Since there was not a Minitor in sight, they had evidently all escaped in time. For a while she watched the flood in silence, and then she spoke again;

"How do we get away from here? What's next?"

"We stop," Lanning said. "Do you mind?"

"Mind? I should think I do! I'm no pole-squatter! How long do we have to stop?"

"Oh, it depends. I usually reckon to stay here for three days and nights—that is, by Earth standards. There's never any real dark on Saturn, as you know. By that time the mud is usually hardened enough to be normal and new trees and things are starting to spring up.... It's not half bad up here. It's warm; and there's always light, be it from the Rings, Titan, Dione, or Hyperion."

Lena looked anxiously about her. The major force of the mud flood had already spent itself. The vast swirling brown river below was moving more congestedly, building up slowly to a solidity, which would mean only a two-inch depth of upper plasma.

"Wash your neck!" screamed George suddenly, flapping his ponderous wings. "Hellish hot! Wash your—"

"Hey, sit still!" Lanning cried in alarm, clutching hold of the platform edge. "Take it easy—"

He broke off in horror as the bird flapped his enormous fantail violently. Even on the ground the wind disturbance from it was tremendous: up here within the short compass of the platform it was catastrophic. The whirl of feathers hit Lena straight in the face, knocking her backwards.

With a cry she tumbled over the platform edge and went hurtling to the turgid expanse below.

"Lena—!"

Lanning flung himself flat on his face. He was just in time to see the girl strike the mud with a dull splash; then she began to strike out desperately towards the distant cliff surrounding the domain of the Minitors. Without a moment's hesitation Lanning dived after her. He struck the mud feet-first and swam towards her.

Struggling through the filth made him feel like a fly in warm treacle. It weighted down every portion of his body. He could see Lena's head bobbing some distance away as she struck valiantly for the cliff base, but it was plain she was becoming weaker. He could tell that by the dragging movements of her mud-caked arms.

Cursing George, Saturn, and women who nosed around where they weren't wanted, Lanning hit out with renewed savagery, using every vestige of his immense strength. By degrees he began to gain, but he realized he had only the gradually ceasing mud-current to thank for it. The stuff was already congealing.

He reached the girl fifteen minutes later, as she was commencing to drag her labouring limbs up the stones of the cliff base. Catching up with her, Lanning grabbed her round the waist, dragged her a little distance, then set her down carefully.

"I'm sorry about that," he apologized. "It was George's fault, of course. Thank heaven you dropped feet first into the mud, otherwise—"

"I'd have been drowned," she finished quietly, sitting up and clawing the slimy mud disgustedly from her hair and skin. "Anyway, would that have mattered so much? After all, I'm here to run you in. You can get ten years on penal Jupiter for illicit trading. Remember that!"

"You can only get me to Green City of my own free will, Miss Tavistock. Your gun won't be any use after the mud bath."

With a start of alarm Lena yanked the weapon from her belt and fired it into the air. Nothing happened. With a rueful glance at the ruined charge-drum she threw the gun away.

"All right, Mr. Lanning, you win." She got to her feet and faced him steadily. Their eyes met—his curiously uncertain; hers completely unafraid. Then Lanning's gaze went up to the cleft high on the cliff face to the rear of the girl. For a brief instant he caught sight of a Minitor who had evidently been watching the proceedings.

"They seem very interested in us, don't they?" the girl asked. "How are the chances of staying with them until the mud solidifies and we can get away from this glorified desert island?"

"The chances are not so good." Lanning's face was grim. "I don't trust 'em, and never have done. They're like precocious children, and damned nasty ones at that! In fact—"

He broke off as there suddenly came the familiar piping voices of the little creatures. In another moment or two the cleft disgorged a horde of them. They came swarming down onto the shingle, chattering and laughing amongst themselves.

"They're armed!" Lanning exclaimed, with a start of surprise. "I wonder what the game is now?"

He and Lena stood waiting as the Minitors came up. The men were carrying spears in their hands, spears tipped with deadly ilifac poison, sap of the most lethal plant Saturn produced.

"What is this?" Lanning demanded, as the ring of the little men closed around Lena and himself; as the women, looking like dolls out of a Christmas store, kept at a watchful distance.

"Well, what is it?" he roared, as they were silent. "Come on, Lifican, let's have it!"

The boss of the seed pickers smiled innocently. His round, cherubic face was as baby-like as ever.

"Mister Lanning, sir, we want you\ You and the lady. To come to our valley. You will? Better, you know!"

"Are you threatening me?" Lanning demanded, clenching a big fist. "If you are, I'll—"

The ogling eyes widened in surprise. "No threaten. Just order. Ask you obey, please, sir."

Lanning glanced in bewilderment at the girl.

"Perhaps we'd better," she said; "though it's the first time I've had an invitation in the form of a poisoned spear!"

Lanning nodded. "Okay, Lifican, we'll come. But make it short. We've got to get away from here as quickly as possible."

Lifican beamed with satisfaction. Proudly he led his file of people up the shingle to the cleft, waving his poisoned spear like a bandleader as he went. The pass was only short, leading down into a wide valley filled to a great extent with the humble hut dwellings of the lazy little people, huts which were surrounded by neatly planted palisades of ordinary trees, with a carnivorous plant here and there for the consumption of carrion, waste, and unwanted foes.

When the centre of the valley was reached, Lifican called a halt. His people gathered around him. Lanning and the girl stood like Mr. and Mrs. Gulliver amidst them.

Lifican bowed politely. "Sir, Mr. Lanning, we have the honour to be avenged! You make us work in plantation, threaten my daylights with prompt bumpings if I do not work. So sorry, but you rule with iron rod and trouble plenty. We do not like that."

Lanning's eyes narrowed. "You blasted, traitorous little devil! So you think you need revenge for the way I've made you and your lazy tribe work, do you? And take that damned deceitful grin off your face!"

"I doubt if he can," Lena put in. "As I understand it, these people are differently constituted than us. They have only one visible emotion—childlike innocence. The rest of the emotions sort of boil up inside them. Something to do with their adrenal glands. They're underdeveloped so they can't express anger. We know already that their pituitary glands are almost nonexistent. That's why they're so tiny; So I've heard, anyway."

Lanning stared at her. "Yet knowing all this about them you

had the nerve to call me Simon Legree! As for you, Lifican, to blazes with you! Come on, Lena—on our way."

Lanning turned in vigorous contempt, but the little man made a quick movement. In response to it both Lanning and the girl found themselves suddenly smothered in the little people. Tiny though they were, there was an unbelievable power in their delicate-looking bodies and doll-like hands, begotten mainly of Saturn's rather heavy gravitation against which they were always labouring.

In the space of a few minutes the astounded Lanning found himself being carried by fifty of the men, and the girl by another thirty. When a corner of the clearing was gained they were hauled to their feet, their hands jerked over their heads, and then fastened by a length of tough creeper to the branch of a tree.

Lifican, at the forefront of his fellows, smiled again.

"So sorry," he apologized. "Tree a Titan-Bender. You know rest, Mr. Lanning, sir. No work hard no more."

He bowed, turned about, and marched off with his men and womenfolk towards the mile-distant abodes at the remote end of the palisade.

Lena twisted her face between her updrawn arms. "What— what did he mean by a Titan-Bender?"

Lanning came to the end of an underbreath of oaths. With a final glare after Lifican he turned to the girl as well as he could.

"It's a tree peculiar to Titan. I've seen it work and it's mighty weird. A carnivorous tree, of course."

Lena studied its drooping branches, in particular the one to which her wrists were fastened.

"Looks harmless enough," she said. "In fact I'd say it's asleep."

"That's just it. It is asleep. Listen, you've seen an Earth sunflower turn its face to follow the sun, haven't you?"

"Surely. What's the connection?"

"This tree's pretty similar. While the moon Titan is below the horizon this tree is limp and resistless—but once Titan rises it comes to life! Something to do with its origin, and maybe a botanist could explain it. The tree came in the first place by seed spores blown across space from Titan's Whispering Forest. On this world it starts to move and consume whatever living prey is near it at the moment Titan appears over the horizon. Clouds make no difference. Radiations from Titan stimulate its inner organs, just the same as the moon affects certain plants on Earth."

"Then it will attack us? Consume us?"

"That seems to be the prospect," Lanning admitted soberly. "It's just like those little devils to think of this. Torture and death rolled into one—and it took those china dolls to think of it! God, if only I could get my hands on them!"

The girl tugged furiously on the vine tethering her wrists. Lifting her feet from the ground she threw her whole weighted body into the effort—but it was no use. The vine only cut the deeper into her wrists.

Lanning tried too, with similar futility. Both of them desisted at last, breathing hard, surveying the twelve-inch length of vine, which separated them from the branch itself.

"No use," Lanning panted. "Let me think now...." He stared at the murky sky. "At the moment we have Iapetus and Ring light. That means Titan will be up in fifteen minutes or so."

"Fifteen minutes!"

Lena gave a gasp and waggled her cramped arms helplessly, staring with Lanning into the vari-lighted scum that was Saturn's perpetual sky. Then suddenly both of them twisted sharply at a faint cry.

"Hellish hot! Seed thief!"

"George!" Lanning yelled. "I'd forgotten him!"

He stared away towards the village. Typical of their race, now their task of revenge had apparently been accomplished, the treacherous Minitors were thinking no more about it. With their usual laziness they had retired to their huts, probably to eat and then fall into a prolonged state of torpor.

Lanning's eyes searched the sky with a feverish intensity, until at last he caught a glimpse of an unwieldy object like a high-flying ostrich.

"George!" he shouted desperately. "George! Come here. *Here!*"

The bird turned at the sound of his voice, and finally swept down in a flurry of wings and feathers. Alighting, it wasted precious seconds pecking at itself, then finally condescended to waddle forward.

"Wash your necks!" he screeched; then his amazing voice suddenly changed to gravelly bass and he added, "No sign of plantation. Where's Lanning? Damn, damn. Where's Lanning? Darn the mud!"

"That voice he's imitating!" Lena cried. "Where'd he get it, do you suppose?"

Lanning was looking puzzled. "I was just wondering the same thing. Matter of fact, it's the voice of my boss. No idea how George happened on it, though—"

"You mean the chief of the opius organization?"

"Yes—but that doesn't matter now. We've other things to worry about. Here, George! Come here, you brute. Nice birdie. Here.... *Here*, you pigeon head!"

Lena watched tensely as George fluttered up and down, Lanning issuing gentle orders, and then changing to plain abuse.

"Up!" he yelled. "Up! Come on— Papa's baby! Up...."

"Oke," George assented, and rose. His beady eyes shone in the pale, vague light as he listened to Lanning's desperate instructions.

"Down a bit— This way. Vine! Bite it! I said *bite* it, you blockhead! Come on!"

Lanning had to try again and again to make himself understood, but little by little the bird's subhuman intellect began to function. Finally it swooped triumphantly, snapped its scissor jaws together, and slashed through Lanning's vine with razor efficiency. Panting, Lanning dropped his leaden, aching arms. Then, ripping out his penknife, he cut the girl free.

"Thanks...," she whispered, nearly tumbling into his grasp. "That's a nicely educated bird you have there."

"Good going, George!" Lanning called. "Remind me to give you some extra sugar."

"Hellish hot," George observed, strutting around with tail outspread in a gaudy fan.

"We'd better get out of here," Lanning said, catching the girl's arm, and she nodded quickly.

They moved quickly through the shadows of the palisade, and even as they did so the Titan Bender behind then suddenly came to life. Its branches writhed weirdly against the scummy sky, continuing their eternal, horrifying search for edible things. Lena shuddered a little. There was something incredulously grotesque about this blind plant, which was a born killer.

"We only just got away with it," Lanning muttered. "George deserves a medal pinning on his ample chest. Here, sit down a bit. You look all in. This fallen tree here will make a rough seat."

Lena settled thankfully, massaging her still aching arms and contemplating the weird, vari-lighted sky. She was silent for such a long time that Lanning finally looked at her in puzzlement.

"Anything wrong? Feeling ill?"

"No thanks; I'm more or less all right. I'm just sort of puzzled. I'm thinking of the voice George imitated. That of your boss."

"What about it?"

"Obvious, isn't it? If your boss is around here somewhere, and apparently he is, I'll have to run him in along with you."

"You certainly take plenty on yourself for one gal, don't you? Any ideas as to how you'll run us in?"

"None. That's what's bothering me. I've no gun. I'll have to think of something."

Lanning gripped her arm encouragingly. "Then take your time about it, sweetheart. Frankly, though I don't want to sound too ungallant, I think you're plain crazy."

"Because I'm in the Space Service?"

"Yes. Women in the Space Service ought to wear number nine gumboots and have shoulders as broad as a man. You just don't—don't *fit* somehow."

"They're not all Amazons," the girl shrugged.

"Having seen you, I can believe it. There's another reason why you're crazy, though. You don't suppose for one moment that a slip of a girl like you, unarmed, could force a tough egg like me—to say nothing of my boss—all the way to Green City, do you? Forget it, Lena. Write us off. In *that* capacity, anyway."

"Admit failure?" Lena's eyes flared abruptly. "Not likely!"

Lanning grinned widely, which did not improve her temper particularly.

"Look here, Mr. Lanning, what do you mean by writing you off in *that* capacity? What other capacity is there?"

"Well, now.… You might try letting me make love to you for a change. That way you could react like a normal woman instead of kidding yourself you're an officer of the law."

"Huh!" Lanning saw her determined little chin elevate against the murky sky. "I should let a great hulking brute like you maul *me*! An illicit trader in drugs, at that."

"I've told you before, I'm only obeying orders! And less of the 'hulking brute,' if you please. If I were that I could have taken advantage of you long before this. Your five-foot-nothing against my six-foot-three wouldn't have availed you much."

"Let me tell you I'm five-feet-six! I have to be to get in the Service!"

Lanning sighed. "Must be my technique that's wrong. Moonlight is supposed to be ideal for romance, and on this planet there's moonlight and to spare. Yet you don't soften up any. All right, forget what I said. Seems a pity for a nice girl like you to be spoiling her natural charm, though."

"I've had enough of this," Lena declared flatly, and got to her feet. "Let's get out of here before the Minitors happen to spot us."

She turned away, indignation in her lithe movements. With a grin Lanning watched her go. Not a second later, however, her dignity was completely upset, literally, as she unwarily trod in the noose of a cotton-reel tree. Instantly the noose, actually the thin, whip-like vegetation of the tree, contracted with reflex action and Lena found herself whirled into the air, the mad landscape twisting wildly before her eyes.

Lanning, who had glanced away for a moment, stared in amazement when he saw what had happened. The girl was dangling helplessly by her right ankle, struggling to escape the other maze of awakened tendrils, which were writhing and uncoiling towards her.

Lanning moved—and fast. Though the cotton-reel tree was not to be compared to a Titan-Bender for carnivorous tendencies, it did nevertheless have terrific constricting power in its tendril branches. It had been known to crack a man's leg by sheer constriction alone.

"Get me out of here!" Lena shrieked, as Lanning blundered to the spot directly beneath her. "*Do* something!"

"Give me time," he panted, whipping out his knife and hacking first at the branches, which were twirling towards the girl.

One went—another—and as each one dropped, it lashed and twisted like a live wire.

"If I may say so," Lanning exclaimed, between gasps as he whirled down the vicious blade, "the expert of the Service is in a most undignified position! Since you're so well able to take care of yourself, why don't you get out of this one? Or do you prefer—" slash! "—the hulking brute to help you?"

"I—I take it back," Lena gasped quickly. "Honest I do! Get me down, quick!"

A tendril coiled relentlessly round Lanning's ankle. He swore savagely and stooped to deal with the coil—and in doing so he took his attention from a tendril near his knife hand. It lashed, tightened, and his knife dropped.

"Hell!" he exclaimed, staring at the undergrowth in the moonlight and striving to see the glitter of the knife blade.

"What's happened?" Lena demanded, in a frenzy.

Lanning made a mighty effort to drag his imprisoned arm free, but failed. He felt circulation ceasing as the awful branch began to constrict tighter and yet tighter. Numbness deadened his leg from the trailer round his ankle.

"I said, what's *wrong*?" Lena shouted, still twirling round upside down and striving to catch at something with her flailing hands. "Hurry up, can't you! I can't hang like this much longer—"

"I've lost the damned knife!" Lanning swore. "And this tree's got me pinned tighter than a vice—"

"Hot again, folks! Hellish hot!"

Lanning's remarks were cut off by a whirl of feathers in his face as George abruptly appeared with his affable greeting.

"George!" Lanning spat feathers out of his mouth. "Bite, boy! Good birdie! Bite vine overhead!"

"Plenty trouble!" George shrieked. "Hellish hot!"

"Call him, Lena," Lanning panted. "Get him to cut you down—"

"But what about you? You're pinned, aren't you—"

"Do as you're told, woman!" Lanning yelled, trying to disregard a third vine sneaking round his throat. "And prepare for the heck of a drop!"

"Nice birdie!" Lena coaxed, too dizzy by now to see straight. "Here, George. Come to mother—"

George flew upwards, perching himself finally on the girl's foot where the vine held it. Lanning watched intently as with his one remaining free hand he tugged savagely at the vine now sliding round his throat.

"Bite vine!" he yelled. "Bite!"

George bit, with the razor-keen abruptness common to him— and instantly Lena crashed downwards on top of Lanning. The impact did two things—it broke the girl's fall and probably saved her from serious injury, and it also flattened Lanning to the ground, producing a tremendous jerk that snapped the vines holding his neck and his right arm.

"The knife!" Lena exclaimed, dragging herself free. "It's here— I just saw it!"

She whipped it up out of the rooty undergrowth and slashed

at the tendrils holding Lanning's ankle. He stumbled free, clutching at the girl, and within moments they had got clear of the danger—but George had not been so lucky. It was his mighty screech, which must have been heard for miles, which caused the two to glance back. They could see him struggling frantically in the grip of the vine which had formerly held Lena's ankle. It was a truncated tendril, certainly, but still deadly because connected to the tree itself. And others had added their numbers.

"George!" Lena shouted in horror, and with the knife still in her hand she started to dash forward—but Lanning caught her arm and shook his head.

"No use, Lena," he muttered, his face taut. "We can't risk that tree again even if it *is* George—"

Lena gave a little shudder and turned away. Lanning put his arm about her shoulders and they deliberately turned their backs. Twice more George's despairing shrieks split the moonlight, and then there was silence.

"Why do such things have to happen?" Lena demanded, coming to a stop. "That bird saved us twice and all he gets for his trouble is to be killed himself! I'd developed quite an affection for him."

"Just the luck of the game," Lanning sighed. "On a planet like this you're alive one minute and dead the next.... And how are you feeling? None the worse?"

"Bruised, that's all. And I'll take care I don't wander into any more nooses like that one, too."

"It would seem," Lanning remarked, as they resumed their slow and cautious advance towards the main clearing, "that the lady officer of the law has become almost human, even if only for a few moments."

"I've had a fright," Lena said. "Maybe that's what did it—but it doesn't alter anything, you know. You're still a crook, and I'm still an officer of the law."

"You didn't look like one a moment or two ago. You were giving a fair imitation of a trapeze artiste!"

"Stop *ragging* me, can't you!"

With a grin Lanning subsided and they went on in silence for a while. Then the girl asked a question:

"What's the name of your boss? The one who's running this illegal racket."

"Davis. He operates from Green City. I told you that earlier."

"I just wanted to refresh my memory."

Lanning expected more, but he did not get it. By degrees they skirted around the back of the huts of the Minitors towards the foothills of the valley cliff.

"Does it signify that you know my boss's name?" Lanning asked presently.

"Not particularly.... I just wanted to be sure."

Lanning got the impression that the girl was deliberately holding something back, but he did not press the matter. Together they made their way along the valley side, keeping a good mile of distance between themselves and the huts of the Minitors. Unseen and unheard, they finally reached the pass. In a few more minutes they were through it.

"Whew!" Lanning whistled. "Thank heaven for that! We're safe enough now."

"I suppose," Lena asked slowly, "you wouldn't be man enough to come to Green City with me and cause no trouble?"

Lanning hesitated, searching her pretty, troubled face.

"Frankly, Lena, I'd go to the ends of the System with you, and enjoy every second of it—but when this particular jaunt would end in fifteen years on penal Jupiter, I'm not so keen. Afraid there is nothing doing.... All this serves the Service right, you know. They shouldn't have sent you out alone."

"They didn't. I had two men with me, but they were killed on the way here. A volcanic rock-fall got them. Two seconds later and I'd have been finished, too."

"Blessed two seconds," Lanning murmured, looking down at her.

Her shoulders rose and fell negatively in the soiled blouse.

"Well, I've only one course then—to go back to headquarters and report failure. And that means I'll be thrown out of the Service. Maybe it doesn't matter much, but I'd rather have retired honourably than be thrown out—"

She broke off in surprise at a booming voice.

"That you, Lanning? Why, so it is! Thank goodness I've found you! I thought you'd gone down in the mud-flood."

In the moonlight a heavily-built man of middle age accompanied by a dozen raft experts—Earthian past masters of negotiating rafts through Saturnian mud-flows—came slowly up, brushing drying mud from his white ducks.

"Mr. Davis," Lanning acknowledged cordially, extending his hand. "I'm mighty glad to see you, sir. Not that it's a surprise though. George gave advance warning."

Davis nodded. "You can thank George for my finding you. I heard him screeching in that unmistakable voice of his, so we headed in that direction. Had a bit of trouble getting here; mud was heavier than usual."

"But why all the trouble?" Lanning demanded. "Why take such a risk at mud-flow period?"

"Well worth the risk, my boy. You see, the Interplanetary Police have agreed to let opius seeds pass as legal merchandise from here on. Earth chemists have just discovered that they are the finest things out for producing a new form of anesthesia for severe operations—anesthesia that produces delightful dreams and leaves no hangover. Because of that, because we are the only two who own an opius plantation, and therefore have first rights, the charges against us have been dropped. Instead, I've a contract to produce as much of the stuff as possible."

"Why—why, that's terrific!" Lanning cried, doing a war dance. "No more scraping, no more—Lena! Do you hear?"

The girl turned from the shadows of the cliff wall and Davis glimpsed her for the first time in the pale light. He raised his hat.

"Hello there, Miss—er—I hadn't noticed you."

"Mr. Davis, Miss Tavistock," Lanning introduced. "She came to run us in, sir, but that's all washed up now by this new order. So you're safe after all, Lena. You can return with dignity to your job, without having to admit failure—"

He broke off in astonishment as Davis suddenly gave a shout.

"Great heavens, Mary, it's *you*! What in tarnation are you—"

"Yes, Dad, it's I," she assented simply, moving into his wide-flung arms. "Oh, Dad, I'm so glad your trading is—is legal. Otherwise I'd have to—"

"You mean to tell me you're a member of the Service?" Davis demanded. "Is that what you've been up to since you left Green City four years ago?"

Lena nodded slowly. "Yes, Dad. I got sick of Green City; it was too slow. I told you I was going on a trip round the System, and sent messages to that effect from various places. Instead I became Lena Tavistock of the Service. They assigned me to this job...."

Pausing, the girl turned to Lanning, "You see, when George used the voice of your boss, I knew it was father. That was a shock to me. My duty was to turn him in along with you—or else report it. To protect father I'd have to admit failure.... But now it's all different! I can return to Service headquarters with a clear conscience."

"And a fresh assignment?" Lanning queried gloomily.

"No. Resignation, without the stigma of failure. I'm getting tired of wandering, anyway. Besides, you're going to need help around here when the fresh opius sprouts.... You'll also need a woman around to look after the cooking department when you import good Earthian labour to take the place of the good-for-nothing Minitors."

"Trouble with them, eh?" Davis asked. "Well, I'm not surprised. I think you're right, Mary—"

He stopped. She was not listening. Lanning had swept her impulsively into his arms.

"There's only one way for you to be respectable and live with a plantation man," he said severely. "Now will you listen to romance in the moonlight—"

"Hellish hot! Hellish hot!"

Lena and Lanning both turned in amazement as that amazing

voice knifed in upon them. Then they both doubled in laughter, in which Davis joined them, as George abruptly landed nearby. Swearing volubly he waddled forward, every one of his feathers torn out and leaving him like a fowl ready for cooking. Evidently he had saved his life at the cost of his plumage.

"Hellish hot!" he repeated, screeching.

"Like that!" Lanning cried. "Hellish cold, more like it!"

MOON HEAVEN
BY DOM PASSANTE

FROM *SCIENCE FICTION* JUNE 1939

In his editorial in the October 1939 issue of *Science Fiction*
Charles Hornig wrote:

> "In our June issue we presented you with a nov-
> elette ("Moon Heaven" by Dom Passante) that you
> seemed to like very much—at least, most of those
> who have written in letters recently. In fact, that story
> was rated first in the issue, by popular vote. Well, I'm
> glad you liked it. Some of you commented upon the
> fact that the story was written in the masterful style
> of the late Stanley G. Weinbaum, which fact made the
> take so enjoyable. But if we gave you a magazine full
> of Weinbaum-type tales, every issue, I think you'd
> soon get tired of them—regardless of the fact that they
> would all be *good* science fiction, So if you like a vari-
> ety of good stories, I don't think you'll ever get tired of
> reading *Science Fiction*—because I try to get as much
> variety into one issue as possible...."

However, there was one English reader, G. B. Woolley, who
strongly dissented, and his letter appeared in the June 1940 issue, and Hornig's reply to this letter (under the heading WE
DON'T LIKE TO GLOAT, BUT—) gave me the solution of

the profound riddle of Fearn's 'Thornton Ayre' stories. Woolley had written:

> "It would be nice if you would keep stories like 'Moon Heaven' out of your so-called science fiction mag. That particularly disgusting specimen of American (it should be written american) writing just stank. You know, the English aren't always saying 'By Jove!' and they are a bloody sight tougher than their degenerate imitators, the Americans.
>
> "I should like you to publish a photo of Dom Passante for me to spit on. The English are the greatest nation on Earth. Heil, Chamberlain!
>
> "I'm sorry, but I had to get that off my chest. If other magazines can keep that sort of filth out, so can you. What's more, don't publish such childish mush.
>
> "I am going to read your magazine again, and keep it up unless it gets worse. You won't publish this—I forgot to say that Americans are cowards."

A number of points are relevant here. Woolley's outburst evidently came under the strain of the outbreak of the Second World War. (Fearn, of course, had actually written the story in 1937.) Whilst it was true that two of the English characters in the story are indeed deliberate parodies of "upper class English wasters," Woolley neglected to note that the *real* hero of the story was Betts—an archetypal *English* butler! Editor Hornig clearly enjoyed responding to this heated missive, writing:

> ("...Now about this international feud! I just can't resist informing you that 'Moon Heaven,' which you claim is so filthy and disgusting—though I'm at a loss to see where—was written by a bona-fide Englishman, who, to my knowledge, has never lived anywhere but in England. His real name is Frank Jones of 70 Portland Road, Blackpool, Lancs., England. He has

written scores of successful science fiction stories under a more famous pen-name. So you see, it wasn't an American—or american—specimen. Too bad you had to pick on this particular story!

"You know, some of our best authors and fans live in England—and some of our best critics—but never before has an Englishman written to a science fiction editor—to my knowledge—to say that American should be written 'american,' that we are degenerate imitators of the British, and that we are cowards. Of course, such comments are not fit for discussion in the public press, but I'm exposing you to any objections that other fans might care to make—and I miss my guess if a lot of your British brothers aren't amongst the most vociferous denouncers of your attitude.

"I am glad that you call Britain the greatest nation on Earth—that shows real patriotism, and I would be disappointed if you had not made that statement.

"I sincerely hope that you take on a more friendly attitude in the near future. And practice the science fiction quality of brotherly love. I wish we Americans and British could mix more frequently, in person. Eric Frank Russell, famous British fantasy author, visited this country last year and I am proud to have met him at that time. I think he enjoyed his visit.

"Oh, yes!—I am not printing this letter to prove that Americans are not cowards—but it is so strikingly different and original in theme that I couldn't miss out on the opportunity.—Editor.)"

Hornig's spirited defence was applauded by the magazine's readers in subsequent letter columns: in the January 1941 issue Ted White wrote:

"—ignore letters like the one you received from Woolley of England. He is a fool and a [censored] to make such rash statements without any reason. As a fellow Britisher, I apologize for him—if he hasn't got the guts to do it himself."

And in a long letter noted Canadian fan Leslie A Croutch wrote of Woolley's letter that it was one

"...which I think no right thinking American—and I say this as meaning every inhabitant of these American continents—should be weak-kneed enough as to let pass without some kind of comment. I refer, of course, to that particularly obnoxious communication of a certain Englishman, to wit, one G. B. Woolley. Really, Mr. Hornig, and fellow fans, I am surprised that anyone who reads science fiction could be so narrow-minded, cheap enough, as to write such an apparently infantile letter!"

What the incident *did* do, however, was to reveal Fearn's cunning methodology in trying to establish Thornton Ayre as an author other than himself, by using the name of Frank Jones and Geoff Medley's address.

However, by the time this story had appeared in print, Fearn had already decided (or perhaps been obliged by the imminence of war with Germany) to give up using Medley's address, and instead have 'Frank Jones' supposedly move into his own home, to live with Fearn and his widowed Mother. Of course, this was a complete invention, the real Frank Jones being no longer involved. Once this change of address became known, the suspicion of the SF fans and authors in London that Fearn was Ayre intensified—led by the always-suspicious Gillings.

Himself a Londoner, Bill Temple could not resist putting these rumours to Fearn in one of his letters in August 1939, which evoked this acerbic reply:

"The boys in London sure think up some pet excuses to account for Frank. I suppose if I was to stay with Hitler, they'd say I was Fearn and Hitler as well? Two guys can't live together without being one, is that it? Gillings met Frank three or four years ago in the Strand Palace Hotel, and Gottcliffe met him last year at my old Abbey Road address. What more do they want? It makes me sick."

Of course, Fearn's continued insistence that he was not Ayre was not just pique: he had very sound commercial reasons for maintaining the deception. It had effectively doubled his sales chances and income, on account of his consistently having two stories in the same issues of magazines—one as Ayre and one as himself or Polton Cross. The longer he could maintain the illusion of Ayre as a separate writer, the more money he could earn!

MOON HEAVEN

Brig Dean and Cynthia meet a mishap in space and are brought down upon Io, jungle-infested moon of the planet Jupiter! Besieged by the weird denizens of this alien world, what hope can they have for survival?

A meteor disables a small ship of the void and Brig Dean is forced to land his party on a wild, unexplored satellite! Bu their safety seems assured—until the primeval inhabitants begin to resent the presence of Earthmen!

CHAPTER I

Two pairs of worried eyes stared apprehensively at the fuel gauge; it was nearly down to zero. The giant rocket exhausts gasped and choked noisily over a fast-diminishing supply of explosive.

"It's that meteor bumping we got coming through the asteroid belt," panted Brig Dean, crack American space pilot, as he swung around from the control board. "I felt her jolt, but I never figured she'd had a crack on the jets. The power's leaking...."

"Well, don't stand there talking like a textbook!" wailed Cynthia Fowlie, flapping helplessly up and down in a sheath of green silk. "We're going to crash! Oh, why did I ever become engaged to an American spaceman? Why didn't I stop in London? Look—look! What's that?"

Her bejeweled white hand pointed through the window and her vivid blue eyes opened wide in alarmed surprise. She was a beautiful woman, and knew it; what she didn't know was that she was vain and exceedingly selfish....

Brig swung around with tight lips. His gray eyes were bright and hard.

"That's Jupiter," he growled; "and it makes it plenty bad, too. We can't escape his gravitational field with this leak. Our only course is to land on one of his moons—if we're lucky!"

"One of the moons!" Cynthia cried in horror. "But—but, Brig, what about my visiting father at the Uranian settlement? That's what we came on this journey for, wasn't it? To go to Uranus and get married?"

"Have to wait," Brig said briefly. He clamped strong hands down on the rocket controls. His eyes studied the whirling moons of Jupiter—Ganymede, Io, Europa, and Callisto. The other five didn't count; they were only derelict rocks, anyway.

"I guess Io's about the nearest," he muttered presently, and giving a lateral blast to the vessel, he swung it rather laboriously away from Jove's titanic field.

"It's our only chance," he went on. "We'll have to ditch for the time being and wait until a regular line vessel passes this way. Won't be more than a fortnight...."

Cynthia stared at the back of his black head for a moment, pushed aside an aluminum-colored lock of hair from her white forehead. Awkwardly, due to the ship's lurching, she went over to the figure lounging in the swinging armchair.

"Monty, what do we do?" she entreated, spreading her arms. "What do we do? We just can't land on this nasty old Jovian moon. Think of the wreck I'll look if we have to stay very long...! Me, the best-dressed woman in England."

The lounging figure, potential best man at the Uranian wedding, disentangled himself. Immaculately clad limbs took their right positions. Lemon-haired Lord Montgomery Stinson, chinless blue-eyed cousin of Cynthia, stood up—then promptly sat down again as Brig hurtled the spluttering vessel around in a curving arc.

"After all, Cyn, there isn't so deuced much I can do," he complained, wincing visibly at the sinking sensation in his stomach. "I mean to say, I don't dashed well understand how to run these confounded space things, anyhow. Come to think of it, it serves you right. If you'd taken an ordinary vessel—"

"And engaged to Brig Dean, crack space pilot!" Cynthia exclaimed, ashy pale with space-strain. "I couldn't do that, Monty. Besides, on an ordinary liner, I'd have to mix with the common rabble. Naturally, that's impossible!"

Monty stared around the control cabin uneasily; finally he looked at Brig's broad, hunched shoulders.

"I say, old fellow, did you say Io?"

"Yeah." Brig twisted momentarily. "Better swing onto something. We'll land in a minute—and pretty forcibly, I'm afraid. Our forward jets are dead...." He broke off and yelled, "Betts! Betts! Come here!"

A momentary silence as the ship hurtled towards the brilliantly gleaming Jovian moon—then a portly figure of medium height, attired rather incongruously in a morning suit, silently entered from the kitchen region of the vessel.

"Yes, sir?"

"Betts, we're going to land. In case of any mishaps, I want you to stand by and help me get all the valuables off the ship."

"Very good, sir. Io, I believe?"

"Right! Know anything about it?"

Betts' three chins quivered momentarily in pent-up pleasure.

His pale blue eyes became earnest.

"Quite a deal, Mr. Dean, if I may be permitted. I understand it is an outpost planet, useless as a trading center, therein differing from Ganymede, Callisto, and Europa, which are, of course, both trading and refueling centers. Io, I understand, turns one face to the primary, Jupiter, with the result that Io has been drawn into valley form on the side opposite Jupiter. In this valley, according to the tests of Murchinson and Snedley, sir—expedition in 2112, I believe—is a breathable atmosphere, ceasing at a height of five hundred feet and there becoming pure vacuum...."

"Nice going, Betts," Brig murmured, tense eyes fixed on the flying moon.

"Thank you, sir. There are other things. Io's gravity is a third of Earth's, and her solar revolution is forty-two hours or thereabouts.... Forgive me, sir. My interest in the moons of Jove rather carries me away at times."

"That's beastly clever of you, Betts," observed Monty, in wonderment. "Funny! To think my manservant knows all that!"

Betts turned deferentially. "The other details are none too clear, my lord. I understand that one Captain Rutter and his wife crashed here some twenty years ago and were never found. Subsequent explorers have found little on Io to commend it. It is a desert island of space, if I have your lordship's permission to use the phrase—"

"Get ready!" Brig interrupted curtly; and simultaneously the ship darted into what little atmosphere the non-Jovian side of the satellite possessed.

Brig stared below. The ship was leveling over a deep, fertile, jungle-infested valley, bathed in the triple lights of Europa, Ganymede, and the distant, disk-like Sun. The valley—drawn thus by the terrific pull of the primary—occupied an approximate half of Io, bounded on all sides by black, cruel mountains which skirted a vast rocky plateau bathed in the sullen green light of Jupiter himself.

There was no time to observe more. Brig held his breath as

the vessel plunged into the midst of the valley, landed with a crash that tore down trees, creepers, and plants in the rush.... There was a violent jolt and a long soggy thud—then the ship began to tremble and started sinking gradually.

Brig glanced out of the window.

"A swamp! We're sinking! Outside—quick!"

He picked the fallen, gasping Cynthia from the floor with consummate ease; she weighed very little in the third-normal gravity. Betts, his cumbersome body comfortable for once, was spinning the airlock screws. Monty rose up and uneasily adjusted rimless glasses.

"Sinking?" he repeated helplessly. "Oh, dear!"

Brig, all action, ignored him. He began snatching at all the light valuables he needed, crammed them into his pockets, his shirt, everywhere he could.

"Step on it, will you!" he yelled, as Monty and the girl looked dubiously outside on a steamy expanse of jungle. "Betts, give them a hand."

"With pleasure, sir."

He stepped outside and tested the ground and jumped back immediately. It was pure bog—nearly ordinary water. Dubiously, he studied the ground beyond; there it seemed to have solidity.

"Here, I'll try it," Brig said, looking with him. "Don't come until I tell you."

He stepped back a little, hugged his various valuables, then vaulted with all his strength. He cleared the bog with ease in the slight attraction, landed in lushy but quite supportable loam.

"O.K.!" he yelled. "Come on!"

There was a stir in the lopsided airlock. Cynthia flew towards him like five-foot-six of green ribbon. He caught her, set her down.... His Lordship dropped short and fell knee deep, floundered out with ruined trousers and revolted face. Betts was last, bearing in his arms the portable electrical equipment.

"It occurred to me, sir, we might need it—for signaling," he explained ambiguously, as he landed.

"Huh?" Brig puzzled, then he shrugged. "Mebbe. You'd

better come back with me. We've got to grab portable tents, spacesuits, and several things before the ship sinks. Let's go."

"Delighted, sir."

Time and again they vaulted back and forth over the morass, accomplishing leaps that would have been farcical on Earth.... Little by little they brought everything portable they could find; the slight attraction made heavy objects simple to carry—but at last it was no longer safe to venture. The vessel gave a heavy lurch, settled down, vanished in a slowly closing eddy of ocher bubbles.

"It would appear to have sunk, sir," Betts commented sadly, flattening back his thinning hair. "Most deplorable, if I may say so...."

Brig shrugged helplessly. "Eighty thousand dollars at the bottom of a morass. Thank Heaven it was a service machine and not backed by my own money."

"Have you got that much?" asked Monty affably. "Dash it, I thought you were marrying Cyn because you were broke—"

"Monty—you idiot!" she flamed, turning on him. "You know perfectly well it's love at first sight.... And in front of your servant, too!"

"I assure you, my lord, that your confidence will be respected," Betts murmured calmly.

"Considering we're the only people on this hell-fired moon, that's no news," Brig grunted. "As for my financial status, I *am* broke. So what? The market crash two years back saw to that.... I'll start over again somehow— But come on, let's get moving. We've got these tents to fix. Betts, you fix the props."

Betts moved with his newly found celerity. Cynthia flapped her white arms helplessly.

"But work, Brig, in this heat!" she protested, fanning herself. "After all, there are certain things a woman of position must remember, even here. Poise, deportment, and dignity. Suppose—suppose my makeup were to become smeared?" she wound up in horror.

"It probably will," Brig assured her laconically, pegging down the tent poles as Betts held them. "Temperature here is far over a hundred degrees; makes Central Africa feel like an icebox. It's solar heat and Io's internal warmth that's responsible. The rest of Io will be void-cold. Jupiter's no use for heat...."

Monty tore off his coat impatiently, laid it reverently with the rest of the equipment.

"May as well help, I suppose," he grumbled; "but I regard it as a damned insult. A slur on the traditions of the Stinsons. Ducal halls—and things."

"Forget your ducal halls and grab the rope," Brig grunted. "Cyn, hold this canvas—That's it. Now we're going places."

CHAPTER II

In two hours a makeshift camp had been erected, split up into sleeping quarters, cooking tent, general and dining tent. Betts came to the rescue with a meal from tins warmed over the electric heater.

During this period, the lights shifted somewhat. Ganymede had set, but Callisto had risen. The Sun had not changed position very much. Since Io takes forty-two hours to revolve, its solar day is roughly twice as long as an Earthly one.

After the meal, Brig went to the tent door and looked around him. The jungle seemed peculiarly silent—a jungle made up of trees and plants totally foreign to his spatial knowledge. It had about it a certain odd, attractive beauty. Its principal trees were feathery, palm-like creations, bolstered around their boles with thick, vividly-hued verdure.

Struck with a sudden thought, he turned back into the tent, regarded Betts as he removed the remains of the meal,

"Betts, I believe you said something about a signal? What were you driving at?"

"Well, sir, it occurred to me that on the Jovian side of this moon there will probably be carbon. If we could obtain two sticks or pencils of the substance, fix them in our electric equipment, and break the electric current at the points of the carbon, we would have an extremely brilliant signal—in truth a carbon arc. No ship could fail to observe it."

Brig nodded slowly. "You've got something there, Betts.... Seems to me you're something of a scientist."

Betts smiled humbly. "Forgive my saying so, sir, but the well-trained servant is the master of many vocations.... I would like to add, I would be willing to accompany you to the plateau in search of carbon."

"So you shall, when we've had a night's rest. In the meantime I don't think it would be a bad idea to see what sort of a jungle we're in. How about an expedition?"

"Too hot," groaned Monty. "The work with the tents has left me a mess of bally nerves."

"I'll come," Cynthia volunteered, rising languidly. "I may be able to find something to use for make-up. My compact went down with the ship." Brig shrugged, turned to Betts, "You'd better come too. We don't know what we may find and the more there are of us—"

"Exactly, sir. Ray guns, of course?"

"Yes, right away."

"I might as well come," Monty broke in, rising hurriedly. "I wish you didn't have to be so energetic, though...."

Brig didn't answer him. Betts reappeared in the tent with four ray guns and the party moved out into the clearing, entered the jungle's steamy, lacy folds.

Monty grumbled perpetually; Cynthia floundered on high heels and bewailed the rents that were being torn in her silken gown.

"You ought to wear shorts," Brig remarked dryly. "There are some in the clothing equipment back at the tent. And flat shoes."

"Shorts!" she echoed, horrified. "Me? Good Lord, do you think I'm a common woman pilot, or something?"

"No, but this is 2130 and it's time you behaved with sense," Brig growled. "I can't make you out, Cyn; our landing here has shown me lots of things I'd never have thought were possible in your make-up—"

"Because you're a penniless space pilot, a space trotter who's always looking for a perfect place to live, doesn't give you the right to insult me!" she said hotly. "Sometimes I wonder what I ever saw in you to—"

"Oh, skip it," Brig sighed wearily. "Come on."

He turned to advance, but Cynthia stopped suddenly and looked up in surprise. "What's that?" she whispered.

The others looked above. Brig stared in wonderment at something quivering in the tree branch just over their heads—then suddenly Betts hurtled forward, clutched the girl around the waist in a flying tackle, and bore her to the ground.

Instantly the others fell back, stared in frozen horror at a snake-like object that had abruptly hurtled forward with bullet swiftness and imbedded itself in the tree beside them. It quivered spasmodically, died from the sheer impact of collision.

Brig stared at is in horror. It was a pure ropy organism, bounded with incredibly powerful muscles.

Betts floundered to his feet and dragged the gasping Cynthia up beside him.

"Pardon my roughness, miss," he apologized. "That object is an Ionian impaler, or more technically, *Impalia diaboli*. It usually kills its prey by behaving like a living javelin—buries its head inside its prey and kills it, absorbing nourishment at the same time. A flesh eater, obviously. If it misses...." He glanced significantly at the dead organism.

"Thank God you recognized it in time," Brig whispered. "How'd you ever come to know about it?"

"Quite simple, sir. I have read the copious notes of Murchinson and Snedley, wherein it is mentioned. There are other things.... Really, sir, Io interests me immensely. Shall we proceed?"

"I'm not too sure," muttered Monty. "Suppose another of these things attacks us?"

"If we keep alert, my lord, we can always dodge them."

"Let's go," Brig said, taking Cynthia's arm.

They resumed their progress, hardly realizing how subtly

their positions had reversed. Betts, though still a servant in essence, had in truth become the leader of the party. His unexpected knowledge of things Ionian had elevated him considerably.

The fantastic wonder of the place held the party silent, for the most part. They were accustomed by now to the intense, cloying heat and lighter gravity—but what they were not used to was the constant shift of lights as the moons went across the sky, outstripping the slower-moving Sun. Everything had three shadows, the constant changing of which formed sinister patterns at times.

"I say, just a minute!" Monty exclaimed, stopping. "What's this?"

He came forward from the rear, holding up a corroded object with an inlaid pearl handle. Most of the pearl had fallen away; the whole thing was near to collapsing in rust—but what was left of it was plainly distinguishable as a hunting knife.

"Where'd you find it?" Brig demanded, studying it.

"Back on the trail there; I kicked against it. Somebody's been here, what?"

"Yeah, but a mighty long time ago."

Betts hovered up, took it courteously—studied it.

"I believe it must have belonged to Captain and Mrs. Rutter," he said slowly. "You notice, my lord, it is the early-type knife in use twenty years ago. The later explorers did not use knives of this type—Murchinson and Snedley, for instance. This trail, then, must once have been traversed by the long-dead Rutters."

He tossed the relic to the ground, dusted his plump fingers.

"So be it, then. I often wondered what happened to the Rutters. They—"

He broke off and turned at a sudden crackling of branches nearby. Immediately he and Brig whipped out their ray guns, then lowered them at the odd, fantastic little creature that hopped into the clearing.

It was perhaps eighteen inches tall, moving with the gait of a baby ape, its face astonishingly like that of a pathetic human child. As it advanced, it chattered and whimpered, began to clutch Brigg's leg imploringly.

"Well, old man, what's the matter?" He heaved it up and studied it, stroking it gently. It was clearly frightened.

Betts cleared his throat. "A baby manape, sir—a curious kind of hybrid, cross between man and ape with an almost human intellect. Rather treacherous when full grown, I believe."

"Let me have him!" Cynthia begged, cuddling the soft, hairy body in her arms. "He's just too sweet! I'm going to make him my pet; I've so missed poor Pogo since we left Earth."

"Pogo?" Brig hazarded; then he remembered. "Oh, that Pekingese of yours!"

"Don't you think we'd better stagger back?" suggested Monty nervously. "I mean to say, apes and snakes and things. We might meet a dinosaur or something...."

Brig nodded. "O.K., we'll go back. We've seen enough...."

Turning, they began to retrace their steps. As they went, they could hear the strange sounds of the champagne flitters—or, in modern American, the 'pop and bubble' birds—odd, fast moving specimens resembling storks, with a chirping note like the pulling of the cork and subsequent pouring of champagne.

In temperament they were akin to moths singeing their wings—but instead of seeking flame, the flitters chose to rise to the airless heights fringing the valley, there to commit suicide in the ghastly cold sweeping in from the little world's Jovian side.

Once they regained camp, the party retired, exhausted with the heat and their activities. Cynthia took her new-found pet to her tent with her, doting over it with almost sickly intensity. By the time she had finished fussing with it, the camp was quiet.

She turned and switched off the portable lamp; the lights of the moons and sinking sun moved slowly across the roughly canvased floor. Abruptly, she turned as the tent flap opened. Monty came in slowly, fully dressed in his mud-stained suit, cigarette smoking lazily between his lips.

"Y'know, Cyn, it's all very idiotic," he complained, sitting on the edge of the bed.

"What is?" She stared at him in surprise in the twilight.

"Your marrying Brig—when we get to Uranus. What do you want to do it for? Hang it all, he's admitted he has no money— and I'm darn sure you don't love him. So, why do it? I'd marry you tomorrow if you'd have me."

"I know, Monty—but if I did that, I wouldn't have nearly so much money as I shall get if I marry Brig. You know, of course, that father's fortune is far larger than yours?"

"Of course, but—"

"Well, when father dies, I shall get the lot, providing I marry Brig, together with a handsome yearly allowance while he lives. Simple, isn't it? Dad dotes on Brig because he's the ace pilot of the spaceways, and since father is himself chief of that organization, I just can't help myself.… You do understand, Monty, don't you?"

"I suppose so. You don't love him, do you?"

"Who could? He's all brawn.… Not like you—"

Cynthia paused in mid-sentence and stared through the gauzy wall of the tent. Something was moving in the shifting lights. Monty stared with her, gulped audibly.

Then something came into fuller view, followed by others— stooping, shaggy forms moving forward slowly, muttering and chanting strangely among themselves.

"Apes!" Cynthia screamed suddenly, clapping a hand to her mouth. "Monty! They're apes!"

He blinked stupidly, uncertain as to what to do—then, as the shambling figures came nearer, he jumped to his feet, intending to head for the interconnecting tent flap joining the other. The lesser gravity tripped him up. By the time he was on his feet, Brig and Betts had appeared, drawn by the girl's cry.

"What's the matter, Cyn?" Brig strode over to her after a mere passing glance at Monty. Betts blocked the inter-flap.

"Apes!" she faltered. "L-look!"

"Manapes, miss," Betts corrected, gazing at them. "Unless I am very much mistaken, they are looking for this little lost one on the bed here. It may mean trouble if we don't give it back."

Brig studied the growing circle of creatures with worried eyes. They were surrounding the entire camp, evidently not only intent on rescuing their lost baby, but on exacting vengeance for his theft also.

Reaching backwards, Brig grabbed the little creature from the bed, flung the tent flap to one side and dropped the baby, whimpering, outside. There was a concerted rush towards it. He watched tensely.

"I ought not to have let you bring it," he muttered. "I might have known the parents and tribe would come after it—just like lions or tigers do.... Trouble is, these things are more brainy than lions and tigers. They might do anything."

Betts disappeared through the inter-door. He returned with four ray guns and handed them around.

"I—I don't know how to use these things," Cynthia wailed, fingering it gingerly. "I didn't know how when we were in the jungle, either. Oh, Brig, I—"

"Shut up!" he hissed. "They'll hear you!"

He was right. With menacing care, the manapes, reinforced now by others from the jungle, closed their circle towards the tents. Every detail of their subhuman faces and hairy bodies became distinctly visible in the changing lights.

"Get ready for a fight," Brig muttered, dropping to one knee to steady his intended aim. "Betts—Monty, down beside me. Cyn, stay on the bed. You may be safer...."

She was crying now, frightened out of her wits. Monty fidgeted with his gun, swore limpidly.

Brig and Betts both tensed, their eyes bright and hard, guns ready as the packed creatures reached the gauzy tent wall; the sound of their labored breathing became distinctly audible—

Then something inexplicable happened. There was a brief sound, almost like the merry laugh of a woman, and it was followed almost immediately by a whirring, buzz-saw note like a horde of bees pouring from a hive. The pale light of the setting sun and the scurrying moons was dimmed by a sudden swirling bit of cloud. The buzzing grew louder.... The twilight dimmed to almost pitch darkness.

"Look, sir!" Betts whispered. "Millions of insects!"

Brig nodded helplessly and got to his feet. He stared out on the disorganized mob of manapes. They were writhing and twisting as though in the grip of something devastatingly ticklish. They were laughing! Actually laughing with uncannily human tones, and the more they were smothered in the whirling cloud of zipping, darting insects, the more they laughed!

They doubled up in insane mirth. The clearing became a mass of hysterical pandemonium, male and female manapes alike rolling over and over on the ground, bellowing until it seemed their lungs would burst.

"What in Heavens' name happened?" Brig gasped, astounded. "Betts, do you know?"

He slid swiftly to the outer flap and gently drew it aside. Instantly, he jerked back as a cloud of the insects came whizzing in like a multitude of wasps.

"Most careless of me, sir!" he panted. "I—I just wanted to make sure. They're laughing bugs, sir...." He brushed them off frantically as they stung his face and hands. "Keep clear of them if you can—"

That was impossible. The things were everywhere. They smothered the screaming Cynthia in one solid cloud, left her gasping and gurgling with revolted horror; then they swept across to Monty and enveloped him—and quickly moved on to Brig.

He felt an extraordinary sensation surge through him; it felt like a dentist's laughing gas.... But this was no nitrous oxide; it was a sudden change in brain sensations. He was prompted by an ungovernable desire to laugh—laugh insanely...for no reason!

Betts' face merged up in the half-light like a kid's balloon, grinning from ear to ear.

"Hysteria termite, sir," he gasped out, fighting for control. "Harmless, but its sting poisons the blood stream—produces a spurious energy and needless merriment. I remember....

Murchinson and Snedley were bitten. Page six, sir, if I remember, of volume one.... Ha-ha! Pardon me! Io and Insects, sir.... Safe enough from manapes, sir, though I don't know how they came so conveniently.... Bugs, I mean., Ha-ha! Ha— Pardon me!"

With a gulp, Betts floundered outside into the clearing, unable to control himself any longer. He mingled with the manapes, but like him, they were too convulsed with laughter to attack him. He was laughing, peal upon peal. He blundered out of Brig's sight.

Brig swung round, still holding onto the threads of control. He went across to the hysterically giggling Cynthia and caught her slim shoulders tightly.

"Cyn, shut up!" he shouted hoarsely. "Control yourself; You've been bitten by—Cyn, please!"

She only yelled the louder, tears streaming down her cheeks. He shook her until the hair tumbled in front of her face; he struck her sharply across both cheeks, but it made no difference. Finally he left her coiled up in paroxysms of merriment.

It was the same with Monty. He lay on the floor, rolling over and over, breathless with hysteria.... Brig breathed hard, felt himself slipping. The next thing he knew, he too had burst into peal upon peal of gusty laughter. He felt as though nothing in the world mattered.

Shakily, quaking with mirth, he clawed his way into the adjoining living tent and sat down, trying vainly to recover control. He laughed so much that it hurt; and as the queer poison of the zipping laughing bugs worked deeper into his system, he began to lose all consciousness of his surroundings.

CHAPTER III

Brig became suddenly aware that his head ached, that he was shaking like a leaf. He opened his eyes and peered around the tent. Monty and Cynthia were there, slumped into portable chairs, breathing hard, utterly disheveled and overcome with reaction.

Outside the tent there was stillness. Sunlight had disappeared, but Europa, Ganymede, and Callisto compensated for the loss.

Brig stirred stiffly. "Whew! What a hangover!"

Wincing, he got to his feet. He was damp with sweat. Vainly he tried to piece together the intervening hours—or minutes, but with no success. The hysteria had gone now, but the reaction was terrific.… Moving across to the kit, he jerked out a bottle of restorative, forced it down his throat. Then he revived Monty and the girl. Groaning, they sat up.

Cynthia, pale and perspiring, looked up with lackluster eyes.

"Brig, what happened?" she asked dully; and briefly he told her.

"Betts!" called Monty wearily. "Betts, where are you? Come here.…"

"He went out into the jungle," Brig told him. "So far, he hasn't come back. I guess I'd better go out and find him."

He turned towards the tent door, mastering his shaking limbs, but at the same instant, Betts came slowly through it. His thin hair was draped over his forehead, his clothes were torn and filthy. Under one arm he carried something like a pink melon.

Unsteadily, he made his way to the center of the tent, the eyes of the others following him in amazement. Reverently he laid the melon down. Only then did it become evident that it was alive! A living organism with a vast, distended mouth gaping weirdly.

"Ohhh!" Cynthia yelped in horror, leaping up; then she sat down again as her head spun like a top.

"B-Betts, take—take that horrible thing away at once!"

"Never knew anything like it," Betts muttered uncertainly, passing a hand over his brow. "Woman.… Laughter.… Now this!" He raised a plump finger significantly to his lips, and whispered, "Sssh! Listen to this!" Then, swinging around to the melon, he barked, "What is two and two?"

"Four!" the melon answered promptly, in a husky voice.

Brig's eyes popped. Cynthia and Monty stared at each other like a couple of drunks.

"Then, Heaven be praised, I am not intoxicated!" Betts breathed in relief. "It does talk! I'm plain, cold sober!" Standing erect, he tried to regain his dignity, but like the ethers he was still quaking from the hysteria's reaction.

Brig strode across. "Look here, what is this?" he demanded, staring at the thing that was devoid of eyes, ears, and nose—that was all mouth and nothing more. "Where'd you get this? Did it actually say 'Four' just now, or do you include ventriloquism among your accomplishments?"

"This, sir, is a true native of Io," Betts observed stiffly. "It is made up of carbohydrates, and consumes carbohydrates for nourishment. Normally we are wont to call carbohydrates sugar, starch, and so forth—but you must admit they can exist in minute quantities in the air—especially here. The invisible mites which are constantly swarming into its mouth are of carbohydrate basis."

"But this thing's a fruit!" Brig yelled.

"No, sir—forgive me. It is carbon, developed along human lines. You notice the absence of chlorophyll, the green substance by which plants break down inorganic matter and so build up organic matter from the simplest constituents. If this were a true plant, it would be green. It is protoplasmic, cellular—carbon, sir! I am given to understand that it is only part of a parent tree, but can live quite comfortably by itself."

"Yeah?" Brig was still gaping.

"It is intelligent. It reasons. It talks by impressing sound waves on the air from its interior bladder; those sound waves resemble human words. Is that so strange, sir? A good musician can make his violin closely imitate a human voice by producing the right sound waves.... Most bizarre, sir—most bizarre!"

Brig came to himself suddenly.

"But where the devil did you get the thing?" he demanded.

"She gave it to me, sir. I met her in the jungle.... A most

delightful young lady. Quite educated, too."

"Young lady! Jungle!" Brig gulped. "What the devil are you talking about?"

Cynthia and Monty got out of their chairs and came closer, staring at Betts wonderingly. He didn't seem very certain of himself.

"When I was laughing, sir—for which I shall never forgive myself—I blundered into the jungle. I came face to face with a young woman, very...ahem!...lightly clad. She gave me a weed of some kind that stopped my laughing. She was carrying this—er—organism under her arm and, after a while, gave it to me. Then she told me all about its origin and life. Finally she suggested we listen very carefully to what it had to say...."

Betts stopped and cast his eyes roofwards. "I wonder, sir, if I dreamed it?"

"You bet you did!" Brig snapped.

"The organism is real enough, but the girl—! Hang it all. Betts! And her talking in English, too! The thing's impossible."

"Maybe, sir; I'm still not too sure."

Brig shrugged. "Well, anyway, we've no time now to bother about your dreams. You'd better scramble some breakfast together—if it is breakfast, that is. We've got to head for the Jove side and collect those carbon pencils. The sooner we get out of this nutty place, the better I'll like it."

"Very good, sir." Shaking his head doubtfully, Betts went outside to the cooking tent.

In silence, Brig studied the mouthy object, and the more closely he studied it, the more it became apparent that it was palpitating slowly with life energy. Its mouth, too, was a mass of fine hairs, evidently flawlessly designed for catching invisible aerial miles and retaining them.

"Two and two?" he questioned suddenly.

"Four," came the prompt answer, but the mouth didn't move. The sound came from inside.

"It's a trick," muttered Monty disgustedly. "Betts must have been drunk and fashioned this thing. Break it open and see what makes it tick—"

"It's no trick," Brig interrupted, shaking his head. "The thing is quite intelligent I'm not overly surprised. After all, there's some plant on Titan that's a natural singer. This isn't so queer.... What's your name?" he finished suddenly.

"Jack Horner. Sit in the corner, eating curds and whey."

"But—but he didn't!" Cynthia said, thinking. "It was Bo-Peep, or somebody...."

"It was Miss Muffet, darling," Monty said patiently.

Brig raised his eyebrows. "Darling, huh? Nice going for a best man...." His lips tightened a little as he turned back to the thing.

"Jack Horner, eh? Anything else?"

"A stands for Atmosphere, not very much here; but if you stop in the valley you've nothing to fear. B stands for—"

"All right, all right," Brig interrupted hastily; and he turned aside, pondering. "Where the devil did this thing pick up such nursery rhymes?" he asked blankly. "Somebody's taught it them, and with a modern flavor, too."

"Perhaps there *was* a woman," Cynthia suggested, languidly.

"But, Cyn, it is so absurd! What woman could there be here, in a crackpot place like this, who'd teach a melon nursery rhymes? The thing's idiotic. Besides—"

"C is for Carbon in so many forms, Io is full of it, life simply spawns," Jack Horner observed. "D is for diamond, which is carbon quite true, money and fortune for me and for you."

"What's that?" Cynthia asked abruptly, gazing alertly.

"He's right," Brig murmured. "Diamonds are pure carbon. It never occurred to me that—"

"There may be something in it, sir," Betts remarked, as he came in with a loaded tray. "I heard Mr. Horner's last words. Possibly there are diamonds in plenty on the Jove side of this globe. It would seem the young lady's request that we listen to Mr. Horner's observations was quite significant."

"You still believe you saw her, don't you?" Brig smiled.

"I do lean to the view, sir, yes. My father suffered from

delusions through excess of alcohol, but acquired traits are not inheritable. Therefore, I did not suffer from delusions."

"Sound reasoning," Brig grinned; then he became serious. "Guess I could do with a handful of diamonds at that. Might repair my shattered fortunes."

"Come to think of it, so could I," murmured Cynthia, giving her brain unaccustomed hard work. "I mean to say, one can be quite independent of parental wishes if one has a private fortune, can't one?"

Monty's eyes brightened at the hidden cunning in her voice.

"By gad, rather! Deuced good, Cyn—deuced good."

Brig regarded them in puzzlement for a moment, then turned back to Betts.

"The minute we're through with this meal, we'll head for the Jove side—all of us. We've enough spacesuits."

"Very good, sir."

Cynthia snickered, "Suits me! I've always wanted to see a diamond naked, so to speak...."

An hour later, encased in clumsy, heavy-booted spacesuits, the four headed away from the clearing towards the valley side two miles distant. Save for occasional encounters with swamp region, and less frequently with the savage impalers, they made the trip without mishap. Then began the long, arduous climb to the five hundred foot summit of the valley side.

Never before had they quite realized the oddity of this world. This valley, drawn by the terrific pull of Jupiter, contained all the air the satellite possessed. At a 250-foot height, it thinned out perceptibly—nothing could live long in it, save perhaps the suicidal champagne flitters.

At 300 feet the air was dehydrated; at 500 feet it was almost a vacuum....

Here, at the summit of the valley, the hot, steamy blue-black sky had become replaced by the virgin, soulless black of space, in which the neighboring moons and newly-risen sun hung with savage brilliance. The further the party moved beyond the valley summit, the lower the sun sank, and the higher vast

Jupiter poked himself over the opposite horizon.

At last they gained the broad, black-dusted plateau itself. Here, Jupiter was pouring forth his complete complement of yellow light, but according to the thermopile, hardly a trace of heat

"Pressure almost zero, sir," Betts remarked, consulting the portable instruments he was carrying. "There is a faint trace of warmth, of nearly non-existent atmosphere. The former obviously comes from Jupiter's cold disk, and the latter is a surplus from the valley...."

"Rather scary, isn't it?" muttered Cynthia, switching on her electric audiophone. "I almost wish we hadn't come."

"You can return if you want," Brig answered briefly, and he smiled a little at her expression behind the glass helmet. Incongruously enough, he suddenly wondered why the devil Monty had been with her in her tent the previous night. Silly thought!

Betts came up, unslung electrical equipment from his bloated shoulders.

"I've just been looking around, sir. Things are pretty much as Mr. Horner intimated, and also as I suspected. This side of the satellite is mainly carbon—in various modifications. There are also traces of carbon dioxide gas collected here and there, probably left behind from the time when Jupiter was at its hottest and thereby produced a considerable amount of carbon combustion. Here, sir, is the residue....."

His massive boot stirred dusty black crystals that faintly caught the light of Jove. Brig watched keenly.

"Guess it might explain Io's relatively high albedo," he remarked. "These things do reflect quite a deal of light."

"Undoubtedly, sir. May I call your attention to that?"

His arm pointed to a small black cliff nearby, riddled with cave entrances, fronted again by massive coal-black boulders.

"Natural carbon cliff!" Brig whistled. "Come on...."

He started the advance with Betts beside him. Once they gained the cave, Betts stepped forward and snapped off two of the thousands of carbon stalactites depending from the cave entrance. With considerable difficulty, he fixed them into the roughly designed clamps of the small electric motor he carried.

"I would advise looking away, sir," he warned, fixing the battery terminals. "Now…let us see."

He moved the small switch that operated the storage battery; almost instantly the separated carbon pencils flared into blinding life at their tips, created entirely by the resistance between them to the passage of current.

Betts fumbled for the switch; snapped it off. He stared at the dying red glow of the carbon points.

"That's terrific!" Brig cried, clutching him eagerly. "Nice going, Betts! No ship can possibly miss a signal of that brilliance.… Of course, it will mean somebody having to stay here to give the signal when a ship is sighted."

"No, sir; forgive me. I have a timetable of the Earth-Pluto space service, and I have also kept a careful check of Earth hours since we arrived here. The next liner is due to pass near here in about four earth days. Therefore, a little in advance of that time, one of us will come here and give the signal."

"Four more days in this ghastly place," groaned Cynthia. "I wish to Heaven space travel had never been invented.… Incidentally," she went on, with sudden keenness, "what about those diamonds? I don't see any."

"I fancy those rocks, miss…," Betts murmured, and turning about, he headed towards the massive boulders fronting the cave entrance. For a while, he studied them in silence in the Jove light, then, removing his ax began to hack steadily. Three heavy chunks fell off into his glove.

"Wealth, beyond imagination," he murmured, his face beatific behind the glass. "These rocks are pure diamonds.… Pure carbon without a trace of impurity."

"You—you mean these entire rocks are diamonds?" babbled Monty hysterically.

"Yes, my lord."

"Then why the devil hasn't somebody collected them before

this?" demanded Brig. "Untold wealth lying here.... It just isn't possible."

"Possibly there are two reasons, sir. For one thing, the dark side of Io has never been explored—not even by Murchinson and Snedley. For another, it is doubtful if anybody untrained in the various forms of carbon would recognize this stuff as pure diamond in the unfinished state. Again, visitors are very few and far between here. The pull of Jove is—"

"O.K., never mind that," Brig interrupted. "We've found them and I guess that's all that matters. Come on, let's get the bags filled."

The two capacious bags were opened up, Cynthia taking on the job of holding them open whilst the rock chippings were dropped into them. Her blue eyes went wider behind the glass every time she saw one fall. Her brain was no longer made up of cells but of surging dollar signs....

When at last both bags were filled, Betts put his ax away with a sigh of content.

"The value is, of course, incalculable," he breathed; "and since we are joint discoverers, the claim will be filed both in the United States and Britain—"

He broke off in surprise as Cynthia suddenly gave a violent jerk, a vigorous movement, and waved her arms wildly. She began to kick desperately.

"Call them off!" she screamed frantically. "Call them off!"

It was immediately apparent what was the matter.... So absorbed had they all been in their collecting efforts, they had failed to notice a small army of curious, dull gray objects, not unlike fast moving tortoises, gathered around them. Now, governed by sheer curiosity, they were crawling over the boots of the party. It needed no imagination to realize they had come from the depths of the carbon cave.

"Life, here! In a vacuum!" cried Brig, threshing his boots wildly. "How the devil—"

"Carbon life, sir," Betts said, struggling hard to keep the things from puncturing his spacesuit. "No—not so improbable....

Carbon is the element on which all life is built.... Remember, sir, that the carbon atom forms the basis of an unlimited number of compounds. Its atoms can form long chains, but these are the skeletons to which other life, of infinite complication, attaches itself.... Here, apparently, carbon has taken a form rare to our knowledge, but by no means outside probability. Maybe a formation of pure carbon, unconnected with any higher form. Carbon life, eating pure carbon, naturally— Damn! Pardon me, sir. I thought my spacesuit was nearly through."

"We've got to get out of here," Brig panted, swinging around. Then he gave a cry. Cynthia and Monty were already well away from the things, were rushing towards the edge of the plateau leading down to the valley.

"Hey!" Brig yelled frantically. "Come back here! Give us a hand!"

"I'll get them, sir."

Betts dashed off after them, and Brig made to follow his leaping floating form.... But in that he was too energetic; the toe of his heavy boot stubbed against one of the things, and he went sprawling. Before he could rise, they were swarming over him actively, tiny little scissor-like mouths working industriously on the fine metal of his spacesuit.

Carbon, of course! It suddenly dawned on him. The metal of his suit had a carbon basis, mixed with innumerable other compounds. Probably the stuff was appetizing to them, something they had never known before. Whatever it was, they refused to be shaken free. As fast as he dusted them off, they came back again. His horrified eyes stared at growing dents and pockmarks.

He whirled round, determined to make a frantic effort to reach the plateau edge—but at that identical moment, the thing he most feared happened. Viciously sharp teeth plowed clean through the mesh, punctured his only protection against the airless void.

Instantly the pressure inside his suit ripped the tooth-hole open wide; air gushed mistily out and evaporated. He fell blindly on his knees, ready for instant death. He gasped chokingly as the air left his lungs. Blood oozed from his nostrils, hammered in his ears and smarting eyes.

He fell flat, aware of a terrific sense of inner pressures, of sudden violent near-apoplexy. He fought and struggled for the air that wasn't there, lay with his suit now flattened to his figure, trying to understand why he still felt warm in this utter emptiness.

Where the devil was Betts? Silly thought now, as he was dying,

He stared through tortured eyes, felt his senses swimming with the absence of life-giving oxygen. Then he saw something that for a split second summoned a vague stir of life back to his brain.

A woman! A woman almost unclothed, save for a fabric of some kind around breast and hips. She was speeding towards him in long, lithe movements, her black hair flat to her head through the absence of air.

Delusion of course! He was dying.... He shut his yes again, felt himself trailing off. Then yet again he opened them as a knife flashed before him in the Jove light. The woman was real. Her nose was bleeding freely; her eyes were starting in sheer torture from her head; yet she still had mastery over her movements.

With what appeared prodigious strength, she ripped off the remains of his spacesuit, tore off his helmet. For some reason, Brig felt momentarily eased for that. Then he was aware of being lifted in strong arms.... Beyond that was a complete and utter dark....

CHAPTER IV

Brig stirred slowly, conscious of only one glorious fact—he was not dead. He was breathing steadily, drawing in deep breaths of glorious air. For a while, he did nothing else; then very gradually the memory of events began to trace back into his mind.

The half-clad girl in the zero cold, her strength, the knife, his unconsciousness.... He opened his eyes suddenly, and for a moment the sun and Europa light dazzled him a little—

There she was!—standing against a tree, watching him, smiling a little. Now that he could see her clearly, he realized he had never seen anybody quite so like a goddess. She was tall, with a snow-white skin, obviously caused by lack of ultraviolet at Io's great distance from the sun.

Her eyes seemed to be violet-colored, her hair black. Her clothing consisted merely of a light garment resembling a modern Earth swimsuit, but made of pulped vegetable matter.

Brig found his voice with difficulty as he sat up.

"S-say, am I nuts?" he whispered.

As her smile widened, he saw that her teeth were very regular and white. "Are you?" she asked, almost mischievously.

"Then you talk—talk English?" He got to his feet and went across to her. He judged she was about five foot seven tall, and muscled like a lioness.

"Yes, English," she assented, nodding her raven black head. "That is, English with American expression. I am an American, even though I've been here for the last twenty years. I'm Elsa Rutter, only child of the late Captain and Mrs. Rutter."

Brig stared at her, fingered the smudge of congealed blood under his nose.

"Of course, you're Brig Dean?" she said decisively.

"Yeah, that's right. You—you must be the girl Betts met up with when we were attacked by the manapes."

"Right!" she laughed. "I gave him Jack Horner...."

Brig shrugged. "Of course, this is all screwy," he sighed. "Here I meet up with you and don't think much of it—just like I might meet a beautiful girl on the sidewalk back at home. I don't have to tell you I don't begin to get it, do I? How'd you come to be here, anyway?"

"Oh, it's pretty simple, really. Father and mother died here without being rescued. I was three when that happened. But I didn't die. Oh, no! You see, the Ionians took care of me—the bladder Ionians, like the one I gave to your friend Betts."

"And?"

"Well, the Ionians are actually trees with the power of loco-motion on their roots. The bladder-mouths that talk are really only their fruit, their offspring, as it were. You may have noticed from Jack Horner that they're not true plants; they have no chlo-rophyllic properties. They absorb oxygen and hydrogen just as you or I, and therefore are made up of the main carbohydrate order—sugar, glucose, fats, and so forth. Therefore, by feeding me on their own substance, which they did, I had food compa-rable, if not better, than any normal child. See?"

"Yeah, I get it. And you live here, you say?"

She moved from her lounging position. Her satiny skin rippled with the action. "Yes, and I never want to leave, Suppose you come with me and see my home?"

"Nothing I'd like better, but I've my own party to think of."

"You're nearer my home than your own camp," she murmured. "Besides, surely you want to know more?"

"Plenty!" he agreed with vehemence, and at that she set the example by striding into the midst of the jungle, following a well-worn trail with unerring accuracy. Brig began to wonder, as he stumbled along beside her, whether he was still uncon-scious, if this was a fantastic dream.

"You are lucky that I've kept my eye on you ever since your ship crashed here on Io," she murmured, glancing at him with her deeply blue eyes. "But for my calling the hysteria termites to a muster, you would have caught it pretty badly from the manapes."

Brig snapped his fingers. "Then it was you! And I'll swear I heard your laugh about the same time, too!"

"Like this?" she suggested, and demonstrated with a peal of silvery notes.

"Like that," Brig agreed gravely; then after a pause, "I still don't figure how you came to be up there on the plateau, in pure void. You saved my life."

"That's why I say it's lucky I've kept my eye on you. I watched where you went. I guessed that, having Jack Homer with you, you would hear him remark sooner or later about diamonds.... But that space walk of mine wasn't so very amazing. I've lived here all my life, and like a swimmer who can accustom himself to long periods under water, so have I, by occasional jaunts to the plateau, accustomed myself to void conditions."

"But the cold!" Brig protested.

"Did you feel cold when your spacesuit ripped?"

"Come to think of it, I didn't."

She smiled. "Of course not. Empty space is a perfect insulator of heat; you radiated heat faster than it could escape. The cold made no impression on you. What did tax you, and me, too, was the lack of air. Lung control in swimming and void experiments helped me to save you. I just managed it—and only just. I cut off your spacesuit to relieve the tremendous strain on the tissues of your body. A body can stay in void without bursting, but not for long. Depends on the strength of the body. I'm far stronger than you, of course...."

"So I noticed," Brig murmured.

"Why not?" she asked quickly. "Io is only a third Earth normal. I have the body of an ordinary Earth woman, all the same muscles, but all my life I've been accustomed to a third the pull. The result has tripled my strength. Then there's open-air life, certain health-giving radiations from the moons, which make up for those the sun is too far distant to give, feeding on carbohydrates.... Well, I'm pretty strong!" she finished with a laugh.

They plunged on for a while in silence. Brig noticed the flawless ease with which she mastered the satellite's slight pull.

"Just how did you learn English?" he asked suddenly.

"Radio."

"Good Heavens, you don't mean—"

"Why not?" she smiled. "Although the ship was wrecked, a good deal of the equipment was in order. When I grew old enough to understand life a little, I started to make myself comfortable. I read the ship's books and learned the rudiments of language, learned all about radio, electricity, the space I live in, and so forth. There was no electricity, so I soon fixed that. I took the ship's electric engines and attached them to a home-made waterwheel. It works as good as a turbine and keeps a generator going. I run it from a stream near my place.... That started the radio. I tuned in Earth, Mars, Venus, Uranus—all the principal planets, and so little by little learned how to talk. Come to think of it, I've heard your name mentioned many a time as an ace spaceman. That right?"

Brig nodded slowly. "I guess so, yes. But I'm rather sick of it. It doesn't bring much happiness. I've made money, and lost it, chained myself up to a girl with a featherweight brain and— Well, I guess that doesn't interest you, anyhow. There's one thing. Why exactly did you give Betts that Jack Horner thing?"

"Well, I usually carry a Jack Horner around with me for company and, when I had cured Betts of his laughing, I thought it might be a good idea if he took Jack with him. You see, I knew Jack would come out with that line about diamonds, and I thought the information would be useful to you and your company. Diamonds are valuable on Earth, of course...."

"That was decent of you, Elsa," Brig said quietly. "Just the same, I don't think I got as big a kick out of finding those diamonds as the others did. Cynthia in particular."

"She's rather good-looking, isn't she?"

Brig shrugged. "I guess so.... Tell me, why the blazes did you teach Jack Horner those nursery rhymes?"

"Not only him, all the Ionians," she laughed. "I used things around them that they'd understand, like 'A is for Atmosphere', and so on.... Well, here we are!" she finished suddenly.

Brig looked up to find that they had entered a clearing—a clearing almost filled with a large ranch-like house fashioned from trees, ship's metal, numberless metal crates and boxes, leaves and vines. Stilts raised it a trifle from the soft ground.

Around it on all sides depended the tree Ionians, slow-moving protoplasm-yellow objects not dissimilar from Earthly beeches, smothered in yellow foliage from the midst of which poked the ridiculous mouthing faces of dozens of Jack Horners....

As Brig and the girl approached them, they set up a chorus of welcome—the oddest chorus, mixed with American slang, obviously learned from radio, the girl's teaching, and their own subtle, peculiar imagination. Feathery branches reached down and caressed the girl affectionately as she passed by. Her slender white hand reached up and stroked the soft, golden foliage.

"Grand people," she said seriously, and led the way into her shack.

Inside the shack, Brig gazed around in approval. The vast length of the single room was perfectly, though crudely furnished, some of it recognizable as ship's material; the rest was homemade. A badly scratched radio of ancient design, skilfully patched up, stood by the glassless window. Tables, chairs, a sofa—even electric light generated from the simple turbine standing over the stream outside—they were all present.

"I shouldn't have thought you'd need light here," Brig remarked.

"Oh, but I do. Now and again there are periods when Io is without light for several hours—when all the moons and the sun are below the horizon simultaneously. Then there are occasional eclipses...."

He nodded slowly, watched her graceful, queenly figure moving swiftly back and forth. She hummed softly to herself as she moved; outside, a group of Jack Horners began with "A is for Atmosphere...." Silly, absurd place, of course! And yet, not altogether. The girl was real enough—very beautiful, very happy, a goddess in a little backwater of peace.

She paused in the business of setting forth a meal of heavy fruits and tree-sap wine and looked across at Brig seriously.

"That was a good idea with the carbon arcs, Brig. When— when do you leave?"

"About four days," he answered slowly. "Then it's back to the old regime. Marriage to Cynthia, fortune from diamonds, enlistment in the coming war with Mars over the Canal Control question. Damned silly, isn't it?" he asked abruptly.

"It sounds it," she admitted. "I'm shut off here from that sort of thing.…"

She went on preparing the meal, finally signaled him to the table.

With an unexpected feeling of drowsy content, he munched the soft fruits, drank the smooth wine. He'd half expected the girl would eat like a young savage, but she didn't. Instead, she used old but serviceable cutlery from the ship.

"Even here, a lady must preserve her dignity," she smiled across at him. "I know just what is civilized from the radio. Incidentally, if you need tobacco, you'll find some tins of it in the corner there. Been sealed for twenty years, and still perfectly fresh."

"Thanks, I don't smoke…," he said absently, then went on reflectively. "Even here a lady must preserve her dignity. I've heard that put in a different way by Cynthia—the girl I'm going to marry."

"Love her?" Elsa asked casually.

"Funny, but I'm not sure. I think she got herself engaged to me, more than me to her. Frankly, I don't think I do love her—now.…"

The girl looked back at her food, said nothing. Brig found his thoughts wandering. The long slumbering idealism in his make-up was beginning to come to life, and with it a certain bewilderment. For some reason, everything outside of this little peaceful place was unimportant.

Diamonds, wealth, Earth, Cynthia.… Meaningless parade. He had already tasted life in most of its phases and found it pretty much the same—drab. Colorless.

Brig stopped through the long Ionian night, made himself comfortable on the sofa. The girl, for her part, took up what she proclaimed was her normal position—a restful pose deep in the gathering arms of a tree Ionian outside, raised high above what-ever insectile life there might be crawling on the wet ground.

Brig slept well, happily. The next morning, the girl showed him the pool made by the turbine stream, demonstrated her magnificent swimming abilities. For an hour, they sported together in the cool depths—and all the time at the back of Brig's mind were troubled thoughts, separated from the immediate delight of this paradise of soft water, friendly childlike organism trees, and shifting, eternal lights—thoughts removed from the soft, alluring beauty of the girl....

"Thinking?" Elsa asked gently, and Brig turned sharply on the warm rock slab on which they were lying. In silence, he studied her beautiful face and still-damp, black, gleaming hair.

"Yes—of things I shouldn't," he admitted bitterly.

"Such as?" she murmured.

"You, mostly."

She lay on her back and clasped white arms behind her head. In silence she watched Europa moving across the sky.

"And why should you not think of me? We're friends, aren't we?"

"Friends!" Brig echoed hollowly. "It's a mighty poor word from my point of view, Elsa. For one thing, you saved my life up there on the plateau. For another, you've shown me something I've looked for all my life. That something is peace and happiness. Here on Io there is so much that could be done—"

"That would mean bringing others, unwanted people," she interrupted quietly. "Here there is peace; others would wreck it."

"Are you never lonely?"

She rose up at that, looked at him steadily with her deep, glorious eyes. "Not often, Brig; but sometimes I think I would like the company of just one other human.... I am still Earthly in being, of course, though Io has molded me. I could never live on Earth—never anywhere except here."

Brig fell moodily silent through an interval, then slid off the rock. Holding out his arms, he helped the girl down, held her for a moment with her face very close to his. With a sigh, he released her.

"I have to go, Elsa," he muttered. "I have my duty to do to the others—to Cynthia, Monty, and good old Betts.... Perhaps someday I might come back."

"Perhaps," she agreed simply. "You're in love with me, Brig, aren't you?"

"Yes. But I still have my duty to do. That's the worst of hidebound convention."

She studied him for a full half minute, then turned suddenly aside. "I have a small compass you may find useful. Your camp is due north from here. Io's north magnetic pole is strong enough for needle deflection...."

She went quietly into the shack, returned with the compass and a small vegetable bag of fruit. Silently Brig took them.

"This isn't goodbye, Elsa," he said quietly. "I really will come back one day—when Cynthia tires of me. I—"

"Goodbye, Brig," she interrupted quietly, and held out her white hand. He took it gently, regarded her delicate, inviting mouth, then turned abruptly away without another word.

Cursing himself with every step he took, he headed towards the clearing, a northerly exit, but upon the very point of plunging into the jungle he stopped dead, listening in amazement to a familiar voice.

"H is for Hut which lies to the south; believe in Jack Horner though he's mostly all mouth...."

"South...South by the stars, of course," remarked an accompanying voice. "H is for Hut.... Young lady? A dream? I begin to doubt. Most certainly I begin to—"

The talking stopped. A portly figure, disheveled and stained, emerged from the jungle's depths, the gaping-mouthed Jack Horner under one arm.

"Betts!" Brig yelled wildly, swinging around. "Betts, you old son of a space bull! Where the devil did you come from?"

Betts' voice trembled a little. "Thank God you're safe, Mr. Dean—thank God! This is indeed a wonderful surprise.... You see, on leaving the plateau, Miss Cynthia fainted from the shock of being attacked by those carbon eaters. By the time his Lordship and I had revived her, some ten minutes had gone. I went back to look for you, but you'd disappeared. I was convinced of the horrible thought you had blown asunder.... You see, sir, I found your ripped spacesuit."

"One can't blow apart in empty space," Brig grinned.

"Dear me, sir! Murchinson and Snedley distinctly stated—"

"Be damned with Murchinson and Snedley. Here—meet Miss Elsa Rutter, daughter of the late Captain and Mrs. Rutter...."

Betts bowed as he girl came slowly up. "Delighted, miss— though I have already had the pleasure. At last I know what happened to the Rutters. They had a daughter."

"That is hardly historical news," the girl laughed; then seriously, "But what brings you here to this place of mine?"

"Well, one reason was that I knew I hadn't dreamt about seeing a young woman in the forest, and another was that Mr. Horner here started talking about a hut to the south. I realized it might lead to your possible abode.... So I came. Then again, though I told his Lordship and Miss Cynthia that you had apparently been killed, I could not rid myself of the idea that you might be alive somewhere. I fancied this young lady might know something about it.... So I came. Forgive me, sir, for monopolizing so much time in explanation."

"That's all right, Betts," Brig smiled, then he shrugged his shoulders heavily. "Well, I guess we'd better be heading back, hadn't we?"

"If you wish, sir—but I feel bound to point out that you will not be exactly—ah—welcome."

"Huh? Why not?"

"Much as I regret it, both Cynthia and his Lordship were delighted when they knew you had been killed. Some trifling matter of diamonds, sir. I understand their possession releases Miss Cynthia from the obligation of marrying you."

Brig stared blankly, past events shuttling through his mind. Little incidents—Monty in Cynthia's tent, her eagerness to achieve independence, their interest in each other....

"I get it," he nodded slowly. "So she was marrying me to

grab her old man's money when he dies and an allowance for life in the meantime. Nice going."

"Yes, sir. When I disapproved of their satisfaction at your decease they—or rather his Lordship, discharged me. My last act was to give them the exact time when a space liner is due, and to extract the assurance that they know how to operate the carbon arc signal.... Then I left, always with the assurance, sir, that I could signal the next liner if my searches in the jungle proved futile.

"I am afraid there is much I do not understand," Betts admitted.

"But you will!" Brig cried joyfully. "All in good time. You'll be able to learn about Io and be the perfect servant and scientist at the same time. Then—" Brig stopped suddenly. "Oh, gosh! Elsa and I want to be married, but there's nobody present to make it legal."

A beatific smile spread over Betts' round face. "Forgive me for my temerity, but I was, in my—ahem—younger days, intended for Holy Orders. By the Convention of 2119, once a clergyman always a clergyman, even though I took to service afterwards. I, sir, can perform that ceremony."

Brig drew the girl towards him. "Betts all over, sweetheart," he murmured. "Servant, scientist, and now clergyman. O.K., Betts, let's go...."

"Very good, sir." He tugged fiercely at his hip pocket and wrenched forth a battered version of the 2100 Bible....

"As I have frequently said, sir, the well-trained servant is the master of many vocations," he murmured. "Now, if you will please join hands...."

FRIGID MOON
BY DENNIS CLIVE

FROM *FUTURE FICTION*, NOVEMBER 1939

Originally entitled "Excelsior," this story was sold to Hornig by Fearn's agent in June 1939, along with three other old mss., appearing in the first issue of *Future Fiction*. The readers' column in the next issue (March 1940) gave it a high rating. The noted fan critic and author Thomas S. Gardner wrote a careful analysis of all the stories, and of "Frigid Moon" he said:

> "—good plot, action and characters. Written in the Weinbaum style. A good B."

His views were echoed by Isaac Asimov:

> "…Second honors go to 'Frigid Moon.' I know very well that it is what fans call a 'Weinbaum imitation' in that it contains the late S.G.W.'s favorite type oif character—a screwy animal in an alien environment. However, I have never really been able to work up any resentment over a Weinbaum imitation. My viewpoint is this. Weinbaum invented a new type of story—the most entertaining of any I've ever read, excluding the heavy super-super science of Smith and Campbell, but he has no copyright ownership of this type of yarn. He is dead now, poor fellow (and poor SF, too), and

that is no reason why this very successful type of story should be allowed to die out. If there are authors who can think up screwy animals after the fashion of Weinbaum, why shouldn't they? Perhaps they can do it as well as Weinbaum could, and wouldn't that be a gain for science fiction? True, no one has yet turned up that even made a patch on the immortal Stanley G., but is that any reason to quit trying—and hoping? No—give us more Weinbaum imitations, provided they are good enough to print, and maybe some day if I'm drunk or filled with opium or for some other reason filled with wild over-confidence, I'll write one myself—you can always reject it."

On 13 November 1939, Fearn wrote to his friend William F. Temple in his 'Frank Jones' (Thornton Ayre) persona:

"Thanks for your praise for *Frigid Moon*. It was written three years ago and never sold until Hornig came into being with *Science Fiction* and *Future Fiction*. I wrote a lot of them, the remaining one being 'Domain of Zero,' which has not yet been accepted (and probably won't be, since I understand Hornig is folding up). He hasn't paid either Jack or I for our latest efforts.

"No, I have no explanation as to how Rope Trick disentangled himself from gas. Though it is unquestionably a true scientific question I do feel many a time that you give yourself needless worry in both reading yarns and in writing your own in your endeavours to find the accurate scientific way out. Be damned to that! Palmer has said 'I want stories of action, not textbooks.' What more do you want? Today, of course, I have abandoned the imitation Weinbaum technique and do either fast adventure or complicated webwork."

FRIGID MOON

The hideous, inhuman zinrots of Ganymede cast icy spires of terrible coldness into the last retreat upon the little moon, throwing Smithy and Eva into the hostile elements and a trap set by an alien intelligence!

Fighting their way through a blizzard of frozen carbon dioxide, Smithy and Eva struggle against impossible odds to reach the one point on little Ganymede where there is a chance of rescue—a weird battle between nightmare creatures spells life or death for the two Earth people!

I.

ROPE TRICK

Barry Smithson—"Smithy"—tossed restlessly on his light bed and finally sat up with a jerk, staring around him in the dull glow of the bedchamber safety lights. Stiffly he stuck out his arm and jabbed the switch that illumined the twenty cold light bulbs set diamond fashion in the glittering *lanium* ceiling.

He recognized the sound that had awakened him almost immediately—the release of the alarm bell by means of a greatly improved photo-electric device outside of this solitary Ganymedian refueling supply station.

For a moment, he sat trying to still his throbbing head. The lonely jitters had gotten into him again, plunging his vitality to the lowest ebb and turning his mind to black despondency. Lonely jitters was the American slang term for the predominant disease of Ganymede, solitarius melancholia, supposedly a nervous reaction from continuous months of solo work in a viciously cruel climate and light gravity.

Grunting painfully, Smithy slid off the bed at last and reeled rather than walked across the shining expanse of floor, passed through the giant machine room wherein the silently working pumps extracted the raw mineral from Ganymede's depths for later pulverization and refinement into fuel for the giant liners on the Earth-Planet XII run, three worlds beyond Pluto. The Planetary Commission of 2316 had extended the known frontier of the Solar System enormously.

Stopping the alarm, Smithy lumbered across the great place, broad shoulders slouched, lank strings of black hair bobbing over his craggy face, furrowed with unbidden despair and melancholy. Tiredly, he ascended a rigid steel ladder and came up under the two-foot thick dome of viltex glass, looked at its arcing smoothness and tried to grin as he beheld the sight of blue vapor contracting and mushrooming on the exterior surface. So the Gasbrain had intercepted the cell-ray with his fantastic misty body and set the alarm going....

"What's on your mind, Rope Trick?"

Smithy called the being that because of its magical ability to form its gaseous body into any desired representation of thought. Rope Trick, a true Gasbrain of Ganymede, composed entirely of carbon dioxide and oxygen under slightly heavier pressure than the surrounding atmosphere, represented the frigid satellite's highest form of life, far in advance of even Terrestrials, each one of his widely spaced molecules being an actual tiny brain working in conjunction with the neighboring molecules. He was easily able to catch and interpret the thoughts of the lonely Earthman under his shelter dome, but Smithy's brain was incapable of receiving thoughts back again.

Accordingly, Rope Trick did the next best thing and formed his astounding body into a series of pictures to represent his communication. Smithy watched him wearily, eyes adroop, as the Gasbrain caught the thought behind his words and began to writhe in the unimaginable cold of the Ganymedian night— minus 200° F.—cold because mighty Jupiter, though so near at hand, reflected little or no heat from his 85,000 miles of surface. Ganymede was no steaming jungle, as the first explorers had anticipated; it was a cruel, ruthless little world infinitely colder than the terrestrial Antarctic.

The shafting beams from the cold light bulbs revealed Rope Trick as a billowing cloud of blue against the intense dark of the Ganymedian night. As he stood watching, Smithy's eyes took on a new light. With magical speed, the gas transformed itself into the unmistakable outlines of a raniac spacesuit, the only substance safe to use in an atmosphere where the minutest fraction of a spark would blow to atoms anything containing a bit of cotton with its gathered charges of unexpended static.

"Spacesuit?" Smithy cried, impacting his thoughts simultaneously. "What do you mean? Want me outside?"

Rope Trick changed from a spacesuit into the outline of an Earthling, unmistakably that of a young woman with her eyes closed.... Smithy scowled with perplexity. Woman? Spacesuit? What the hell—?

The only women on Ganymede were those at the Settlement beyond the Mountains of Excelsior, the wives and daughters of the relay pilots who drove the huge space-liners on the savage tugging run past Jupiter's attraction field to the further planets. What in insanity was the Gasbrain driving at? No space-suited woman in her right senses would surely risk crossing the Excelsiors, especially with the Carbodox Blizzard season due at any time!

"Make it clearer!" Smithy bawled, his gray eyes brightening and his attack of jitters fading before this new interest. "What woman? Where? Use words, you featherhead! You know how!"

Receiving the thoughts, Rope Trick obeyed. He palpitated weirdly, then formed himself like a trick airplane exhaust advertisement. Smithy gazed in blank wonder at the misty message quivering on the dome.

"Earth woman twenty miles from Excelsiors. Senseless. Alone. If the zinrots see her, she's finished. Better come."

"Oke!" Smithy cried eagerly. "Thanks a lot, Ropy! I guess I don't know what I'd do without you to nose around outside."

Rope Trick telescoped into his normal hazy ball and left the glass. At top speed, Smithy clambered back down the ladder and raced across to the spacesuit closet.

It was a matter of seconds to scramble into its roomy, automatically heated interior and spin the viltex helmet into place. Then slipping his jet pistol on his belt, he moved through into the valve-chambers giving egress to the surface.

In ten minutes, he had passed through four chambers of successively lower temperature, and so out into the barren rocky landscape of the satellite itself. Immediately, Rope Trick whipped like a sapphire Catherine wheel from the higher air and glowed by his side, writhing slowly through the poisonous atmosphere as he clumped along.... Odd indeed the understanding between these two—worlds apart in knowledge and formation, yet held together by the common unity of science.

Gaining the top of the little slope leading to the refueling station, Smithy paused for a moment. Ahead of him, stretching to the near horizon, was the empty plain, coal black under the terrible cold, marred only by pits and craters where the deadly zinrots, second highest form of Ganymedian life, had burrowed underground with their claw nails and scissor teeth.

Touching the eastern horizon loomed vast Jove, visibly turning slowly in the cloudless star and moon-riddled sky. To the west stabbed the upper peaks of the Mountains of Excelsior, dominated by the Thunder Molar rearing to 8,000 feet. Selby, the Earth explorer, had called it that because it had reminded him of the back tooth of mythical Jove, God of Thunder....

These were familiar sights to Smithy as he started to plod on again, but he had the advantage of knowing that the Excelsiors were not really true mountains, but vast glaciers, flung to their great heights by Ganymede's slight gravity. Upon them rested the whole secret of the satellite's small colonization. By electrolyzing the water frozen into their masses and adding to it an element with scant nitrogen content, both Settlement and refueling station—by underground pipes of lanium metal—possessed breathable atmosphere. Jong, the Martian engineer, was responsible for the miracle.

As Smithy clumped onwards, he adjusted the neutral shields in his boots from Earth-normal to Gany-normal. Immediately, his speed increased. Rope Trick twisted constantly in front of him, directing the way.

Ever and again, Smithy sailed clean over the zin-pits, finally covering nearly three miles—then suddenly the Gasbrain veered off to one side. Smithy promptly followed him and quite abruptly came upon a prone figure in the jovelight.

The bright rays slanted through the viltex helmet onto the pale face of a girl, completely unconscious, apparently from exhaustion, since there were no traces of bodily injury.

In a moment, Smithy had her over his broad shoulder and, Rope Trick beside him, began the return trip—but he had hardly covered a mile before he caught sight of perhaps eight squatting, catlike things lined up ahead of him, their wicked faceted eyes glowing with unholy fires in the joveshine.

Smithy stopped and smiled inside his helmet glass.

"Zinrots, eh? Wondered how long they'd be...."

He tugged out his jet pistol, leveled it, and marched on again. The zinrots held their ground, standing in characteristic fashion with sharply clawed front paws widely straddled.

The ape-like faces filled with a demoniac ferocity and cunning, easily made them the most dangerous-looking, hostile creatures on the satellite. Added to this was their keen intelligence, level with an Earthling's, but warped by a queer glandular secretion that stifled all traces of sentiment. The outcome was inhuman ferocity and implacable intellect.

With steady tread, Smithy still moved forward, eyes narrowed menacingly, right arm clamped round the bloated legs of the girl over his shoulder. Then he halted and fired deliberately as the leading zinrot suddenly charged— It vanished in a blinding flash, its basic atoms changed into energy.

That was sufficient for the others. With terrible claws distended in cat-like fashion, they hurled themselves on the struggling Earthman. Two-inch steely talons scratched and raked on the viltex helmet; teeth bit furiously and futilely at the metal mesh of his spacesuit. Nothing short of an explosive could get through it, however.

"Damned blasted little devils!" he raged, plowing through the midst of them. He kicked and slammed around with his heavy boots, bringing his jet pistol into action wherever he could, until its constant recoiling kick began to make his arm ache.

He changed his tactics suddenly, put the gun back and flicked a button inside his huge glove. Immediately, a curved scimitar blade sprang from its sheath on his arm. He gripped the handle tightly and slashed with ruthless malevolence, literally hacking his way forward. He sliced the blade through the neck of a nearer zinrot and glimpsed the savage head jump clean from the body, which immediately spouted fast-freezing humor.

Another one he carved in the belly and hurled it writhing to the ground; still another he kicked in the face and sent spinning fifty yards.... And all the time Rope Trick writhed in impotent fury, a blue fog, unable to lend assistance for the simple reason that the two major life forms of Ganymede were so utterly opposite in physical properties that they could not attack each other....

Further decimating sweeps finally cooled even the inhuman courage of the zinrots; this raging Earthman was too dangerous. The survivors turned and fled in vast leaps, vanishing at last down the nearest zin-pit half a mile away. Smithy breathed hard and watched them go; then, resheathing his scimitar, he went on again, weary and drenched in perspiration.

"Wish I could figure those damn things out," he muttered, and his thoughts impacted to the rolling light beside him. "They've got the brain of a man and the savagery of a tiger. The two make a hellish combination...."

Rope Trick did not essay any written response. Going ahead, he curled up in a palpitating haze outside the external valve of the refueling station. Smithy came up at last and twisted the lock-switches. In five minutes he was back in the warm interior and laid the girl gently down on his own bed.

Once he was out of his spacesuit, he began to unscrew her helmet, soon had the heavy protective suit sinking like a pricked balloon on the floor beside him.

II.
LONELY JITTERS

She lay very still as he bathed her white face and tried to force a draft of vita-acid between her pale lips. She swallowed hard and stirred as the strong fluid went down her throat.

Smithy sat down on the bed edge and contemplated her. She was blonde, with regular but not beautiful features and a slim, well-built body—obviously refined, he decided. He couldn't recollect having seen her before on his rare visits to the Settlement.

At length, the vita-acid had the desired effect. She threw a well-rounded, black-clad arm over her forehead, moved weakly. Then her blue eyes opened suddenly and settled on Smithy's lean and puzzled face. The sight of him jerked away the last traces of lethargy.

"You're—you're Smithson, aren't you?" she asked, with the noticeable accent of a New Yorker.

"Yeah, I suppose you're one of these confounded Ganymedian tourists who lost your way?"

His laconic tone did not nettle her; she sat up with a serious expression.

"I'm no tourist; I'm Evania Dodd, daughter of Commandant Dodd of the X-16. I—er— You rescued me, I suppose?"

Smithy laughed shortly. "What do you think? You were out there on the plain as flat as a Plutonian buzzard. How the hell did you get there, anyway?"

"Walked," she said naively. "How'd you come to find me?"

"Rope Trick did that."

"Whom?"

"Skip it." Smithy rose to his feet and plunged his hands in his pockets, scowled down at her.

"Mebbe you'll tell me what you're doing away from the Settlement?"

"You're not very sociable, are you?" she pouted, lifting her slender legs and planting her feet on the shiny floor. "What's wrong with you? Jitters?"

"Perhaps," he admitted briefly. "Chief snag is that women aren't allowed at this refueling station. You ought to know that by now. The 68-Y will be here soon and Dawlish is a stickler for rules. You'll have to be gone by then."

She smiled oddly at that, watched him as he prowled around her.

"Where'll I go?" she asked slowly.

"Where? Back to the Settlement where you came from, of course!"

She said quietly, "There isn't one anymore, Smithson!"

That halted him with an amazed gasp. Twirling around, he gripped her slim shoulders.

"Isn't one!" he shouted hoarsely. "What do you mean? Quick! Tell me."

Again she brushed the arm over her forehead.

"I guess I'm still a bit rocky," she whispered. "Had nothing to eat for ages...."

Smithy cursed his forgetfulness and strode to the provision chamber. He held his patience as he watched the girl eat and drink avidly. The color slowly returned to her features.

"I'm the only survivor," she said after a while, between munches. "Something happened. Something queer came into being under the Settlement floors—clean through six feet of lanium metal. The stuff came up in frozen spires and produced terrific explosions by the fusion of cold and warm air.... Somehow I got away, though I hardly remember how I managed it. I'd no time to bring food, gun, or—or anything."

Smithy stared at her fixedly. "You mean that every scrap of the Settlement was destroyed?" he insisted incredulously.

"Yes. Space machines and everything. Four explosions finished the business...." She regarded him with a level, half-challenging gaze. "Maybe you'll apologize for being so rude to me when you know that I tried to get here in order to warn you. Your air supply comes from the Settlement; your reserve cylinders will exhaust themselves anytime."

"Suppose we call it quits, since you had no place else to go?" he suggested; then smiled. "Thanks all the same, Eva...." His brow furrowed and he stroked his chin. "This is damned serious!" he declared finally. "We—"

"There's something else too, though it may not be important," she interrupted him. "After the first explosion, I ventured to look at the spire that caused it, and believe it or not, I got the worst attack of lonely jitters I've ever known! Gosh, I wanted to kill myself right there and then."

Smithy's eyes had a faraway look. "You did, eh? I'm just beginning to wonder if solitarius melancholía is all the experts claim it to be. They say it's the planet's frigid climate; now I'm thinking it may be deliberately induced depression. Maybe those damned zinrots are trying to make us kill ourselves; maybe it was they who blew up the Settlement—"

He broke off suddenly and gazed with the girl through the open doorway of the adjoining power room. From within it had come a slight sound—a low, subdued crackling that was something quite different from the usual rhythm of the engines.

"What the hell—" Smithy began, then he jumped to his feet and strode forward. The girl came quickly behind him, but before their reached the doorway, they were both suddenly hurled into the center of the living room by the blast of a tremendous concussion.

Superheated air gushed momentarily around them; for an instant their eyes were blinded by intensely brilliant light. Smithy picked himself up with a throbbing head and twitching eyes, wiped a trickle of blood from his gashed cheek. Quickly, he hauled the alarmed girl to her feet.

"Hurt, Eva?"

She shook her head quickly. "What happened in there? Sounded like—"

"Like a frozen spire, eh?" He looked at her grimly for a moment, then went forward again. Standing on the threshold of the immense pump room, he stared at a solitary spire of slate-gray material, innumerably faceted, projecting through the midst of the shattered center-aisle floor. Even as he watched, he could feel intense waves of biting cold ranging from it; at the same time a crushing conviction of lonely jitters descended upon him.

"It is a spire!" the girl cried, coming to his side, "the same sort of thing that blew up the settlement.... You—you feel the jitters?"

"And how!" Smithy's eyes narrowed; he found it an effort to control his will. "This sort of thing is deliberate, Eva; I'm convinced of it."

He turned abruptly and snatched his jet pistol from the rack. The girl shook her head moodily.

"No use. We tried that at the Settlement. You'll only slice off a bit of the stuff, at the most—"

"That's all I need," Smithy answered, tight-lipped, and leveled the pistol at the spire. The jet snicked off a small lump and sent it clattering to the floor, but before Smithy could move towards it, another devilish spire suddenly burst into view with a thunderous explosion at the far end of the place, toppling over a massive generator and instantly stopping the main power supply of the pump room.

Smithy gazed for an instant in alarm. He found himself suddenly drawing breath only by extreme effort. Twisting around, he found Eva slumped wearily against the doorpost, her breast heaving frantically in the struggle for air, her face suddenly shining with perspiration.

"Air—air supply stopping!" she managed to gasp out. "Your reserve tanks must be...be empty...." She gulped, reeled dizzily. Instantly Smithy caught her in his arms.

Half-dragging her, he moved to the spacesuit closet, lifted her limp body into one of the heavy coverings and screwed the helmet into position. The moment the air cylinder was switched on, she began to recover.

Scrambling into his own suit, he linked up his outer microphone and spoke quickly.

"Better?"

His words came clearly in her earphones. Her head nodded behind the viltex glass. "I'm all right now, but what are we going to do? You realize that this place is as doomed as the Settlement, I suppose?"

He nodded. The dull heaviness of the jitters was still in his eyes.

"Yeah, I realize that, but I'm not leaving here without taking a closer look at these spires."

With that, he returned to the power room and picked up the lump of material he had sliced earlier on, lifting it carefully in insulated clampers. Back in the living room, he thrust the substance into the super-microscopic analyzer and switched on the current, gazing intently at the reflecting screen.

Eva's eyes widened in surprise as she watched.

"Why, it's electrical! Internally, anyhow."

Smithy nodded quickly. "These darn things are connected somewhere underground to powerful electrical engines. Quite a good device for destroying anything made of lanium. Lanium's molecular constitution is such that it breaks down before intense electrical fields. By the same token, these things radiate electrical waves, which have a dampening effect on the slight electric constitution of the brain. Result—jitters."

The girl stared at the magnified metallic fragment.

"But—but jitters were here long before these things put in an appearance," she pointed out.

"I know, but the dampening effect, with the correct machinery, could easily be generated without these devices. This is simply a prize idea to cause destruction. Only one explanation is possible. The zinrots are at the bottom of it. They live Heaven knows how far under Ganymede's surface; they've got an intelligence easily level with a human's, and they're fiendishly jealous of anybody invading their territory. Our mineral fuel-bores have driven deep and perhaps caused them plenty of upset. Now they've gotten rid of everybody on Ganymede except us...."

He straightened up from the screen. "Guess they're too smart to deal with single-handed," he muttered. "I just wonder how they generate their electric power...."

He stopped and glanced quickly across the pump room. Two more spires had explosively appeared. Then he started violently as a sudden thought struck him.

"Outside—quick!" he yelled hoarsely, and spinning the bewildered girl around in a fierce clutch, he whirled her to the inner valve, snatching his provision satchel and jet pistol on the way.

As the valve opened, the lights suddenly expired; the power had stopped. Smithy flicked the button on his belt battery and his headlamp came into action. With frantic speed, he dragged the girl through the locks, left them open behind him, and, with boots tuned to Gany-normal, they vaulted away from the refueling station in wild, desperate leaps, hardly noticing the fact that Rope Trick uncurled from the ground nearby and kept them company.

At two miles distance from the station, Smithy at last came to a halt, listening to the whistle of the girl's hard breathing in her microphone. She looked back with him, rather wonderingly.

They had not long to wait. Abruptly the distant dome of the station vanished in a blinding sheet of flame; a deeply reverberating concussion shook the black ground....

Smithy smiled bitterly. "Exit!" he commented shortly. "There goes ten years of good American construction."

"But what happened?" the girl asked, mystified. "The place went up like a powder magazine."

"What else did you expect? I happened to notice that that latest spire was pushing itself upwards directly towards one of the seven fuel storage tanks. Once its point punctured the tank, the itterbim inside would immediately explode. We'd have gone too if we hadn't scrammed out as we did."

"I see.... Guess that makes us quits, doesn't it?"

"Quits?"

"Certainly. I saved you and you saved me. Now, where do

we go from here? We've no spaceships and no friends—all nice and peaceful with a million enemies under our feet."

Smithy didn't answer her. He stood looking around him in the weak light of the risen sun, well above the horizon like a bright star. On the opposite horizon, vast Jove still loomed in all his frightening majesty, part pf his disk hidden now by the ridges of the Excelsiors.

At length, Smithy turned. His face was curiously set.

"To reach me you came through the Excelsiors, of course?"

"You bet I did! Why?"

"I was just thinking it's a good thing you have mountaineering knowledge, because you're surely going to need it. Our only chance of escape from this infernal place lies in our reaching the table top at the summit of Thunder Molar!"

"What!" She stared at him incredulously. "Why— You're crazy! It's three thousand feet up, and absolutely sheer!"

"It isn't sheer; pioneers have made steps and acclivities all the way to the top. Don't you see, Eva, it's the only way? We've no spaceship to get away in. In roughly twenty-four hours, at 39-12, to be exact—Gany time, that is—the 68-Y will be here for refueling. We've got to be somewhere we can signal, and the only place is on top of Thunder Molar, if we can make it in time."

"But why not stay by the demolished fuel station until the 68-Y lands?" she demanded.

"Because the zinrots will be after us. Don't you see that the moment they find they haven't bumped us off in the station, they'll turn out in force to get us?" Smithy glanced up at the beclouded Molar. "It's the only way," he muttered. "We've got the necessary rope cable and boot-spikes in our spacesuit kit, so there's nothing to stop us."

Eva shrugged. "O.K. Since we're liable to be killed in any case, we may as well make it spectacular."

She turned and began to clump along beside him. Ahead of them, Rope Trick twirled and writhed uneasily, suddenly formed into a written question and hovered in the now slightly windy air.

"What about the Carbodox Blizzards?"

"Got to chance it," Smithy mentally returned.

"They're due any day. You'll never make Thunder Molar."

"We've just got to, Ropy—unless you've a better idea?"

Rope Trick hadn't. He elongated into a streamer again and kept the two company as they moved along.

III.
A HOSTILE WORLD

After a while, Rope Trick went on a little distance ahead, came back again at top speed, twirling into a further message.

"Zinrots closing in on you in a circle!"

Smithy came to a stop, lips compressed. He stared at the girl's anxious face.

"Just what I expected," he muttered. "If they make a really determined effort to wipe us out, we're sunk. All the jet pistols and scimitar knives on Ganymede won't avail us anything.... And you're unarmed, too...."

The girl looked quickly around her. At the moment, the barren unimaginably cold plain was deserted, but that did not fool her. Years on Ganymede had taught her, as it had Smithy, all the answers with regard to the zinrots—their crafty methods of approach, their almost non-reflecting black bodies against the barren ground. Rope Trick had seen them, and he was to be implicitly relied upon.

At last Smithy strode forward again. "Have to keep going and fight for it when the time comes, that's all. Come on!"

But he stopped once more as Rope Trick became a sentence.

"Don't advance. Stand still. I'll fix this. Wait."

Then he was off towards the Excelsiors like a luminous air serpent, traveling with the demoniacal speed for which, when under stress, he was phenomenal.

Smithy frowned and looked at the girl.

"Can't see what he can do. Gas-heads and zínrots are as apart as Mercury and Pluto; can't harm each other...."

She said nothing, then after a while her gloved hand gripped his arm. She pointed quickly. Straining his eyes in the various lights, Smithy could discern a distant circle of black moving slowly inward on every side. He caught the jovelight reflecting from deadly claws; here and there the facets of merciless eyes flashed like transitory diamonds.... The advance of the zinrots had come very close, moving with the implacability that spelt certain death.

Smithy tugged out his gun. His lips were a tight line.

"Guess Ropy can't sort this one out," he breathed. "Here goes!"

Dropping on one knee and pulling Eva down beside him, he leveled his gun at the approaching line, but as his finger quivered on the trigger-switch, he stopped and looked up in amazement. The Jove-filled sky was suddenly thick with clouds of twisting blue vapor. Not one Rope Trick, but literally thousands were writhing and twisting there in a gyrating scum, oozing and flowing downwards with gradually thickening density.

"I get it!" Eva cried, jumping up so swiftly that she nearly overbalanced. "Ropy and his comrades are changing into a fog—a smoke screen, Zinrots can't see through fog."

Smithy grinned happily as he scrambled up beside her. "You're dead right! They're sunk!"

They stood waiting eagerly, and at length the vast conglomeration of interwoven Gasbrains had enveloped the zinrots entirely, leaving one long corridor stretching across the plains to the foothills of the Excelsiors.

When that happened, Smithy and the girl started to run, covering the ground in huge flying leaps, listening to the wails and subhuman shrieks of the vicious creatures from the murk as they traveled. Now and again, a piece of fog detached itself from the main bulk, formed briefly into a directional arrow, then reassembled into mass unity.

At the end of forty-five minutes of frenzied effort, they

covered the length of the corridor and gained the lowest foot-hills of the Excelsiors, emerged from the clinging vapors and looked back on a blue opacity stretching for a vast distance over the plain. Then as they went on again, the Gasbrains began to disperse.

The zinrots, courageous and jealous though they were, would never risk the slippery foothills; they were physically unfitted for the task.

The way now lay ever upwards—first through Echoing Pass, then into Whirlwind Canyon, and so up to the defiles and tortuous ascents of Thunder Molar. It towered above the two as they stared up at it. Its white frozen escarpments glittered in the faint sunlight and stronger jove-shine.

From this point, the acclivities were invisible, but Smithy knew that indomitable Earthmen had found a way to the top of the mountain—a top that was invisible from below. Clouds were writhing around it, hurled from the range's opposite side where the Twin Winds gathered. They gave promise of the Ganymedian season of the Carbodox Blizzards, smothering downpours of frozen carbon dioxide from which the abbreviated name was derived.

Smithy's face was grim as he stared up.

"Excelsior is right!" he murmured feelingly, then he looked up sharply as Rope Trick, detached from his fellows, floated into view.

"Thanks a lot, Ropy. You got us out of a hell of a jam."

The Gasbrain made no effort to form an answer. He kept up with the two as they resumed their careful advance along the glassy ground.

By the end of two more hours of rough, hard going, they reached the outskirts of Echoing Pass and, from common knowledge, headed for the nearest cave for rest and food.

They found one easily enough and experienced no discomfort. Their spacesuits were perfectly warmed and regulated; the food traps in the helmets functioned faultlessly and provided them with all the food and drink tablets they needed.

Outside the cave, Rope Trick curled into a ball and slept. Beyond him was the view of the mighty sheer-faced North Glacier, its upper notches lost in the swirling clouds. Jupiter was out of sight; the Carbodox was about to break.

The moaning of the Twin Winds came back from the nearby Echoing Pass in a million forms, and as usual, owing to the eternal caprices of the air currents, the sounds were never reflected in the order received. Sometimes they were utterly reversed. Men in the pioneering days had been known to go insane when they lost themselves in Echoing Pass; its weirdness unbalanced the brain....

Smithy and the girl slept many hours. Weak sunshine sifted through the clouds as they 'breakfasted', but by the time they had fitted the spiked clips to their boots in readiness for the ascent of the Molar, the brightness of day had gone. Instead, the first big whirling flakes of the Blizzard were whisking past the entrance to the cave.

Once outside, the flakes plastered to their glass helmets, flakes of frozen carbon dioxide driven by a raging tempest that was steadily growing stronger.

Drawing his cable-steel rope from about his waist, Smithy knotted it loosely around the girl's waist. He caught her faint smile in the dim light.

"All set?" he asked, purposely refraining from mentioning the dangers ahead.

She crossed two begloved fingers. "All set!"

Turning around, he started the advance, digging his spiked boots hard into the glassy ground, sole-shields fixed to third Earth normal to give his feet added weight on the treacherous surface. By his side, ragged tendrils of mist whipping in the wind, came Rope Trick, expanding and contracting weirdly as he drew in the poisonous atmosphere for his nourishment.

In twenty minutes, they reached the center of the Pass, high atop a rocky ledge leading around to Whirlwind Canyon three hundred feet higher up. And it was here that the first mishap befell them.

Eva, in endeavoring to make a small leap, suddenly slipped. Her wild scream re-echoed strangely in the chasm, and the steel rope suddenly tautened as the noose slapped up under her armpits. The jerk sent Smithy sliding to the edge of the glassy defile.

He dug his heels savagely, clamped his hands over the rope with despairing effort. The ice shaved into brittle shards under the digging rip of his spikes—but for all his frantic effort and tension, he wasn't quick enough to save the girl.

She vanished over the edge of the defile, dragging him after her.... He dropped slowly, thanks to the slight gravity, felt himself torn and whipped by the gale until he finally landed on a broad ledge some distance below.

In a moment he was on his feet. "Eva! Are you hurt?"

"Hurt you.... Are Eva...." flung back at him from the unseen walls of the Pass.

He stumbled forward in the whirling scurry of flakes, following the length of rope backwards until he came upon the girl getting to her feet. Her face was white in the dimness; she laughed nervously.

"Darn silly trick, wasn't it?" she asked shakily. "I sure thought you'd have to send me flowers that time."

Smithy gripped her ballooned body tightly to him. Somehow he hadn't realized until this moment that that body was very precious to him. He stared anxiously about him. The sheer face of the cliff loomed in the smother, utterly unscaleable.

"We're stuck!" he whispered hoarsely. "No way up and no way down!" He stopped, aghast at the discovery, then struck with a sudden thought, he adjusted his outer microphone to full volume and yelled, "Hey, Ropy! Where are you? Rope Trick!"

"Trick Rope.... Eerope!" cackled the Pass. "Eerope! Are you where...."

Nothing happened. The echoing ceased. The Gasbrain didn't appear. Smithy fumed and stared down into the wild Carbodox-flaked chasm. Time and again he called; fifteen minutes slid by.

"Damn!" he swore at last. "He would do this, just when we

need him! Where in hell can he have gotten to...? Hey, you slithering, Catherine wheel, give us a hand down here!"

"...here down hand.... Slither here.... Earslith...."

"Blast these echoes!" Smithy glared around him. "About the most idiotic thing on an idiotic world. Might tickle a tourist pink, but I'm no tourist. Ro-py!" he bawled.

And suddenly the Gasbrain appeared, shooting out of the snowstorm along the ledge from some distance ahead, apparently emerging in the first place from the solid cliff face.

Smithy blinked in amazement. "Now how in hell did you...?" He didn't finish his sentence but watched as Rope Trick, hiding from the direct force of the wind in a slight curve of the wall, conveyed a tattered message.

"Way through cliff! Tunnel. Leads to Whirlwind Canyon. Safe way out. Follow...."

Without hesitation, the two complied, clinging to each other and picking their way carefully. To their amazement, Rope Trick was right. They moved into a fairly wide tunnel entrance some distance further on. Flaking the snow from their helmets, they studied the place in the light of their lamps.

The tunnel went on an obvious rise for nearly a mile, then its ragged floor was suddenly broken by a pit perhaps fifty feet in width. When they reached it, they peered cautiously over its smooth, obviously machine-made edge.

Just for a moment, they could hardly credit the thing they saw. The pit went down, bottomless, an immeasurably deep shaft at the base of which reposed the unmistakable outlines of some sort of city. Tiny though it was, the biting thinness of the air rendered every detail crystal clear. It was possible to see a certain ordered symmetry of buildings, floodlit from a source unknown, together with streets and squares.

Smithy drew a deep breath from his cylinder. "Now I get it! That city must be where the zinrots hang out; this thing is some kind of ventilation shaft. Nobody has ever been able to find how deep down they live. That city is proof alone of their human intelligence. No doubt they resent our interference in drilling for mineral as much as New Yorkers would resent an air raid.... Bet they use the water of these glacier mountains for their electricity generation."

"Correct," affirmed the body of Rope Trick, hovering over the pit. "Zinrots below. This tunnel leads to Whirlwind Canyon. Air current through mountain necessary for zinrots' city below. They made it. I found this by accident. Come...."

Smithy unhooked the cable from his belt, gathered himself together and leapt the fifty-foot gap with ease. In another moment, the girl had whirled to his side. They went on again, once more in harness, and after a distance of nearly three miles through the twining white tunnel, they emerged into the thick of the storm high on the main acclivity of Whirlwind Canyon, Echoing Pass lost far below in the tumult.

The darkness of the storm had deepened to that of night. Their headlamps were the only illuminants that reflected on the glassy, frosty wall close beside them. On the other side was the sheer nothingness of that dreadful gulf, lashed by the Twin Winds battering from one side of the Excelsiors to the other, a hurricane so terrific that when it occasionally snatched savagely at them if they moved too far from the wall, it threatened to hurl them into the seething depths.

The Carbodox Blizzard whirled thicker and thicker, plastering their helmets so heavily that they moved as though blind, massive gloves wiping incessantly at the glass to reveal only more hurtling flakes.... Time and again the struggling Rope Trick, battling with all his weird form to stay consistent in the gale, descended swiftly and guided them over particularly difficult points.

Once around the corner of the Canyon, they were open to a brief mile of level, glass-like plain until they started on the final dangerous ascent to the summit of Thunder Molar.

IV.

FIGHT TO THE SUMMIT

On the plain, the driving blinding cataract of flakes hid from sight the sudden attack of a flock of armobats, deadly vulture-like birds inhabiting the higher ramparts of the Excelsiors, only venturing from their icy homes when the Carbodox season made it unsafe for them to stay any longer.

Almost before they realized what was happening, Smithy and the girl found themselves in the midst of whirling, savage darts of flying fury, things that were a cross between an armadillo and a bat, moving with bullet swiftness and provided with deadly pincer teeth in top and bottom jaws.

Smithy tumbled and fell knee-deep in snow; the pull on the cable dragged the girl down too. In that position, he tore out his pistol and fired desperately, flicked one bird in half and sent a sizzling gust of destruction amidst the descending billows. Another armobat hurtled down from behind and pecked fiercely at his helmet, left a distinct scrape of razor teeth on the viltex glass.

Smithy let out a yell. "Keep going, Eva! If we stop still, these devils'll get us!"

He got up and floundered onwards, dragging the girl with him. This time Rope Trick could do nothing. He was not big enough to form into a protective fog by himself, and even if he had been, the Twin Winds would have made the feat impossible. All he could do, and did, was to swirl in and out and confuse the armobats' projectile sweepings.

Two of the flying horrors were split into pieces by the flaying jet pistol; yet another one dashed its head clean into its scaly body by plunging too savagely at Eva's metal-mesh spacesuit. The impact left a dent in it and momentarily brought the girl to her knees—then she was up again, battling and plunging through the piling snow.

For an hour, the fearful things whirled and whizzed in the raging storm, then as the plateau was gradually left behind and the ascent of the last Thunder Molar acclivity began, the things became scarcer and finally disappeared.

The two were left alone again—save for Rope Trick—in their whirling world of blinding snow, darkness, and the ever-eternal roaring of the Twin Winds....

For another hour, they struggled onwards, having no idea of what distance they had covered, since everything was enveloped in the same blanketing dark—but at the end of that time, they gained a slightly more protected ledge and paused to rest. Rope Trick curled up behind them, palpitating visibly with the vast strains to which he had been subjected.

"Think we'll make it?" the girl asked, wiping the plastered flakes from her glass.

Smithy looked gloomily at the hurricane. "Mebbe," he said pessimistically. "Our lamps are beginning to run out. The batteries are going down...." He stared at the yellow glow of the girl's lamp and fell to thought.

She said nothing. Like him, she was wondering if, even when they reached the top of the Molar—if they ever did—it would prove worth the effort? Suppose the 68-Y didn't come? Suppose the— But what was the use of vain, despondent surmise?

They went on again at last, somewhat refreshed by the rest.

Minutes and hours seemed negligible things in their vast struggles. They were commencing to feel exhausted, and with every foot they went up, the danger increased by reason of their almost exhausted lamp batteries.

They became mechanical, slipping and sliding, constantly ascending automatons, plugging up frozen, brittle steps that went higher and ever higher. They almost forgot that the faithful Rope Trick was always with them, doing what little he could in his loyal way to assist them—

Then with amazing suddenness, they were in the midst of clear air with the dense clouds below them! The Twin Winds ceased their fury and dropped to gale strength. Almost overhead loomed vast Jupiter, and, at the zenith, the weak sun. The 7-day Ganymedian day was halfway spent.

The sky at this height was black, scattered with innumerable brilliant stars, dominated apart from Jupiter by the remaining eight moons.

Smithy stopped and drew a deep breath of relief. He and the girl were almost at the top of the Molar; immediately above them, clear against the stars, was the flat tableland summit.

"We made it!" he yelled. "Eva, we made it!"

She turned and looked back on the woolly clouds of the Carbodox Blizzard in the sun and joveshine below. The words she intended to utter were interrupted by another shout from Smithy as he stood directly above her on the slope.

"The 68-Y! There! Help me signal! Do something!"

The girl was just in time to see a vast smooth-sided 500-foot monster of the void, port lights gleaming, go sliding noiselessly over the summit of the Molar, heading directly for the ruined refueling station hidden below the clouds.

A hollow groan escaped Smithy. He waved his arms frantically and yelled through his full-volumed microphone— But it was no use. The giant liner passed on.

Then the girl caught up with him. "Quick! To the top! If the 68-Y goes away, we're done for. Come on!"

He floundered along beside her, speaking in gasps.

"Even then I'm wondering if it will be of any use. It'll be like a couple of ants on the top of Everest."

"We need a beacon, or something," she said worriedly.

Smithy became silent, flogging his brains for an idea. He was still flogging them when they gained the flat tableland and sank down to rest.

Rope Trick quivered up beside them. The girl regarded his gaseous form speculatively.

"We might get him to make a written signal," she suggested, but Smithy shook his head gloomily.

"I guess not. It's not very likely that the 68-Y will come back over the Molar. When Dawlish finds the station's gone, he'll head for the next nearest on Io and we'll be left behind. What we need is a flare—something to really attract attention."

He clubbed his gloved hands together in frantic thought, but ideas just wouldn't come. He was mentally and physically worn out.

Then suddenly Rope Trick glided forward. In a few seconds he wrote his message.

"Your thoughts tell me you need a signal. Right?"

"And how!" Smithy affirmed feelingly. "Any suggestions?"

"Yes. It is easy when you understand the chemistry of this world as I do. There are plentiful supplies of liquid oxygen on the floor of this tableland, at a temperature of slightly above 300 degrees below zero. You know that?"

"Sure," Smithy growled, frowning. "So what?"

Rope Trick resumed. "This plentitude of liquid oxygen makes some substances, such as cotton fabric, as dangerous as explosive, if ignited. That's why your boots and spacesuits are made of materials non-inflammable on this world. What you have to do is to find a piece of cloth and put it on the floor here. When the 68-Y appears, fire the cloth with your jet pistol. The friction of the jet alone will be enough. There'll be a tremendous explosion visible for miles—a perfect signal."

"By gosh, he's right," Eva cried excitedly; then her face fell. "But where do we get cotton fabric from?"

Smithy grinned and rose to his feet. He withdrew his arms from the folds of his spacesuit sleeves and tore a piece out his shirt, putting it in the small external valve of the suit. Once his arms were back in the sleeves, it was a simple matter to extract the fabric from the small trap.

"Like getting out of your vest with a coat on," he commented, dropping the jagged square on the floor at his feet. Then he and the girl watched in silence as it changed to a frozen gray appearance in that inconceivably cold atmosphere.

They had not long to wait. Fifteen minutes later the huge ovoid of the 68-Y vomited up in the distance through the clouds, pointed directly towards Io.

Instantly Smithy fired the jet pistol in his hand, struck the explosive cotton clean in the center. He had no idea of what really happened after that. The universe seemed to vanish in a sheet of blinding fire.

He was hurled backwards by a terrific blasting explosion, glimpsed Rope Trick vanishing in a blaze of light, saw Eva turning somersaults as she came towards him.... Then everything was dark—

When he moved his aching head again, he found himself staring into the rugged face of Dawlish, commander of the 68-Y. He smiled a little.

"O.K., Smithy," he murmured. "You and Miss Dodd are all right—nothing worse than a broken leg for you and a broken arm for her. We got your signal all right and picked you up in a safety ship. But say," he asked wonderingly, "what the hell were you doing on the Molar? Where's the refuel station?"

Smithy winced, glanced around the cool hospital ward.

"Tell you later mebbe," he answered, then a sudden thought struck him. "You didn't see anything of a gas around the Molar, did you?"

"Gas? No; why?"

Smithy made no reply. So loyal old Rope Trick had been ignited and destroyed by the very explosion he had himself suggested! That was loyalty surpassing Earth's own....

Eva? A broken arm? Smithy grinned faintly. Well that would not stop him putting a ring on her finger when they reached the American settlement at Io—if she'd have him.

She did—fourteen hours later.

LUNAR CONCESSION
BY THORNTON AYRE

FROM *SCIENCE FICTION*, SEPTEMBER 1941
& *NEW WORLDS* #2, (OCTOBER) 1946

This Weinbaum-flavour story was almost certainly written towards the end of 1937, but at first did not sell in America. Fearn's correspondence reveals that he had retyped the ms. from his carbon and had submitted it to the UK magazine *Fantasy*, where it had been provisionally accepted in September 1938. *Fantasy*, however, folded after its third issue, and the ms. was returned to Fearn. He then submitted it to John Carnell for *his* planned new UK magazine, *New Worlds*, in March 1940. Carnell readily accepted it—only for *that* magazine to be aborted before publishing a single issue! Over in the U.S., the American version of the story was eventually accepted by *Science Fiction*, where it copped a fine Frank R. Paul cover for the September 1941 issue.

Usually that magazine ran 'unrelated' Paul covers—*i.e.*, imaginary compositions that were not based on any particular story in the issue. This time that rule was changed. Paul also illustrated the story inside with a beautiful double-page spread.

As noted above, Fearn had first sold the story in the U.K. to John Carnell, who was compiling stories for a new English SF magazine, to be called *New Worlds*. In fact, Fearn wrote and placed with Carnell at least four stories, the other three being "Solar Assignment," "Memory Unlimited," and "Domain of

Zero." Had *New Worlds* been established at that time, Fearn (who was then the *only* full-time SF writer in England) would undoubtedly have become its leading contributor under his own name and various aliases.

Fearn had written two versions of "Lunar Concession" with both American and English settings, Apart from numerous minor grammatical and adjectival changes (Fearn had become adept in writing 'American-style' English) the story was essentially unchanged. Simply because it appeared first, I have reprinted the American version here. Of the other stories, "Memory Unlimited" was fated never to appear (though there is a good chance that Fearn completely rewrote it as "The Unbroken Chain" which he sold to *Startling* in 1946) and "Solar Assignment" would eventually see print in *New Worlds* six years later in the U.K.

John Carnell was no quitter, and he still possessed a burning zeal to edit an English SF magazine. However, his plans to find another publisher had to be put on hold when he was drafted into the Army, and was posted overseas.

When the war ended in September 1945, and Carnell returned to civilian life, he lost no time in trying to revive his ideas for *New Worlds*. His chance came early in 1946 when a close friend from prewar days, journalist Frank Edward Arnold (himself a long time SF fan and published author), introduced him to publisher Stephen Frances (later to become notorious as sleazy gangster writer 'Hank Janson'), the owner of Pendulum Publications. This fledgling company was one of the many small U.K. publishers who had 'mushroomed' into existence in the aftermath of the war. Arnold was editing a series of science fiction paperback novels for Pendulum (including the novel *Other Eyes Watching* by 'Polton Cross', alias Fearn).

At that time there was no indigenous science fiction magazine being published in the U.K., and the canny Frances (himself a fan of the genre) scented a good publishing opportunity. Frances commissioned Carnell to produce two trial issues of *New Worlds*, as quickly as possible.

It was well known within British SF fandom that journalist and prominent SF fan Walter Gillings (former editor of Britain's first-ever SF magazine *Tales of Wonder*, which had ceased publication in 1942, a casualty of the war-time paper shortages) had been compiling a new SF magazine for an established publisher, Temple Bar. Gillings' magazine, to be called *Fantasy* (for which Fearn had also been writing stories) had been held up for three years because of paper shortages, but was finally set to appear towards the end of 1946.

Frances naturally wanted to beat Gillings and Temple Bar to the punch, and so Carnell wrote to all his old contributors, urgently requesting material.

Fearn quickly responded by resending him not only all of the mss. of the old stories Carnell had accepted in 1940, but also copies of three of his latest new stories: "The Vicious Circle," "Sweet Mystery of Life," and "White Mouse." These had recently been written for the U.S. magazines *Startling Stories* and *Thrilling Wonder Stories* (who of course purchased only U.S. rights, leaving Fearn free to resell the stories in the U.K.) Whilst the American magazine had accepted only the first two stories, Carnell accepted all three, plus another three of the old ones.

Thanks mainly to this substantial injection of mss. by Fearn, Carnell's *New Worlds* easily beat Gillings to the punch, appearing in July 1946 (*Fantasy* was eventually published in December). The first issue of *New Worlds* contained two novelettes, by Maurice G. Hugi and William F. Temple respectively, and four short stories, every one of which had been written by Fearn. This multiplicity of stories required Fearn to quickly invent two new pen names, and the published short story line-up was: "White Mouse" as Thornton Ayre (new), "Solar Assignment" as Mark Denholm (an unpublished 1940 ms.), "Knowledge Without Learning" (another unpublished 1940 ms.), as K. Thomas, and "Sweet Mystery of Life" a new John Russell Fearn story (which can be found in Fearn's Borgo collection, *Dynasty of the Small*).

The second issue of *New Worlds* was released in October,

1946, and contained Fearn's "Lunar Concession" as Thornton Ayre (the original 1940 UK ms. version), and "The Vicious Circle" a new Polton Cross story. (This story can be also be found in Fearn's Borgo collection, *Dynasty of the Small*.)

Science fiction had began to change quite a lot during and after the war, and some of the 1940 stories in those first two issues of *New Worlds*, by Fearn and other writers, such as Maurice G. Hugi and W. P. Cockcroft, showed their age, contrasting unfavourably with the new stories by Fearn himself, Temple, and John Beynon (John Wyndham).

"Lunar Concession" in particular was a story of its time, with its premise of breathable air and lunar life existing on the far ('hidden') side of the moon. The idea had originated in SF before the war—in stories by such 'ideas men' as Edmond Hamilton and Raymond Z. Gallun—postulating that Earth's gravity might have 'scooped out' the far side of the moon that is forever turned away from the Earth, and that whilst the Moon had otherwise long since lost all of its atmosphere, some residual air might still exist deep in this imagined lunar basin, hidden from the view of Earth astronomers.

By 1946, with increasing attention being paid to scientific accuracy, the idea was becoming passé. The space travel aspects of the story were also slightly quaint and outdated, and the alien life forms of the story were clearly modeled on the prewar stories of Stanley G. Weinbaum.

However, its structural faults notwithstanding, the story is not without considerable interest today. Written shortly *before* the outbreak of the war, Fearn's story—despite its outdated lunar setting—was essentially concerned with the eradication of war on Earth. Its chief interest for modern readers is that Fearn actually anticipated the main factor that led to the ending of the Second World War—the threat of the atomic bomb! It was also an ingenious and exciting story, and Carnell still liked it well enough to include it, six years after his initial acceptance of it. It is even just possible that because of his overseas war service, Carnell did not know the story had already been published in 1941 in the American magazine *Science Fiction*.

In "Lunar Concession" Fearn imagined a naturally occurring rock-like substance on the far side of the Moon, a form of crystallized energy with tremendous explosive potential, accidentally discovered by space explorer Dagenham Pye:

> "...I call the stuff *Potentium*. A piece the size of a pea will drive a space machine to the Moon and back. I've proved it. That was all the fuel I needed to break the record."
>
> "What!" I cried incredulously. "Why, that sounds almost like atomic force!"
>
> He shook his head slowly. "No, Clem—*potential* force. Hence the name I've given it...."

The enemies of democracy realize its possibilities for superbombs, but our hero—with help from his alien pet—wins the day, and *Potentium* is harnessed by western forces, and superbombs are made. The story ends on an amazingly prophetic note:

> Then, purely as a matter of defense, we demonstrated the bombs' efficiency to a world council of war. The result was immediate. Approaching hostilities were tempered; bickering slackened off. No nation could afford to tackle such a supremely destructive agent. The threat of war vanished—but in the laboratories of the Drew Space Corporation there still remains enough substance in the raw state to blow to atoms any nation that dares break the World Peace Pact of 1994.

Substitute the atomic bomb for the imaginary *Potentium* bomb, and you have a pretty accurate forecast of how the Second World War was ended, and further world war avoided so far!

In 1960 Fearn dusted off the unscientific but fascinating

idea of explosive rocks from "Lunar Concession" and utilized it as a sub-plot in *Ghost World* in order to rekindle a dead sun. Followers of the Golden Amazon series may recognize a resonance here with a very similar substance, *atomium*, which the Amazon and Abna employed to resurrect the nuclear fires of our own sun, in *Conquest of the Amazon* (this novel is now available from Borgo as *World Beneath Ice*). But, in typical Fearn fashion, all of the stories were developed differently.

LUNAR CONCESSION

There was power enough in that Lunar mining claim to blow the Earth to pieces—and Randi, the warmonger, worked his way into the confidence of Ann, owner of the concession—though he didn't for a moment fool Clem. But Randi held a secret that meant disaster for Democracy!

Ann was just a foolish little heiress, and her desire to spend four million to own a mining claim brought tragedy and disaster into the lives of herself and Clem, manager of her Lunar Concession—for Randi, the warmonger, meant business when he learned of the power hidden beneath the claim....

CHAPTER I
POWER AT AUCTION

Something of the usual round of international squabbling, bickering over colonial rights and economic differences, was thrown in the shade in early 1987 by Dagenham Pye's amazing record flight to and from the Moon. It was not the space trip itself that was so remarkable—after all, space travel has been in vogue now for over ten years—but it will be recalled that his meteoric speed certainly aroused interest.

He revealed that he had a new type of fuel, a little of which went a long way; that was the sum total of the information he would give to persistent radio, television, and press representatives. The fuller details of his record flight were only for the privileged few—and because at that time I had done quite a little knocking around in space myself, I was present at the banquet given in his honor in the home of Ann Drew, recently become the heiress of the Drew multi-billions and owner of the powerful Drew Space Corporation by the sudden death of her father.

I hardly need to describe the lionizing and feting—you will remember the televised details—but I can take you behind the scenes to matters of a very different nature as, for instance, when Ann, Count Vaston Randi, Pye, and myself all got into a huddle on the terrace. I remember that we were all very eager—except Count Randí. I couldn't quite weigh the fellow up.

He was foreign; even though he spoke perfect English. I had been given to understand he was of Russian and French extraction—a pale, dark-haired immaculacy, faultlessly mannered; the kind of dress-suit Romeo it pleased a girl like Ann to have around. Beyond that he seemed harmless.

Then there was Dagenham Pye—dark and quick, with a hint of mystery in his manner and speech, a legacy of long service in the Interplanetary Secret Service before he had taken to space racing with his new fuel.... Ann herself, incredibly blonde, incredibly fluffy, and sometimes incredibly senseless, listened most of the time to Pye's statements with her very kissable red lips parted in amazement....

And me? Well, I'm a pretty ordinary guy—not quite six feet, black-headed, and blue-eyed, with a pile driver fist and feet big enough to tread any planet in God's great universe. My name wouldn't make you turn handsprings, either—Clem Dixon, bestowed on me some thirty-three years ago—

Well, there we were on the terrace with Pye talking with his usual machine-gun rapidity.

"The stuff's dynamite plus!" he declared, thumping his knee. "You see, I happened to be lucky. I spent a bit of money in buying a plot of territory on the Moon's other side, but directly under this territory I found this fuel. I'm as lucky as a man with an old time oil gusher in his back garden. Five feet below the surface of the Moon are tons of fuel. In fact, most of the Moon is hollowed out, only it happens that I have an edge over the others because I have a special way in. Besides, it looks as though my particular concession is the main fuel source."

"Whereabouts is your plot, Dag?" I asked.

He tugged out a small but perfect scale map of the Moon's other side, traced a stumpy finger along it.

"Here are the Dawn Edge Mountains, that's where the view of the Moon from the Earth ends. Now, down in all this space there is, of course, air—pulled into the deeply sunk valley caused by Earth's perpetual gravitational drag. Nothing active or dangerous living in the green stuff except, of course, the *Diggers* and *Flame Bugs*. Here's Devil's Nose Rock. Two miles to the east of it"—more finger jabbing—"is my plot. Just here. I bought it from the Government and I figured I might make a tidy profit out of it as a trading center, until I found this stuff below at five feet depth. That altered matters. I got samples of the stuff, had it analyzed and— Well, a record!" he wound up blandly.

"But what possessed you to look underground?" I demanded.

"Quite a commonplace thing, really. You see, the lunar night is hellishly cold, and I noticed that the *Flame Bugs* and *Diggers* all trekked to some part of my plot at sundown. I followed them in a spacesuit on one occasion—I'd have been frozen to death without its protection—and I discovered a fairly wide fissure leading below. I got down and had a look round—found the *Diggers* and *Bugs* all as cozy as you please...." He shrugged a little. "Well, I found the fuel anyway. Being a chemist, I put two and two together when I saw an eruptive crater in the under-ground cavern.... But that's another story," he finished, with a guarded smile.

"So wonderful, don't you think?" Ann asked brightly. "It must be marvelous to have such a scientific mind.... You know,

Daggy, you're much too clever to just pilot a space machine and break records! You ought to be settling affairs of State and all that," she wound up vaguely.

Nobody spoke for a moment. For once she'd come near truth. War was right on our horizon, blowing in from Europe in close alliance with Asia.… Then Randi spoke in his slow, calm voice, fingertips together.

"Since this stuff is so valuable, Pye, why don't you find a company to take it up? Expand it into a business? We need a fuel like that, not only for space travel but for armaments and war materials. The possibilities are— Well, limitless!"

Pye shrugged. "I've been thinking of something like that, Count. Up to now I am the only one who has the ownership of the lunar plot, the only one who knows exactly what the stuff looks like. Naturally, now I've proved the stuff's worth, I intend to cash in on it. I'm going to start looking for a bidder as soon as possible, somebody who will take over the whole concession and mine the stuff. It'll turn in a vast fortune. I call it *Potentium*, by the way A piece the size of a pea will drive a space machine to the Moon and back. I've proved it. That's all I used."

"What!" I cried incredulously. "Why, that sounds almost like atomic force!"

He shook his head slowly. "No, Clem—*potential* force. Hence the name.…"

"One moment," Randi broke in thoughtfully. "Would you consider a private bidder for your concession? Need it of necessity be a space company who buys?"

"Why no, I've no objection to a private bidder. The check is my main interest, I guess. I don't want the job of mining the stuff anyway—I'm not the type. The Interplanetary Secret Service made me something of a rover, you know.… I only said a space company because I figured they're the only people likely to pay my price."

"And it is?" Randi murmured, surveying the ornate ceiling.

"Two million dollars, outright sale. Profits will multiply a thousand-fold in no time."

"Two million. So!" Randi looked momentarily rueful. "You are a businessman, my friend. But suppose...."

"I'll give you three million!" Ann exclaimed suddenly, and giggled a little. "I've always wanted to do something big—like this. I'd just love to own a—a dynamite factory! Daddy was always sure I'd make a businesswoman if I had the proper chance."

Randi sat up as she broke off into another snigger. I fancied that for a moment a queer light had come into his dark, somber eyes. He flashed a glance at Pye, then back to Ann.

"But Ann, my dear, what would you *do* with this concession?" he asked gently. "Think of the details! Expert spacemen, miners, Governmental details, thousands of pounds in labor alone...."

"I'll handle that," said I, turning to her. "If you'd let me?"

"But of course!" she cried. "Oh, Clem, that's awfully decent of you, really it is. And you shall have a nice fat salary too."

Funny thing about Ann. For all her feathery, cockeyed ways, she had a ring of something regular about her. A bit of a chump yes, but she had a quality that made a guy like her.

"You really mean this?" Pye asked at last, keenly.

"Why not?" Ann demanded. "I'm wealthy enough...."

"I'll give you three and a half million!" Randi said suddenly. "That's my limit."

Ann hesitated a moment then she shrugged her bare, creamy shoulders and sighed, "Oh well, make it four million. I believe in paying for things that interest me. After all, Vassy, you don't mind very much, do you?" she pouted. "I do so want to be a businesswoman...."

Randi looked back at her steadily, and I thought I never saw a man kill a girl so effectively without physical force. His eyes had lost that pet dog quietness and went strangely brittle and cold—but when it made no effect on Ann his shoulders went up resignedly and his hand gently patted her arm.

"Of course not, my dear," he smiled. "I only thought I'd like to invest. Your gain is my loss. But just the same...." He stopped and demurred, smoking absently.

"Well?" Ann asked.

"Would it interfere with your business sense if I helped you? Just as your very devoted friend?"

"Why—why no." Ann looked at me. "Would it, Clem?"

"I suppose not," I answered briefly, but I was thinking of that look in Randi's eyes. "Do what you like, Count, but just the same I'm still going to handle the man's end. I know all there is to know about mining for explosive. I've had a year collecting *ampite* compound from Pluto...."

"You're quite indispensable, I'm sure," Randi conceded, airing his unblemished rows of ivory. "Ann is very fortunate."

I didn't reply because I was thinking I was pretty fortunate too. I needed a job, for one thing. A spell of space sickness had knocked me off the payroll of my old company, and space jobs soon fill again. Illness in my racket means long unemployment. Though Ann was a close friend of mine, of any man's for that matter, I couldn't ask her outright for money, though she would probably have given it to me by the truckful if I had. It was better to earn it this way. Besides, there was that nasty look in Randi's eye, something in the acid flattery of his smile....

"Then it's a bargain?" Pye asked suddenly.

"Of course!" Ann got to her feet and left the terrace. She came back with her checkbook. She scribbled with the ease of a girl with too much cash and too little sense, handed the check over. Pye nodded slowly over it and pulled out his wallet, laid a recognizable Interplanetary Concession form on the wicker table, filled out the space provided for endorsement and receipt.

"And this endorses the concession over to you," he said, handing it over. "I'll come with you on the first trip, of course, to show you the exact nature of the stuff you're to mine. Now, here is the formula of quantities for safe usage, which you'd better hand over to your laboratory experts. And here is the map...."

I looked over Ann's shoulder as she studied the various papers. Precious little went into her carefree head, I imagine, though she looked dutifully solemn. Still the papers were O.K.; I could tell that at a glance. Then Randi came silently forward—but he wasn't soon enough. I folded the papers just as he arrived and he shrugged a little, regarded me steadily.

"Surely, if I'm helping—?" he asked.

"To help doesn't mean to know everything," I retorted. "The formula and concession are Ann's personal property—not even the property of the Drew Space Company unless she wishes it. It was your private account, wasn't it, Ann?"

She nodded proudly. "All my very own!"

Randi still looked at me. "You are most cautious, Mr. Dixon," he observed.

"I guess life's made me that way...." I went over and pushed the bell, told the butler to find Sykes Henson, the Drew Company's own lawyer. He came in, bald and perspiring, from the ballroom—but before he left he'd legally finished off the details, got Pye's signature to numberless ready printed forms, and fastened the formula in a heavily sealed envelope signed in Ann's own hand. Without her instructions—or mine, as her manager—nothing could be done.

And Randi was anything but pleased, even though he tried to be as courtly as ever....

At last I managed to get Ann away from him, left him talking to Pye. We wandered away to the edge of the rooftop terrace and gazed over the sprawling, lighted haze of New York.

"Don't you think it's wonderful, Clem?" she said wistfully, resting her elbows on the parapet and clasping slender fingers under her chin.

"You need a keeper," I growled uncivilly.

"Keeper?" Her big blue eyes were astonished. "Oh, Clem, how could you—"

"You nearly chucked four million dollars down the sink," I said, trying to be patient. "Count Randi did his utmost to muscle in and see what was written on that formula. You ought to be more careful! And see that Randi confines his interests to Earth, too! Frankly, I don't trust him."

"Oh, you men!" she chided, and smiled in that irresistible feminine way of hers. When she smiled like that I wanted to stop being tough and scoop her up, frills and perfume and all, into my arms. Since I couldn't stop being tough, I went on talking.

"This thing's got to be properly organized, and I'm the man to do it. I'll run the expedition myself. Have I your authority to do that?"

Blonde waves nodded. "Of course. I just wouldn't know *what* to do without you. But I'm coming on this expedition too, you know."

"But, Ann!" I protested. "There may be danger—"

"Daggy said there wasn't. Only fleas and things— Or was it bugs?" Her nose wrinkled distastefully, then she straightened up. "Anyway, I'm coming!" she announced decisively. "I'm a businesswoman now...."

I couldn't help but laugh. I couldn't picture anything further removed from either a businesswoman or an explorer—but she had a determined kink in her that I think was a relic of her old man.

"All right, I'll fix it," I promised. "I'll have everything underway in a week or two.... Now let's forget it. You owe me a dance."

Instantly she was close against me, and I felt as we floated into the ballroom, with her blonde lead so close to me, that I had a sudden task a life—to protect this generous little fool against the subtle courtesies of a gentleman who had a smile about as friendly as pack-ice.

CHAPTER II
SUICIDE?

In three weeks I had things pretty well sorted out, had made all the necessary plans for a preliminary investigation of Pye's lunar concession. If it was all it was claimed to be, it would be a simple matter afterwards to transport the necessary mining engineers.

I fixed it so that I was to be the pilot of the investigation ship. Pye was also to come along, of course, as adviser. Then there was Ann: she made it clear she would not take any refusal. Last, but not least, there was my pet swamp-hound from Venus—'Snoops'.

Queer little chap, Snoops—not unlike a Chow in shape, but there any similarity ended. He had webbed feet, one very serious blue eye in the middle of his forehead, a coat as soft as eiderdown, and a fanlike tail. Normally, he had a temper like a dove, but he could be unbelievably savage when roused, and never forgot a harsh word or an injury.

Since he had been instrumental in saving my life in an ill-starred Venusian swamp expedition, I felt it almost a duty to look after him, and, to my gratification, Earth and space life seemed to suit him perfectly....

That was the sum total of our party. We fixed the date for July 7th, 1987, and since I had ordered the strictest secrecy, there were only a few mechanics to watch us when we took off from the Drew space grounds.... Once we were free of the atmosphere, I put the automatic pilot into action and turned back into the main living area.

You can imagine my indignant amazement when I saw a long, dark-haired figure murmuring flatteries to Ann. Pye, taking no part in the proceedings, was seated in a comer regarding Count Randi with a rather disgusted stare.

"How did you get aboard?" I demanded, coming forward. "Without wishing to give offence, Count, you were not invited!"

He smiled at me; an ill-disguised smile of triumph; "But I was," he murmured. "Ann herself saw to that. Didn't you, my dear?"

She flushed a little as she turned to me. Shyly, she said, "Well, you see, Clem, Vassy was so persistent in his wish to help me that I just had to be a regular fellow. I—I mean— Well, we had a spare cabin, and— Oh, why do you stare at me like that?"

she broke off tearfully, as I stood grimly listening. "One might think I—I had no say in this thing at all!" Out came her square inch of silk and dabbed her watering eyes.

I looked squarely at Randi. "In other words, Count, you just muscled in," I stated bitterly. "I might have known it! You twisted Ann around your little finger to get in on this expedition and find out all there is to know.… Well, I'm in charge here, and if there's one hint of anything suspicious from you, I'll fix you so the authorities can take care of it when we get back to Earth. So long as you behave yourself, you can string along. But watch yourself!"

"One would imagine you do not like me," he sighed.

"I don't!" I snapped. "And neither would Ann if she'd had many men to deal with!"

That started her off properly and the waterworks went into overtime. Randi gave me a slimy sort of grin and started to console her. I gave it up and went back into the control room. I was beginning to feel fed up already with the whole darned business, mainly because I couldn't figure out what Randi was driving at, and also because Ann had such a crazily generous streak in her.

I took a good look at our objective floating serenely in space, almost at the full—then Pye came banging in and regarded me dubiously.

"Look here, Clem, I hope you don't think I had anything to do with Randi coming along," he said anxiously. "I only—"

"You're all right, Dag," I interrupted him. "But it sure looks as though this concession is starting trouble already. What exactly, I don't know, but we'll soon find out."

He nodded slowly, moodily switched on the radio. The same old Earth jargon came floating through on the ultra short waves.

> *"War is imminent! All Europe and Asia stand ready for a supreme conquest! Every man must stand to arms—every woman must prepare for sacrifice…! Today the American authorities rounded up a ring of*

European espionage agents. The ringleader, the noto-
rious Valon Kintroff, is still missing and—"

Pye savagely switched off, stormed up and down the little chamber.

"War! Espionage!" he shouted bitterly. "What the hell's the use of anything any more? The whole damned world upside down.... It makes me sick!"

He turned and went glumly out. Randi, who had heard his outburst, made an observation about killing being an art. That seemed to set Pye thinking, for the next time I saw him through the glass partition, he was seated in the living-area with his head buried in his hands, musing.

Ann's display of tears had stopped and she was playing a game with Randi—the current craze of 'Give and Take,' not unlike a great-grandchild of mid-century 'Monopoly.' From what I heard, Randi was winning. The game finished with Ann owing him an imaginary continent, and following the rule of the game she gloomily signed the paper admitting her likewise imaginary debt.

Idly I watched Randi push the paper laughingly in his pocket, then I turned back to my observation window and stared out on the velvet dark of space, the glowing silver of our goal.

A sudden antithesis swept over me. Squabbling on Earth, for *what*? And out here the sublime, indescribable glory of infinitude—that had been, that would be, long after man had become a wisp of dust in eternal time. Out in space it is quite impossible to believe in tawdry humans. They just haven't any part....

* * * * * * *

We measured our days and nights by clocks, of course, and they went quietly enough at first.

Pye, for his own amusement, typed out a daily log of events, one of which included our intersection at the halfway line by the ever-active Space Patrol. We were searched, asked to produce every legitimate reason for our moonward journey, then allowed to proceed....

But for the most part Pye seemed intensely preoccupied about something, and all my efforts to get at the root of the trouble were unavailing. Then, on the fourth morning out, we met up with tragedy. While the rest of us had been asleep poor Pye had committed suicide!

There seemed to be no doubt about it—there was a typewritten letter in his quite orderly cabin, a letter that intimated he was too afraid of world crisis and war to live any longer. He would rather be out of it all.

He must have opened the emergency airlock and jumped outside into the void. Anyway, there was a dark gray speck keeping close to the ship all the time, which could only be Pye's corpse caught by our attraction field.

It hit me badly; I'd liked Pye. I recalled his outburst in the control room, his recent thoughtful mood—but even then I couldn't somehow reconcile the facts with his natural space-roving toughness. The business got me worried—but there it was. What could I do?

Randi seemed sorry, but that was all. Poor Ann had a great chance to go prostrate over the matter and stay in her room with an attack of grief. I do think, though, that she *was* deeply sorry. She loved most people with genuine, sex-free affection, and Pye's untimely end struck her deep. It put a new face on the expedition, too. We would simply have to trust to luck that we would find the right stuff. We had all the directions, except the most vital one of all....

Ann and I tried our best to avoid looking at the gray corpse behind us—but I saw Randi studying it once with a faint smile.

* * * * * * *

With ordinary fuel, such as we were using, it is about six and a half days' journey to the Moon, and after Pye's decease things passed fairly quietly. Ann was much quieter, and Randi spent a good deal of time with her. I spent mine either playing with Snoops or watching the great globe of the Moon riding through space, the notched fingers of shadows cast across its waning disk....

And finally it came time for the landing....

We dropped within a mile of Devil's Nose Rock. The sun was halfway to the zenith, just clear of Dawn Edge Mountains, a range entirely encircling the huge valley that forms the Moon's other side.

From our position part of the valley was spread out before us, sweeping down into a deep, verdure-filled cup. Here and there amidst the sprawling green—day vegetation only, withering in the bitter cold of the fortnight-long lunar night—smoked and fumed carbon dioxide geysers, connected by natural shafts to the dying fires of the Moon's core.... Carbon dioxide, broken down by the plentiful supplies of ephemeral green stuff, formed into breathable oxygen of almost Earthly density. Such a thing could only exist in this gravity-drawn valley—for, as science has proved, the Earthward surface of the Moon is dead—airless and finished.

Here in the valley the shadows had lost their savage black and white aspect; they were softly tempered as an Earth shadow, and through the midst of them swarmed the strange lunar *Flame Bugs*, myriads of them, a little larger than dragonflies, sweeping in endless hordes in and out of the glancing, pouring sunshine, reveling in the protracted day.

And then there were the *Diggers*. We couldn't see them from the ship, but from record—and Pye's own observations—the place teemed with them—savagely active, mole-like creatures, forever burrowing with a seemingly blind purposelessness, but probably because being heat lovers they were always trying to get nearer to the Moon's still smoldering internal fires.

"Interesting," observed Randi at last, his eyes fixed on the distant, but unmistakable formation of Devil's Nose Rock. "Just the same, with all these thousands of clefts and ruts in the valley side, it is going to be difficult trying to find Pye's fissure. He could have taken us straight to it...."

"It's wonderful," Ann broke in excitedly, the business of our mission right over her head for the moment. "I've never seen anything away from Earth before. Just look at those darling little Flame Fleas.... It makes me want to go out with a net and catch some. I brought one, you know—on the off chance."

"We didn't come here to hunt those things, Ann," I said, a bit tartly. "And you'd better get into suitable clothes, too. We're going outside. And don't forget a topee, too."

She nodded promptly. "I'll wear a dark blue silk blouse to match the sky," she said thoughtfully, and with that she tripped off merrily. I turned from watching her to find Randi eyeing me.

"Suppose, Dixon, we come to grips?" he suggested levelly.

"Meaning what?"

"That you drop your high-handed attitude and include me in on this investigation! Be reasonable, man, and stop trying to freeze me out. After all, I'm not trying to do anything except help Ann."

"I don't believe you!" I answered bluntly. "However, I have to admit that I can't very well stop you helping us. Just the same, I'll watch that you make no use of anything you may learn."

"Always looking ahead," he said regretfully. "What a pity we haven't got Pye to help us."

His gaze rose for a moment to the spired heights of Dawn Edge Mountains. I knew in that moment that he was thinking of the gray speck that had dropped there as we had landed— Then he turned aside without a word and went off to dress.

CHAPTER III
TRICKERY!

Half an hour later we were outside in the blazing sunshine. Ann fell over twice in her excitement, forgetting the lesser gravity after the ship's attractive plates—but it didn't dampen her spirits and rather pointless vaporings.

Randi and I walked silently together and Snoops came up behind us, sniffing suspiciously. In fact, I never saw him quite so perturbed. His absurd tail was standing upright, an action I had learned to interpret as the prelude to his rare fits of passion. Glancing around, however, I could see no reason then for his mood. Everything was quiet. The hot sun, the distant verdure, the scorching rocks....

I pulled out Pye's map and studied it carefully, made measurements, pointed out directions, but although we wandered for nearly two hours, we could not find that one elusive fissure that gave ingress to the underworld. As Randi had remarked, the surface around Devil's Nose Rock was cracked into millions of fissures, nearly every one of them blind, and to find one in particular that went clean through to below, without a specific guide, was a next to impossible feat.

"We might never find it without assistance," Randi remarked as we halted to review the situation. "Unless we wait until night, when the *Diggers* and *Bugs* head for below."

"And that means working in space suits because of the cold," I grunted. "Wasting valuable hours of time...."

"There is one other way," he said, thoughtfully. "Pye said the underworld begins at five feet down. If we get out the drilling apparatus there's nothing to stop us drilling a shaft of our own and be damned to the fissure."

"Now why didn't I think of that!" Ann exclaimed.

"Guess you're right, Randi," I had to admit; and we returned to the ship for the equipment, set it up in the approximate center of the area Pye had owned....

Starting up the automatic driller, we watched it commence its steady biting into the rocks. A slow haze of dust began to rise in the quiveringly hot atmosphere. The three sat down thankfully on the rocks and relaxed.

"Just look at those flame things!" Ann exclaimed presently, shading her eyes. "Millions of them! Don't you think it would be wonderful if we collected some?"

"What the deuce for?" I asked blankly. "They're already

classified in the Planetary Museum, anyhow."

"I know—but think how lovely a score of them would look, professionally dried and hardened, on an evening frock. I'd be the rage of New York!"

I just couldn't answer that. Here was a girl with four million pounds backed on us finding *Potentium*, and she had to talk about evening frocks! It was clear, though, that the things fascinated her. Chasing about in the lesser gravity with a butterfly net would be just about her idea of a thrill…. She went on vaporing idly, but I didn't listen.

I was eagerly watching the drill's slow progress as it bit a two-foot wide circle in the rock and hardened pumice. I turned to make a comment to Randi, then paused at a sudden bass growling from Snoops. The three of us looked up sharply. Ann was the first to cry out.

"Look! Moles like lobsters!" she shouted. "Oh, Clem, aren't they cute—?"

"*Diggers*!" I interrupted her, watching them. "I might have known it. They seem to scent when anybody or anything starts to dig downwards. Take it easy. They're harmless enough."

We studied perhaps a score of the strange looking gray shapes as they came towards us on their crab-like feet. Their mouths, fitted by Nature with a naturally sharp drill in swordfish fashion, were opening and shutting spasmodically, following the usual custom of biting invisible mites in the air.

Then all of a sudden there was confusion. Snoops' growling abruptly veered off into a hoot of fury. He shot upwards like a gigantic muff and charged at the advancing creatures. Immediately they scattered, then came back to the attack. Inside seconds Snoops and *Diggers* were mixed up in a snapping, snarling mass of dust and flying pebbles.

Randi grinned sardonically. "Evidently that swamp hound of yours doesn't like *Diggers*," he commented, obviously enough. "Sort of cat and dog act—"

"Snoops, come here!" I bawled, racing down into the melee. "Come here, damn you—!"

I plowed through the midst of the drilling little devils, kicking them to one side, tore off those which had fastened their pincer-claws into Snoops' fluffy body. He was bleeding a little. A drop or two fell on my trousers and the *Diggers* flew for it right away until I clubbed them off with my revolver.

Breathless, Snoops hugged tightly to me. I stumbled back to Randi and Ann. Instantly she took Snoops from me, cuddled him under her arm and softly stroked his head.

"There, now, poor little Snoopy. Did he get cross, then...."

"Better keep him locked up after this," Randi suggested dryly. "He may get hurt if you don't, and I'd hate to have that happen."

If Ann hadn't been present, I'd have called him something. As it was I looked back at the slowly returning *Diggers*—then Ann went into action with a very feminine, but very deter-mined, 'shooing' act. Her warlike leaps and noises were enough to keep the Diggers away. In the intervals she took Snoops to the ship and gradually bound him up with lint tied in chocolate box bows.

* * * * * *

In two hours our drill had gone down three feet, moving more slowly now on account of the tougher material packed below. There was little to be gained from just watching, so we returned to the ship for a rest and a meal, leaving the apparatus to its own devices.

With some astonishment we found that we had been at work for eight hours. Time is like that on the Moon. The protracted day—the slow movement of the sun across the heavens—the lesser gravity. They all play havoc with one's sense of timing.... It was the meal that showed us how the burring heat had tired us.

There were no objections to my suggestion that we should get some sleep before restarting work. My last vision before I securely closed the airlock was of the *Diggers* nosing round our still functioning drill and the eternal *Flame Bugs* swirling in the sunshine. Then I went off to my cabin to grab some rest, leaving Snoops in the control room on guard.

In fact, it was Snoops who awakened me—his snuffling, prodding muzzle dug insistently into my ribs until I was forced to take notice of him. I sat up yawning, saw through the port that the sun was considerably higher in the sky. According to my watch another eight hours had passed. The drill ought to be through by this time.

I washed and tidied myself up, then I became aware that Snoops was remarkably agitated about something. He ran in and out of my cabin, finally clamped his teeth on my trouser-leg, and began to pull me insistently.

The moment I entered the control room I got a shock. The airlock was wide open—open to the drowsy stillness of the lunar midday. That started me on a wild search, and within three minutes I had found it was Ann who was missing! Randi wanted to know what was wrong, but I'd no time to waste on him. Instead I followed Snoops' anxious prowling, went with him across the burning rocks towards our now deserted drilling equipment.

As I'd expected, the work had finished itself and a bottom-less, narrow hole lay beneath the automatically stopped drill. I stared at the shaft, then started at a sudden cry from its dark depths.

"Help! Is somebody there? Clemmy, is that you?"

"Ann!" I yelled, both in relief and amazement, flinging myself down flat on the shaft edge. "Where the hell are you?" I shaded my eyes.

"Down here, of course!" came her indignant retort. "I'm not tall enough to get up and the shaft edge is too smooth. See— here's my hand!"

I watched intently and saw something vague and white twisting in the gloom. I reached to the limit of my capacity and grasped it tightly.

"How did you get in here?" I demanded, staring at the smudge

I took to be her face.

"I—I fell in—and I'm scared! Help me up and stop asking silly questions."

I reached down with both hands, gripped her upflung wrists, and heaved. The weak gravitation and her own natural lightness made it a simple job. In a few moments I had lifted her bodily into the sunshine and sat her down on the rocks.

She was filthy dirty, her bare arms caked in dust, her hair and face smothered. For a long time she sat with her knuckles crammed in her eyes, accustoming herself to the blinding light. Then, by degrees, she looked at me, and I just could not help bellowing with laughter at her comic appearance.

"It isn't funny!" she complained, shuddering as she surveyed herself. Then she said, "You see, Clem, I couldn't sleep properly. I was too hot. I could see the *Flame Bugs* through my window and I got to thinking about that evening frock.… Well, I got out my net and decided to hunt them. I went quietly and took Snoops with me for protection against the *Diggers*. I found when I got here that the *Diggers* had gone and that this shaft was finished.… I leaned over to look down, but I think Snoops imagined I was playing a game. He lunged playfully at me, I lost my balance, and in the shaft we both went. I wasn't hurt much because of the slight gravity—but I could not get again without help. I'm too small."

She stopped and looked at me ruefully, wiping her face. I tried not to grin and asked politely, "And what happened then?"

"Well, I wandered about a little, trying to decide what to do. There were a lot of *Flame Bugs* flying about, and since they give a phosphorescent sort of light I could see pretty well—so I went along the narrow tunnel into which I'd dropped. This tunnel ended in a huge cave, and I think it's the one Daggy Pye was talking about."

"It was!" I cried eagerly. "Then you—"

"There were other tunnels and more caves beyond it," she went on seriously. "Sort of all the insides of the Moon. But there was something else, Clem—something that scared the wits out of me—a great rumbling and roaring noise from somewhere deep inside the Moon; and there were hot winds and things too. I saw the reflection of white light cast on the walls and in the shadows were thousands of *Diggers* crouched round a kind of luminous crater. I think our newly made shaft provided an easier way into underground than the fissure they usually use.... But around the floor there were little chunks of brittle gray stuff. Like this...."

She fished in her blouse pocket and tugged out a shiny piece of stuff like extremely battered aluminum.

"Then I lifted Snoops up our shaft in the hope he'd find you and bring you," she finished, handing the lump of stuff to me. "Think it might be the stuff we're looking for?"

I studied it intently and as I was doing so, footsteps came crunching up and Randi appeared.

"Interesting, isn't it?" he asked slowly, squatting down. He glanced at Ann. "I heard most of what you had to say as I came up," he remarked. "Sound carries very well in this still air."

"Think this might be what we're searching for?" I asked, handing the lump over.

He shrugged, studied it, then stood up. With a sudden effort he heaved it an enormous distance. We all watched its flight— then the three of us were abruptly lifted from the ground and pressed back hard against the rocks by the force of a terrific explosion.

It looked as though the whole verdure-filled valley rocked and swam under the stunning impact. *Flame Bugs* went hurtling like driven mist; the distant trees swayed and bent. Then all was still once more.

Very slowly I rose from shielding Ann. She was nearly crying with alarm. I noticed in that moment that Randi was not over startled; he was looking towards the scene of the explosion with a dreamy expression in his eyes. I saw his thin hands clench momentarily.

"It *is Potentium*!" I exclaimed at last.

"Exactly," he agreed thoughtfully. "*Potentium.* Crystallized energy, stored up through millions of years. Release of natural forces."

"What the hell are you talking about?" I demanded, scrambling up. "Did you know it would explode like that?"

"If it was *Potentium*—yes."

"And I wandered about with that awful staff in my pocket!" Ann cried, suddenly shaking. "If I'd trodden on the stuff, or slipped or something— Oh, Clem! Do you realize...."

She didn't finish; the thought was too awesome for her, though I decided the light pull of gravity wouldn't make her doll-like weight very heavy on a piece of *Potentium* anyway.

"You see," Randi said, looking at us both, "I'm rather more of a scientist than you two think—and I also believe in turning Nature's efforts to good use if possible." He pointed to the ten-foot crater the stuff had blown. "Look at that—from a piece the size of a Brazil nut! Imagine, then, a shell of *Potentium*, dropped in the middle of a civilized city! Nothing—absolutely nothing—could stand against it. Whoever owned such a power could dominate all nations, all Governments—perhaps all planets...."

Ann gave a little gasp of alarm. "Vassy, whatever do you mean? You talk like a warmonger—"

"I am!" he said steadily, regarding her with a cold smile. Then with lightning suddenness, he whipped his revolver from its holster, covered us both steadily. Stupidly Ann and I raised our hands.

"We came for fuel," he went on calmly. "And we've found it rather more quickly than I expected—thanks to Ann's fool blunderings with a butterfly net. As an explosive material for rockets *Potentium* certainly has no equal—but I'm not interested in rockets. I regard the stuff as a supreme war weapon!"

"You mean you're working for some foreign power?" I grated out.

"Yes. You may have heard of a missing espionage agent— one Valon Kintroff? That's me.... You see, my Government has ways and means of learning things. They found out when

Pye made his space-record trip, he was using hardly any fuel at all. Before he set out from Earth, paid agents—in the guise of mechanics and so on—removed a small quantity of his fuel and sent it to our laboratories for analysis. It was found to possess an enormous amount of stored energy, released by the action of friction or heavy successive blows. A lump the size of a pea, as Pye told us, was quite sufficient to drive him the 480,000 miles to the Moon and back...."

"Then?" I asked bitterly.

"I was assigned to learn all about the fuel—to obtain it by any possible means without exciting suspicion. As you know, the Space Patrol prevents us doing anything but legitimate business on any planet. No amount of bribery or corruption can get a paid agent into the Space Patrol. I could not, therefore, by any stretch of ingenuity, jump a concession on Luna—nor could I import the necessary machinery. The only thing to do was to line up with somebody who *had* a legitimate purpose and then work things in my own way. I went to work, found but by devious means that Pye was prepared to sell his fuel secret, that its source was on the Moon.

"I realized he would sell to the biggest company—the Drew. So I struck up an apparently amorous acquaintance with you, Ann. Pye did as I'd hoped, and I tried to get the concession to save further trouble. You outbid me, Ann, so I let you have it, but kept by you just the same.... All very simple, isn't it?"

I looked at him helplessly, said savagely, "Are you fool enough to think you can get away with this, Randi? You—"

"I know I can," he answered me, complacently. "Accidents on the Moon—death of a famous heiress and young space explorer.... Very easy. Oh, yes! Pye was the fly in the ointment. He did not suspect anything until I gather he heard something over the radio about a missing espionage agent—Kintroff. As you know, Pye was once in the Space Secret Service. He'd unfortunately seen my record photograph and started to recognize me.... He came into my room to know the truth while you two were asleep. We fought it out. He ended up through the emergency lock.… You see, of the two evils of him giving me away, and losing him and the exact location of *Potentium*, the latter was the lesser. Naturally I typed his suicide note. I remembered his outburst about war and kindred things. Perfect link up for me."

"So it *was* murder!" I roared. "You damned, rotten snake! I suspected it, but I couldn't prove it.…"

Randi grinned a little as I glared at him. Ann looked at me helplessly. Behind us Snoops snuffled impatiently.

"You know, Dixon, you're something of a fool," Randi commented. "If you were anything of a scientist—such as I am—you would have seen the possibilities of this fuel for yourself. Don't you see what's happened here on the Moon? The titanic craters and mountain ranges could possibly have been caused by volcanic and internal upheaval—but not *probably.…* Nature is ever expending her force. Some of it passes away into space, some of it changes into invisible radiation—but quite a quantity of it is stored up in materials.

"Coal, for instance, discharges long accumulated solar energy. In the ultimate state of a world like this one, vast amounts of energy are liable to be stored up in the rocks themselves in a locked, potential form. The forces that blew these vast craters are no longer active—they're inert, awaiting powerful impact to release them—just as coal seams will not burn until the coal is removed and placed on a fire.… That is the nature of this fuel—locked energy—a planet with great areas of its under-world holding enormous supplies of leashed force—*Potentium*, as Pye so aptly called it. Control of that stuff—"

That was about the limit of what I could stand. Randi's sneering voice, his supercilious expression, his absolute belief in his mastery of the situation, did something to me. With an almost mechanical impulse I suddenly dropped my hands and charged forward. Against the lesser gravity I was on him in a second; his revolver went off violently and fell a few feet away. In the confusion I saw Ann snatch at it gingerly.

Then Snoops joined in, lips drawn back over his teeth, his

single eye flaming hate. He'd never liked Randi anyhow, and my sudden attack was sufficient to release his terrific temper.

I punched and pounded Randi with all the force I could muster, and that was plenty with muscular power rating so high—but in Randi I was dealing with a man of unsuspected strength. He was no boxer, but his wrestling holds were wicked. Before I knew what had happened, I was underneath him with his crushing fingers at my throat.

Snoops charged in with snarling muzzle, only to fly backwards as Randi lashed out his heavy boot. The blow hit Snoops clean on the head, stunned him completely with its violence.... That incident lent me added fury and I struggled again with the force of a maniac.

Out of the tail of my eye I saw Ann dancing round frantically with the revolver butt foremost in her hand. Down it came, aimed unerringly at Randi—but at that identical moment my struggling succeeded and I came uppermost, got the full force of the revolver blow on my left temple. I saw a soundless flash of fire—

CHAPTER IV
POWER AND PEACE

A deep, rumbling, beating roar thundered in my ears. The ground was shaking underneath me. Stiffly, I twisted round and tried to bring up my hands to my head—only I couldn't. They were bound securely at my sides. In fact my whole body was bound so tightly I could not even bend my knees.

For a moment I lay passive on rough stone, gazing at a remote lofty ceiling of rock, lighted by the eternal dancing of the *Flame Bugs*—and something else. A vast, distorted wavering shadow was cast on the wall in front of me, the ragged outlines of a man, his head bent as he looked downwards.

I twisted round at that, and the first thing I beheld was Ann beside me, similarly bound. She flicked her eyes towards the figure of Randi standing some little distance away.... The scene rather awed me for a moment—the vision of him staring down into some kind of crater, its creamy glow casting upwards with the radiance of white hot fire. Hot winds were swirling through the cavern; the deep, remote muffled boomings gave a little insight to the titanic battle of forces still being waged deep in the Moon's core, probably at the bottom of that colossal shaft.

"What happened?" I whispered, wishing my head didn't ache so abominably.

"I'm sorry I hit you," she muttered. "It was a complete accident. He overpowered me in a moment, brought me down here, and then brought you as well. He tied us up together with his belt before he went to the ship and got some rope.... Funny thing, he saved a length of rope for something, and also brought a bottle of acid from our supplies."

"Acid!" I cried.

My voice carried to Randi. He turned and came slowly forward, smiling complacently.

"So you've recovered, Dixon," he murmured. "And are wondering about my acid bottle, eh? Well, you'll soon see its purpose. At least I shall be able to spare myself the thought that I ill treated either of you. It will be so swift—so sudden—that there can be no question of lingering pain.... However, first there is work to be done."

He turned and went swiftly out of the cavern. The moment he'd gon,e I set to work on my ropes. Ann and I sat back to back and worked with desperate energy, she pulling at my knots and I at hers—but we might as well have tried to open a bank vault with a toothpick for all the good we accomplished. Those knots were so damned tight it would take hours to unfasten them working under such conditions.

The idea of rubbing the rope against a stone was ruled out, too, in case we happened to choose a piece *Potentium* and the friction would blow us to eternity....

So by the time Randi came back we were pretty exhausted. He had only that same smile on his sallow face. With him he had brought four ordinary metal chests from the ship, carefully lined with cotton wool and waste rags. Ann and I watched in silence as he moved about the cavern, picking up gray metallic hunks of the explosive rocks and laying them with gentle care in the boxes, taking supreme pains to wrap up each piece separately. As each crate became full he departed with it, walking on tiptoe to avoid all chance of jarring—and thanks to his precautions and the lightness of the gravitation, he got all his crates full and removed them, presumably to the ship.

Then he came back with three strong poles, which he proceeded to erect with significant silence in the cavern's center. By the time he had finished, he had a stand like a camp-fire tripod with a massive hunk of rock suspended from the center by the surplus length of rope. He regarded it like an artist finishing his masterpiece, just glanced at us amusedly, then searched round until he found a large, odd piece of *Potentium*. Carefully he placed it on the floor directly under the suspended rock.

"I wonder," he said musingly, turning to us, "if I need to explain this?"

"You know damned well you don't!" I raged. "If this is your idea of fighting for your country, you've some plenty foul ideas! Why can't you and I fight it out? Leave Ann out of it! She—"

"Knows everything, like you," he murmured. "And that, unhappily, is a chance I cannot afford to take. You see, this piece of rock is large enough to weigh pretty heavy even in this gravity. Now, if I sprinkle nitric acid on the supporting rope, it will rapidly eat through it. Down comes the rock, explodes the *Potentium* underneath, and—! Well, I can imagine my reporting a tragic lunar accident in which two well-known people lost their lives.... And I have three crates full of *Potentium*, enough to make bombs to blow all enemy civilizations from the face of the Earth.

"Then, in the future, I may return here with others. This cave will assuredly be blasted to dust, but not all traces of *Potentium* will vanish from the Moon. I shall dig for it again, be the heir to it, because it was your dying wish, Ann, that it should be so."

"You—you can't do this, Vassy!" she screamed frantically, lashing her bound body. "You just can't—"

"Who's going to believe you, anyway?" I broke in furiously. "You'll be caught by the Drew Company and made to explain!"

"Which I shall—very satisfactorily," he smiled. "You see, Ann, you made the entire lunar concession over to me. It was your dying wish!"

"I—I didn't! It—it isn't!" she stammered despairingly; then she took refuge in tears. I lay glaring up at Randi.

"What in hell are you talking about?" I grated. "You've got no authority, and never will have,"

For answer he tugged out a sheet of paper from his pocket and held it up for us to see. Both Ann and I stared in speechless amazement at a statement in Randi's handwriting that the entire concession and formula were under his control. That was plain enough, but the extraordinary part about it was Ann's unmistakable flowing signature at the end.

"You see, it is not a forgery," Randi commented dryly.

"But—but how—" Ann gasped. "That's my signature, yes. Even my bank manager would swear to it! But—"

"A little game of 'Give and take'," Randi said softly, refolding the paper. "You remember how we played it on the journey? I believe I won an imaginary continent from you. In accordance with the rules of the game you gave me your signature for it, just as an I.O.U. I wrote the statement of the game debt at the top of the sheet and you signed at the bottom. To you it was just a game of fun—to me a game of reality. I had merely to tear the top off the sheet and substitute these other vital words underneath.... Need I remind you that the Expeditionary Clause in the new Space Law makes it legal—as to the constantly existent case of a soldier—for a dying person on an expedition to make a last will without the presence of witnesses, provided the signature is approved by experts...?"

"Why, you infernal swine!" I yelled. "You dared do that? Is there nothing safe from your rotten fingers? And if you wanted to kill us, why resort to this? You killed Pye without compunction: what stopped you on our account?"

"Well, I wanted to be sure that *Potentium* could be found first, otherwise my accident tale and false concession would have been useless and I'd have found myself in difficulties. But as it is—"

He shrugged and turned aside, pulled a bottle from his pocket. Ann and I could only watch helplessly as an oily, corrosive fluid poured from the bottle on to the rope suspending the improvised pile driver. At the finish of his performance Randi threw the bottle away with a flourish, regarded the wisping smoke already rising from the rope into the disturbed air.

"I should say…about fifteen minutes," he commented, glancing at his watch. "That will give me ample time to get away from the Moon into space—and I have an idea that the Moon's surface will change a deal in the upheaval, enough anyhow, to substantiate my story of an accident. Later, even, your bodies may be found." He stopped and regarded us. "It's been nice knowing you," he chuckled, then he went softly from the cavern and vanished in the outlet tunnel beyond.

* * * * * * *

It seemed that Ann and I lay gazing for an eternity at that gently smoldering rope before the full horror of our predicament hammered in upon us—then we both started to thresh and struggle with desperate energy, straining and struggling until the skin round our wrist ropes was bleeding and broken.

Disturbed by our activities, one or two *Diggers* came out of the warm shadows. I called to them as a last desperate measure. If only I could get them to work, they'd drill through the ropes in a moment, but all the little devils did was sit like rats and watch us, basking in the warmth from the central crater shaft.

"No dice," I panted at, last. "They haven't the brains to know what I mean. We'll have to try rolling towards the tripod—"

"No—no, wait!" Ann screamed. "You can't pick your way like you can when walking. There are bits of *Potentium* all over the floor. If your weight crushes one of them we'll go sky high."

"And what do you think we'll do when that blasted rock drops?" I demanded desperately. "This is the lesser of two evils—come on!" and I started rolling with frantic speed, digging my bound heels into the floor to help me along. I could not have stood upright anyhow: I was too tightly bound for that.

Little by little I edged my way along, moving towards the *Potentium* under the tripod in the hope that I might be able to somehow push it away—but the distance! It seemed like hundreds of miles.... And suddenly the rock swayed ever so slightly as one strand of the rope parted smokingly.

"Clem, it's going!" Ann screeched. "It's going!"

"Keep rolling!" I ordered, and made myself sound savage to stop her going hysterical—though I knew it did not matter much anyway. The rate I was going at I would never reach the darn thing in time, anyhow....

Then, halfway in a roll, I stopped at a sudden sound down the outlet tunnel. A second later, Snoops came into view, limping badly, blood dripping from a battered jaw, a deep gash across his skull where the fur had been torn away. I stared at him in momentary horror. In the intensity of the moment I had forgotten all about him.

"He's hurt!" Ann cried. "Look, he's bleeding—"

"Come here, Snoops!" I ordered sharply, making motions with my body. "Bite! In God's name, animal—*bite!*"

Bite! That was the last thing the affectionate old fool did! He lay down, plainly exhausted, and licked my hand languidly. I felt the warm drip of blood drops from his jaw as he made the action.

"Bite!" I screamed, "Dammit, Snoops—*bite!*"

He licked my bound right hand again, more affectionately than ever—and also more wearily. I couldn't figure how he had gotten into such a state, why he had been so long coming. Unless that devil Randi—!

Then my thoughts were interrupted by a violent commotion in the shadows. Like a sudden tide, a mass of *Diggers* came swarming into view, eyes glinting fiendishly, their terrible drilling muzzles projected for action. Ann and I watched in blank horror as they swept towards us—but they left her alone entirely and instead plunged for me.

Exhausted though he was, Snoops was on his feet again instantly, snarling defensively, and this time there was nothing I could do to save matters. Fighting began immediately— a swearing; snapping mass swarming about the cave, piling thick and fast on to poor old Snoops until he went down with a crash.... But I noticed something else too. Savagely sharp drills were boring into my right hand, through the rope that pinioned it. Almost before I realized what was happening, my hand was free!

"It's the blood—Snoops' blood!" Ann shouted wildly, staring at me. "In that other fight the same thing happened—when it got on your clothes, remember? It's on your ropes.... The *Diggers*— attracted them—enemies...." She got no further, collapsed in her ropes, utterly overcome.

I didn't wait to ask whys and wherefores. I hurled off the remaining *Diggers*, ripped my hand free, tugged out my left arm from the loosened rope, then dragged myself as fast as I could go along the cavern floor, fell flat by the tripod.

With infinite care I dragged out the *Potentium* from beneath. Hardly had I pushed it to a safe distance than the supported rock came down with a bang that made a dent in the soft floor and sent dust swirling wildly....

I was shaking with reaction, had to lie prone to still my slamming heart. Then at last I was calmer, tore the remaining ropes from my body and released Ann, raised her in my arms.

I was glad she didn't see the damage I was forced to gaze upon—the swarming masses of *Diggers* over the corpse of poor old Snoops. I knew in those moments that all aid I could give was unwanted.... Slowly I went out of the cavern.

As I neared the surface opening, Ann recovered again, but I still carried her. Without saying anything, I lifted her up to the rim of the surface hole and she scrambled outside. With my greater height, I got up without assistance, just as Randi must have done.

"Even though we've got out of that mess, we're not much better off," Ann remarked moodily, gazing at the blue-black sky. "I don't see the ship anywhere up there, so I guess he's gone.… Taken all the drilling apparatus too," she went on, surveying the deserted space. Then she looked at me quickly. "Where's Snoops? We must have left him below—"

"For good," I said seriously. "Anyhow, he died being loyal."

We began to walk aimlessly; then she said, "Well, I was right about the blood on your rope attracting the *Diggers* anyway. They and Snoops were sworn enemies—" She broke off.

"Look!" she cried in amazement, as we turned the corner of the rock which gave access to the main valley side.

I saw immediately what she meant. Our ship was where it had been all the time—but that wasn't the main point. I raced forward in long leaps to land beside the sprawling body of a man—Randi! Ann turned away with a little shudder as I turned him over. Just for the moment I felt pretty squeamish too. His neck was lacerated mercilessly from ear to ear. Across his face were the unmistakable marks of canine teeth.

Gently I let him fall back on the crimson stained dust.

"Snoops!" I breathed, suddenly understanding. "Ann, don't you realize—? That was why Snoops was so long in joining us. He hated Randi: he hated him more after he stunned him so violently. He must have waited his chance and then sprung— probably from this very rock. And he made no mistake—got the jugular.…"

"But Randi made a lot of trips," Ann reminded me. "Why did Snoops choose the last one?"

I shrugged. "Probably because he was still unconscious during the interval and only recovered as Randi made his last trip to the ship.… That accounts for Snoops' condition. There must have been the hell of a fight.…"

She nodded very slowly, gripped my arm in eloquent silence as we turned towards the spaceship.

* * * * * * *

At least Randi had guessed right in one thing—his belief in the potency of *Potentium*. When we got back to Earth and had the stuff analyzed and formulated according to Pye's methods, we adopted Randi's own scheme and had a considerable amount of the raw stuff made into bombs.

Then, purely as a matter of defense, we demonstrated the bombs' efficiency to a world council of war. The result was immediate. Approaching hostilities were tempered; bickering slackened off. No nation could afford to tackle such a supremely destructive agent. The threat of war vanished—but in the laboratories of the Drew Space Corporation there still remains enough substance in the raw state to blow to atoms any nation that dares break the World Peace Pact of 1994.

Today, of course, the Moon is entirely under the control of the Drew Concessionaries. The stuff is mined by trusted experts and used for peacetime super fuel.... None without absolute authority may venture near that lunar storehouse.

Ann has gained more sense since her experiences—but there are times when we both wonder, during the all too slack intervals of our busy married life, how much of this power and peace would have come about but for the supreme loyalty of an ugly, one-eyed mass of fur from the swamps of Venus....

LOCKED CITY

BY THORNTON AYRE

From *Amazing Stories*, October 1938

At the beginning of 1938, Fearn (as Ayre) had received John W. Campbell's letter suggesting that he should change his style and abandon the Weinbaum slant. He had "chewed things over" and then decided to go to the other extreme. He devised a type of story that was entirely new to science fiction—"webwork" mysteries, wherein seemingly disconnected events were cleverly woven together in the style of detective fiction master Harry Stephen Keeler. He also wrote more "Cross" stories that owed nothing to Weinbaum.

Beginning with "Locked City," Fearn injected strong mystery and detective story elements into his Ayre stories. But instead of sending his new ms. to Campbell, as Fearn had intended, Fearn's U.S. agent Julius Schwartz submitted them to new *Amazing Stories* editor Ray Palmer (a personal friend of the agent). Palmer gleefully accepted every story, with a request for more, delighted to have successfully poached one of *Astounding*'s leading writers. They were an immediate success, and Fearn became established at *Amazing* under all three names—Ayre, Cross, and Fearn.

After Palmer had accepted "Locked City," he invited the author to give the background to the story in the October 1938 *Amazing Stories*' new "Meet the Authors" department:

"…Wrote some awful stuff at first, science fiction being right off my line—my ordinary line being articles. Then sold 'Penal World' and after a gap managed to sell 'Whispering Satellite'. Some said I imitated Weinbaum; some said I was original. The first guess was right. At that time everybody was Weinbaum conscious, and as a newcomer I tried to emulate him. Ran into a blind alley doing it and tried to hit on a new mysterious style all my own—hence, 'Locked City,' which embodies mystery with adventure. Other yarns I have done since have also had the mysterious ingredient, which seems one thing so far missing from science fiction.…

"Referring again to 'Locked City.' Though it is a story of Mars—and how many yarns about that planet have been written!—I have tried to give an entirely new explanation for the disappearance of Martians. Maybe it's an improbable explanation, but I personally don't think so. As to the Living Keys in the form of Martian children, the idea came from watching a child do a remarkable mathematical analysis on the Blackpool Pleasure Beach. If mathematics, why not a key combination?

"The sight of a doddery old man, and my own thirst in the summer heat seemed to supply odds and ends. Anyway, 'Locked City' emerged and travelled pronto to *Amazing.*"

This first new-style Thornton Ayre story was an immediate hit, and the approving letters to the magazine's "Discussions" column in the following issue included one by no less a luminary than Isaac Asimov. After remarking that Ayre was a consistently good author whom *Amazing* would do well to feature, Asimov added:

"'Locked City', by the way, was the most imaginative story of the issue and I'll bet you find it is one of the favorites. That'll show you that your readers aren't afraid of a thought-provoking story."

Even without such an endorsement, I have no hesitation in including this story to close this book. Fearn's central plot premise of a mysteriously vanished alien civilization has become an iconic image in science fiction, frequently imitated, especially in television (*Star Trek*) and cinema (*Forbidden Planet*). Of course, Fearn's original story was itself based on the story of the *Marie Celeste* (actually mentioned by a character in the story). His stated belief "that the classics of ordinary fiction all have the basis of science fiction if they're skillfully changed" was an amazingly valid insight indeed (page *Forbidden Planet* and Shakespeare's *The Tempest* for instance!). In the same 1938 article Fearn also astutely predicted that within ten years science fiction "will be an accepted branch of everyday literature, encompassing the book market and films with the regularity of drama and comedy today."

How right he was!

LOCKED CITY

Death faced them on the deserts of Mars, then they found an incredible locked city.

Exiled from Earth, and facing certain death, they found the Metropolis of Mars deserted, except for 7 strange characters.

CHAPTER 1
Sentences of Death

"Rodney Calab, Eva Calab, and Boris Rengard—you stand accused and convicted before this court as traitors to the cause of world progress—as defeated leaders to an effort to overthrow world government...."

The cold, impartial voice of Baxter Holroyd became silent for a moment. Every eye in the packed Hall of Judicature turned to where he sat—a grossly fat, vulgar, bald-headed man half leaning on his high and solitary desk, his pale eyes fixed in gloating triumph on the three in the dock before him.

This was no normal trial, no matter of espionage, but the final act of ruthless injustice that spelled doom for the vast, down-trodden bands of Earth who had seen in the vigorous, intelligent Rodney Calab a new savior from oppression.

Democracy, fascism, communism.... Together with hundreds of other distinct policies they were all merged onto a common dust in a record of nearly fifty years of desperate slaughter and struggle. First Europe and Great Britain; then the United States (with her isolation scheme in pieces) sank too. Japan and Russia rolled into the whirlpool. Across the world raged war at its vilest. Democracy and liberty were swept out of all knowledge. Iron dictatorship had won.

For ten years now, Baxter Holroyd, better known as the Iron Dictator, controlled the Earth's peoples with a severity and cruelty that had no parallel with the past. Science went on, cities were rebuilt, civilization picked itself up again—but all for the good of Holroyd. Anybody daring to raise a finger against him or his retinue knew the answer was always instant death.

Rod Calab and his wife, Eva, defied that possibility. Together, with the young chemist Boris Rengard to help them, they strug-gled desperately and in secret to devise ways and means of scientifically undermining Holroyd's power; were within an ace of success. Then came exposure, trial, and now—

"There are various means this court could adopt to dispose of you," Holroyd resumed smoothly. "You could be shot, you could be burned slowly with heat rays, you could be exiled to the new Polar continents.... All those things we could do, but we shall not.

"Today, it is science that definitely holds sway, that bows

down before the rule I have instituted for the common good of the people. To the end of furthering that science you shall be given a chance to live...."

The three remained silent—Calab, tall, lean-limbed, dark-haired, with a resolute jaw; his wife upright and defiant, blonde-headed and blue-eyed. Both of them moved only slightly. Boris Rengard did not even do that. Small and lofty-browed, unruly hair as red as a sunset and eyes so dark they seemed to have no pupils, he stood gripping the rail in front of him, knuckles white through the taut skin of lean hands. Whether facing death or life, science was his only stimulus. He waited expectantly, almost coolly, staring up into the grinning, flabby face looming above.

"Yes, a chance for life," Holroyd repeated softly, but it was a softness that had the bitterness of nitric acid. "You may be aware—you in particular, Rengard—that our science now is faced by two major problems, atomic force and the feasibility of space travel. I say 'feasibility,' because space travel by rocket ship is an accomplished fact.

"The work of Calva Neil, your close ally in your attempt to overthrow me and whose life I now spare only because of his genius, has unlocked the void for us. But where are there lives we can sacrifice in the first experimental trip across such a vast gulf as, say, forty million miles? Criminals are too useful; ordinary citizens too valuable.

"That the journey can be made, we know full well, but the strain of such a long journey on a human frame has yet to be ascertained. You three will make the initial journey!"

A heavy silence dropped on the hall as the Dictator mused for a moment, rustled his papers.

"The chosen objective," he resumed, "is Mars. Principally because it is obviously a dead world; also because its conjunction is favorable at the moment; and again because a forty million mile journey will tell us all we need to know if a longer trip is ever attempted.

"You three will be rendered unconscious for a period of two

weeks. During that time the rocket ship carrying you will cross the gulf, controlled as on previous occasions by the Neil Remote System. I need hardly add that, in view of his recent collusion with you, Neil will be heavily guarded during the process.

"It is certain you will land on Mars without mishap. If you have succumbed to the strain, you will obviously be dead. If you have survived, you will awaken. When you do that, certain concealed microwaves networked across the interior of your cabin will react on photoelectric cells as your bodies intercept their paths. The cells will in turn actuate along a remote-controlled beam and produce a response back here on Earth.

"We shall know by that means that you are alive—that interplanetary space travel can be accomplished by human beings. Because you do not know the position of these beams, because you will be too dazed on recovery to even bother thinking about them, you will be quite unable to prevent the signals going forth. Is that clear?"

"And if we do live?" asked Rengard stonily.

The Dictator smiled icily. "Then, my friends, Mars is all yours!" he grinned. "A mostly waterless, airless planet to do with as you will. It is one world we shall never trouble to colonize, but if you can reach it, it makes us secure when we decide to take over Venus and other possible worlds. Then outwards—to the Galaxies!" Holroyd paused, oozing for a moment that spellbinding power that had made him the ruler of a harassed, post-war world.

"Your ship will have enough fuel to reach Mars—no more," he resumed. "You will have no provisions, and no water. If you do awake, you will soon die…horribly, as you deserve—"

In the jammed hall outside came a commotion.

"I won't do it! Damn you, Holroyd, I won't!"

The Dictator and three in the dock turned. In an instant they recognized the blond head and ruddy-cheeked face of Neil, their defeated friend, perhaps one of the cleverest young electronic geniuses of the age. He shook his fist savagely across the astonished mob of the people.

"I'll not guide any ship containing my friends!" he roared. "They are my friends, always will be, and no radio control of mine is going to send them to such a death as that!"

"No?" Holroyd's thick lips were sneering. "We will see to that later, my friend. Guards, take him away! Hold him under strict observation until further orders. Take these three prisoners away too. Sentence is passed!"

He leaned back and watched complacently the prompt execution of his commands.

Just after sundown he was watching again from his apartment window in the Executive Building, the departure of a rocket ship climbing in a streak of sparks to the cloudy sky. Languidly he turned to the televisor and switched it on. It gave him a picture of the remote control radio room in another quarter of the vast Executive Building.

Young Calva Neil was hunched over the controls of his amazing apparatus. Every moment was clearly one of extreme, helpless bitterness. Time and again he looked up at the iron-faced guards around him with their leveled ray guns...then with a hopeless shrug of his shoulders turned back to his task.

Baxter Holroyd switched off and smiled the smile of a being who has more of the snake in him than the man.

CHAPTER II
The Deserted City

Rod Calab moved dully, heavy-headed, aching. His body throbbed as though it had been subjected to an interminable succession of hammer blows. Wearily he opened his eyes, found himself gazing at a roof of curved metal illumined by weak, reflected sunshine.

Little by little remembrance seeped back—the anesthesia on Earth in the prison cell, the memory of a last helpless struggle. The journey to Mars? Forgetful of his pains, he eased off the soft spring bed against the wall—eased rather too rapidly indeed, for the lesser gravitation instantly made itself evident and sent him sprawling.

After a minute's careful effort he found just how much energy he needed. Gently he picked his way to Eva and Rengard as they lay motionless on their beds, eyes closed, faces white and rigid. Anxiously he felt their pulses. They were still alive, sluggishly so in the grip of unconsciousness. There was nothing could be done for them but wait for the awakening.

His head clearing a little, Rod stumbled to the window, clutched the frame and stared outside. It was a view that brought hopelessness into his gray eyes. The vessel had landed in the midst of a near-horizoned desert. It stretched away, uneven and bumpy, totally empty of life. Overhead the sky was blue black, powdered with brightly gleaming stars, the blue spot of Earth itself visible low down in the west—or what Rod judged to be the west.

"Grand place to have a thirst!" he whispered, licking his dry lips The stimulus shot into him at the time of the anesthetic had kept his body nourished during the two weeks, but now he felt the ravaging pangs of thirst and hunger. Wearily he rubbed his aching head. Then he turned about and looked at the fuel gauge.

There was still some explosive in the chambers—about enough to cover 2,000 miles. No more. Return to Earth was an absolute impossibility. With fingers that ached he operated the external air devices, made a wry face at the readings. The atmosphere outside was unbreathable in its thinness, approximating that of Earth's stratosphere.

"Damned lousy place!" he growled bitterly, and licked his lips again.

"I agree with you, Rod."

He turned in swift surprise and found Rengard sitting up on his bed, his red head in his hands. Savagely he ruffled his flaming locks, then looked up with a faint grin.

"Well, we made it," he commented. "Guess Holroyd's aware of it by now, too. Our alarm signal will have reacted, I suppose. Not that it does us much good, of course," he finished moodily.

He tested his weight against the gravity, moved to Rod's side and sourly studied the instruments. Then, shrugging, he flung wide the doors of the storage cabinet and gazed at the empty shelves with bitter eyes.

"Nice going!" he sighed. "Holroyd certainly kept his word. If we're to get out of this hole we've plenty of fast thinking to do."

"There isn't a way out," Rod growled. "Holroyd knew that when he sent us here. We're just prize guinea pigs, that's all."

He turned aside at a low cry from Eva. Gently he supported her as she began to recover consciousness. In ten minutes she was fully awake, in possession of the cheerless facts.

"Wonderful!" she shrugged; then with a whimsical smile, "What a pity space didn't make an end of us. Not much sense in being wakened up to die, is there?" She turned and looked at Rengard. He was standing by the window now, hands deep in pockets. "Any ideas, Ren?" she asked. "You're usually the one to get 'em."

"Maybe I have," he mused. "Come here a moment...."

When they had come to his side he pointed across the desert towards the horizon. "Notice anything out there, against the sunlight?" he asked quietly.

"You mean that tremoring effect against the light?" Rod questioned, staring steadily. "Looks to me as though it's coming out of the ground—"

"Yeah, and if it is, it means warmth," Rengard pointed out. "It would rise rapidly in this thin air. Warmth from inside the planet might mean anything. Might as well go and see what it is. We've fuel enough for two thousand miles, so let's go...."

He turned actively to the switchboard, remembered the gravity and shuffled forward slowly. In a moment or two he had disconnected the automatic radio devices and flung in the main power switches. Instantly the tubes fired, drove the ship upward in a cloud of dust and sand grains. Against the lesser gravity it moved with consummate ease.

Rod and the girl remained at the window, holding onto its frame. The terrific speed of the vessel and the slight attraction played the oddest tricks on their sense of balance.

"Why, it's—it's a dead canal junction!" Eva cried suddenly, pointing below to the skimming desert. "Or is it?" she frowned. "Looks like a pit of some sort...."

Rengard stared into his own observation window, took in a view of five dead channels, which had obviously been canal systems at some remote period, all running into a common convergence in a vastly deep, sunken circle. It took him a few minutes to realize that he was actually gazing at a shaft—that the darkness of the hole was not caused by the black shadows of the desert, rendered intensely dark by lack of diffusing air, but by tremendous depth going down heaven knew how far.

"Warm air out of that, huh?" he murmured. "That's interesting! You two ready to take a chance?" He glanced across the room.

"If you mean to go down the mine—yes," Eva said, seeing Rod's look of agreement. "Guess we can't be any the worse off, and we might find a lemonade or hot dog stand somewhere below Go to it!"

"Oke!"

Rengard slammed in more switches, flew round in a sweeping semicircle, then tilted into a dive that sent the vessel whizzing downward with breathtaking speed. For an instant Rod and Eva cramped their eyes shut; it seemed a certainty they were going to crash into the shaft's side; the gravity was so light it was hard to control the machine properly....

But Rengard knew what he was about. With a dexterous swing and a roar of exhaust he plunged into the abysmal dark of the place, slowed the speed, found the shaft wide enough to carry the ship broadside and so teetered down little by little with his ground blasts belching below to prevent a sudden fall.

With anxious eyes he watched the throwback meter—an instrument designed to show exactly how far away the ground was. He stared unbelievingly.

"Thirty miles!" he gasped. "A shaft thirty miles deep! It isn't possible...!"

But he was wrong there. The shaft was all the instrument claimed it to be. The ship descended in jerks for nearly an hour before it finally burst out of the eye-crushing blackness into a titanic, brilliantly lighted expanse that jolted the retinae with its sudden effulgence.

The three stared out on the amazing emptiness. Apparently it was chiseled smoothly by unguessable forces out of sheer virgin rock. A cavern, of stupefying size, illuminated at opposite ends by two blindingly brilliant balls, their heat becoming evident on the meter registers, but not through the proofed windows and walls.

"Energy, I'd say," Rengard murmured, fingering his controls. "Energy cores of some kind, slowly eating their way through the rocks perhaps. Probably the original forces that started this cavern going. Maybe natural, maybe man-made, I don't know—"

"Civilization!" yelled Eva suddenly interrupting him. "Look down there!" She pointed excitedly below.

Rengard and Rod stared with her, down upon the amazing sight of a solid, invincible-looking metropolis, its topmost heights reaching nearly to the cavern roof. In all it covered several square miles.

The buildings were of bluish metal, almost like chromium in their odd tint perfectly architectured and studded with gleaming windows. The streets were orderly and spacious, the squares broad and imposing. There were pedestrian ways, traffic ways, monorails, subway entrances, every conceivable adjunct of a highly advanced city, and yet—

Not a thing moved! The place was utterly empty and deserted!

"Odd," Rengard muttered, staring over the silence. "Damned odd! Looks as though everybody's gone for a holiday...."

He looked beyond the immediate city and found it was almost surrounded by a small jungle, in the midst of which were splashes of yellow which revealed themselves into fruit trees as the vessel dropped lower. Fruit like melons. In between the trees was the gleam of water in the twin sunlight.

"Water!" Eva gasped thankfully. "Thank heaven for that!"

"If it's drinkable," Rengard said pessimistically, and hardly dared glance at the instruments. Then he said brightly, "We're in luck. Air pressure down here is about the same as Earth's. Only explanation is that the Martians, if any, trapped it down here when things got too thin on the surface. Surface air now represents the equivalent of our stratosphere...."

He brought the ship down in a little clearing, facing a miniature lake lined with the heavy trees. It was shadier here, hidden from the glare of the suns.

Rod turned to the airlock, unfastened the heavy screws and flung the cover wide. The air that entered was hot and moist, but otherwise little different from Earth's.

Almost instantly Rengard vaulted like a kangaroo through the opening and headed in flying leaps towards the pool, flung himself down on the mossy ground and plunged his face into the shining coolness. He drank noisily. For a scientist he was amazingly lax in making no preliminary tests; but then thirst had overcome all prudence. He straightened up at last and wiped his trickling chin.

"Swell!" he observed, sighing contentedly, as Rod and Eva looked down questionably upon him. "Try it!"

They lay on their faces to follow his example, but before their lips touched the water they looked up sharply as Rengard gave a hoarse cry.

"For Pete's sake, look!"

Slowly they stood up again, staring amazedly at the first evidence of life they had so far seen. Surprising life indeed!

Little creatures, so human in form it was hard to distinguish them from Earthlings, save for their blue-tinted skin and large vividly blue eyes, were moving timidly from out of the shadows of the trees. In all there were several of them, clad in loose, sleeveless garments that reached to their knees. Their hair, the color of ripe corn, flowed in bushes round their heads, caught up in some cases with a blue band, but in others left to flow wild.

Rod stared at them, blinked as he saw that in their slim-fingered hands they held the melon fruits, extended forward as though in the form of a gracious offering. The feet of the little creatures, encased in soft, vegetable-like shoes, made hardly any sound on the mossy turf.

"Why, they're—they're only kids!" Rengard cried. "They're not even fully developed yet!"

"You're right," whispered Eva unbelievingly.

Certainly the limbs of the little people were quite childlike. The arms and legs lacked all signs of maturity; they were lissom and supple, free from all sinew. From the difference in form of three of them, and the bangles on the hair, it was pretty obvious that three were girls, and the remaining four boys.

"Say, is this a Martian kindergarten, or what?" Rod whistled. "I don't begin to—"

He broke off as one of the girls held out her fruit more boldly, jabbed a rounded arm towards the pool. *"Juzaf!"* she observed, making a pained grimace and rubbing the region of her stomach. *"Ulfa juzaf!"* She thrust the fruit out again.

The rest of the children nodded seriously at her remark and Rod scratched his head.

"The pool," he said, taking the fruit, "is *ulfa juzaf*—whatever the hell that is."

"Yeah...." Rengard looked serious. "Wish I knew what it meant. Tasted all right to me."

Pulling out his knife, Rod cut into the fruit vigorously. The juice instantly began to stream out and he held it over his mouth. Appreciatively he drained it.

"Gosh!" he whistled. "Melon, port wine, champagne, and a highball, concentrated!" He cut the thing into pieces and chewed it gratefully. "Good as beef steak.... Try it. You can't go wrong."

The children looked on in pleased interest as Eva and Rengard took the rest of the fruits and made an attack on them. The stuff was surprisingly satisfying, appearing to have tremendously nourishing properties.

"There's something wrong here, all the same," Rod commented, when he had made an end of eating and put his knife away. "These kids, on Earth, wouldn't be fixed at more than ten years old. What are they doing so far from the city? May have seen our ship dropping, of course, but even then—"

"Point is," interrupted Rengard thoughtfully, "do they even belong to the city? As we saw it, it was totally deserted...." He turned to the pretty little group and showed them the metropolis through the trees. "City?" he asked. "City yours? You come from there?"

Their blue eyes looked towards it. They smiled to reveal white, even teeth. They even danced a little; nothing more.

"Big white chief's palaver no dice," said Eva solemnly.

Rengard shrugged. "Guess you're right. I'll have to learn their language. Sooner I know what *juzaf* means the better I'll like it—"

"The language can wait," interrupted Rod briefly. "I'm going to take a look at that city and see what's wrong with it. There must surely be somebody? The parents of these kids, for instance? Let's be looking.'"

"It's sure got me puzzled too," Eva said thoughtfully. "It stands to reason these kids didn't just 'grow' like Topsy. I'm for finding out now."

CHAPTER III
The Seven Master Locks

The party headed through the queerly fashioned, fruit-laden trees. The Martian children seemed to regard the whole business as some kind of pleasure jaunt, skipping and jumping along behind the three Earthlings

The nearer they came to the city, the more they were puzzled. The jungle led directly down onto one of the main entrance streets, thence into the city center, yet as they progressed slowly along they saw no signs of anybody. Not a thing moved: the giant metropolis loomed around and above them, the very quintessence of power—with nobody to look after it! There were not even any more children, apparently. The seven who danced and giggled with amusement, watched with wide-eyed innocence, were the only guardians.

For an hour—two hours—the party wandered in and out of the great open buildings, found machines set out in orderly array, machines of such complexity that they defied comprehension. It was pretty obvious that they were electrical, and in perfect condition, their controls all being centered on a massive switchboard.

But there was the funny thing. The master switch was locked! It was fastened around with bars of metal slotted into combination wards that no power could conceivably break—except the knowledge of the actual combination itself.

"Talk about burglar alarms," murmured Rengard. "This city looks like one plus." He looked helplessly at the smiling children, patted the head of the nearest boy in controlled exasperation, then turned about to continue the tour.

Yet everywhere they went, every building they looked in, things were still locked up. In one edifice was a vast army of robots, standing motionless. In another there stood a solitary machine—a gigantic circle of metal, its surface finely filigreed, its entire bulk supported by gracefully arched metal arms. It was not unlike a vast gong. Only a vague idea of its purpose could be gathered from tremendous horseshoe magnets grouped above and around it, which in turn linked up to a baby forest of glass tubes, insulator banks, wire wound drums, and finally by far the biggest switchboard yet. Puzzled, the three moved forward and studied it silently.

It was dominated, amongst a stubble of plugs and buttons, by seven massive switches, all of them combination-locked.

"Looks to me," said Rod slowly, "as though this switchboard is the key board to the whole lot. The others we've seen are probably released when this one is. I don't pretend to know how to begin—"

"Look!" breathed Eva suddenly, with a hoarse little gasp.

The urgency in her tone forced Rod and Rengard to twist

round. The children gave little cries that were unmistakably of surprise. And there was a reason; for lying close to the wall of the huge place was a broken skeleton.

Immediately the Earthlings were beside it. Rengard hovered over it with brooding brows; Rod fingered the dusty bones. Though it had fallen apart with age, the skeleton's outline was still distinguishable. It possessed a surprisingly large skull, big chest, spindly legs, and had probably been owned by a man seven feet tall.

Rod stroked his chin thoughtfully; Rengard scratched his fiery mop.

"The only remaining evidence of people outside of these children," he breathed, gazing at them as they squatted on their haunches watching the proceedings. "Just what is the inside story on all this, I wonder?"

"Only way to find out is to adopt your method and learn the language," Rod answered briefly.

"Yeah—later on. More exploring to be done yet. Come on."

They left the building slowly, and as usual the children followed them in their journeying. They examined buildings obviously designed for residence, others for storage, then one that was a masterpiece of telescopic and radio skill. The entire mass of apparatus was quite recognizable—but locked.

Still another building was piled to the roof with armaments. There were tens of thousands of searchlight objects that were probably heat rays. Crate upon crate of blue metal contained gray cylinders that looked suspiciously like bombs, but because the lattice tops of the crates were locked, there was no way of finding out.

Then in an adjoining hall was something that made the three Earthlings stop dead, catch in their breath in amazement.

"Gosh! Spaceships!" Rengard cried, staring on nearly fifty or so long ovoids placed in orderly lines on both sides of a narrow gangway. Only for a moment did he stand drinking the scene in, then raced forward to the nearest one, and fell back in bitter disappointment before the closed airlocks.

"Locked again!" he groaned. "Did you ever see a city with such terrific knowledge and resources so completely fastened? Everything in apple-pie order—Lord knows how much power waiting to be tapped, and we can't do a thing about it."

Tireless with interest they wandered on again, the children chattering their strange language beside them. They went from one end of the city to the other, glimpsed power rooms that housed locked engines of incredible power—and so finally arrived in an immense laboratory. Here again the machines were locked, but the numberless bottles and phials on the shelves were free. Rengard glanced at them, then turned to survey seven small tubes standing in a frame on the floor, tubes which were of some glass composition, shattered now from top to bottom with shards and splinters flung in all directions.

"Seven tubes," he muttered; then a giggling laugh made him swing round impatiently. His expression changed. "Seven tubes—seven children!" he breathed tensely.

"Great Cat, yes!" Rod gasped, "You—you mean you think that these kids perhaps came from these tubes?"

Rengard did not answer immediately. In silence he went round and peered into the phials and jars.

"I'm not so hot on the chemistry of Mars, but carbon's the same the universe over," he remarked at length, turning. "These phials and things have carbon in its various forms inside them. Life is impossible without carbon, of course—flesh and blood life, for instance, like these kids and ourselves.

"I believe it isn't impossible for Martian science to have created life—these children—with the machinery we see about us. Possibly the children were born in these tubes, burst them open, and stepped out like a bird breaks from its egg, only to find.... Only to find themselves alone," he finished, thinking.

"Then why didn't they die?" demanded Eva. "I never heard of a baby looking after itself from the moment of birth."

"Perhaps these weren't ordinary babies," Rod pointed out.

"The more I see of this place, the more I'm reminded of the *Marie Celeste*," Rengard observed. "I'm starting in right now to learn the language. We'll make our headquarters here and eat fruit. Until we find out what *juzaf* is, I guess we'd better leave that water alone. Juice can take its place."

He turned to the children, motioned them to him. They came forward readily enough, and squatted in a circle around him as he sat down on the floor to begin his laborious task.

Picking the things around him as examples, he began—and persisted.… And persisted.

In the course of the next few days, reckoned from Rod's watch (since day was, of course, perpetual), strange changes came over Rengard. For one thing he ate three times as much fruit supply as Rod and Eva; he drank juice until it seemed he would never stop

Nor was it entirely explainable by the terrific heat.

Outwardly, too, he was different. He exuded a sense of radiant well-being and activity, slept but little, spent endless hours questioning and cross-questioning the often sleepy children, who now seemed to have come to regard the laboratory as their new home.

Their intelligence was by no means outstanding, and that was why it seemed so extraordinary to Rod and Eva to behold Rengard's mind leaping all the defective gaps. He conducted himself like a genius, hurdling with incredible mental agility from one point to another, piecing together the Martian language in double-quick time. The first thing he discovered, to his discomfiture, was that *"ulfa juzaf"* meant "death liquid," though exactly why he couldn't then determine. Trouble was, the children still had a good deal of baby talk, which rendered his task all the more difficult.

Nonetheless, he could speak it haltingly within two weeks. In a month, still giving off an aura of accomplishment and purpose, he was proficient enough to teach Rod and the girl. They found it more difficult, were only assisted in understanding by Rengard's brilliant little touches to bridge the hard gaps.

When he rested from his linguistic activities, he roamed the great empty city alone, and seemed to arrive at certain conclusions. For on one occasion he remarked,

"It's pretty obvious where the Martians got their power from. Those machine rooms give the answer. The whole planet can be used as a generator. The site of the master plant is directly in line with the Martian north Magnetic Pole. The planet in its revolution against the time-space ether generates power like the armature of a dynamo. That means endless and terrific power, more than sufficient to drive the city's many mechanisms."

"And how do we use it?" Rod asked bitterly. "We still don't know, and these kids can't tell us anything even now."

"That's the trouble...." Rengard leaned against a bench and rubbed his brow, mystified. The children gathered round him quietly. Again he asked them the question he had so often repeated.

"Where are your parents? How did you get here?"

As usual, the shrugging of slender, blue-tinted shoulders; the frankly innocent looks and giggles.

"The machines!" Rengard persisted. "How do we make them work? Where did the men go that built them?"

"Drinking—much *juzaf*," answered the pretty little girl who seemed to have appointed herself as leader. "They died."

"Huh?" Rengard looked at her sharply. Catching her hand he drew her to him. "Listen, youngster, I know by now what '*juzaf*' means—that it's a death liquid. But why? Can you explain that?"

The child screwed up her face in thought, seemed hard put to it. Then struck with a sudden inspiration she pointed to Regnard's temples. "*Juzaf*' cause that," she said haltingly.

Rengard stared in wonderment, then Rod gave an exclamation:

"Say, Ren, looks like some radiation's getting at you, else you're worrying too much. You're going gray around the temples!"

"So you are!" affirmed Eva wonderingly, pulling a hand mirror from her blouse pocket. "Here, take a look."

Rengard stared at his flaming mop, his rosy face, and bright eyes. The whole picture reflected back at him was one of almost marvelous good health. But certainly gray hair was creeping along the sides of his head.

"Old age," he growled, handing the mirror back. "Not that it matters anyway."

He pondered for a moment, said slowly, "You know, I'm beginning to get the hang of several of these machines, and yet I don't know exactly why I should. I've had no experience of them. Just the same, something's happened to my mind recently. I'm able to figure out quite a lot of things I couldn't manage before. Notice how easily I learned the Martian language, for one thing? It's as though I've suddenly turned into a genius for no particular reason, and—"

He broke off, stopped dead, clearly struck by a sudden amazing thought.

"Lord!" he breathed. "I wonder...!"

He straightened up suddenly. "You two carry on; I'll be back in a while. I've an experiment to make that may settle this mystery once and for all."

He took an empty glass phial from the rack behind him and went out of the laboratory with swift strides. The children went skipping merrily after him.

For several days afterwards Rengard became completely absorbed by mysterious work of his own. Eating ravenously at intervals, swallowing quarts of fruit juice, he essayed but few remarks. His whole concentration seemed to be absorbed.

He worked with phials of water from the lakes and pools in the surrounding jungle, and brought all his newly found strange genius to a problem that was entirely his own.

Day by day he was visibly different. The vigor seemed to be going from him. Streaks of gray had passed from his temples to encompass most of his red hair. The taut freshness had gone from his face; it was haggard and curiously worn.

Investigating the city on their own, Rod and Eva felt profound concern for their comrade. They knew something was radically wrong with him—something outside the scope of normalcy.

"Can't be anything in the air," Rod commented. "If it was, we'd look the same, and we're both all right."

"Can only be that water he drank," the girl said worriedly. "I think that's what he's analyzing now. Remember that we were interrupted before we drank any—"

"But surely it couldn't produce genius?" Rod meditated over that possibility, then shrugged. "Oh, hell—I give up!"

He stared round the great space ship hangar into which they had come. "If only there was a way to unlock all this," he sighed regretfully. "We thought knowing the language would do it, but I guess we're as far off as ever. A whole nation's resources tied up! Think what we could do to Holroyd if we could get this stuff into action!"

"I know…," the girl said quietly; then, tugging a pencil from her pocket, she started to check off the inventory she had been making of the city's resources—mainly for her own amusement. "This city sure has everything," she murmured, ticking off her items.

"Space machines, robots, synthesis apparatus, laboratories, radio, telescopes, armaments—"

She broke off in surprised annoyance as the boy beside her suddenly snatched eagerly at her pencil and started to examine it quickly.

"Hey, give that back!" Rod snapped, in the child's own language. "Come here!" He lunged forward, but Eva caught his arm tensely.

"No—wait a minute, Rod. He's never seen a pencil before, remember. He wasn't with us on other occasions. Seems silly for a lead pencil to interest him in such a city as this, but—"

She broke off and tore a leaf out of her notebook, handed it over. "Draw…," she encouraged.

The boy looked at her with his big blue eyes, then with a slow nod squatted on the floor. He thought for a moment, then rather haltingly began to draw the clumsy outline of an object that was entirely obscure—at first. Eva stooped and watched intently.

"Look here, is this a drawing lesson, or what?" Rod demanded impatiently. "We'll get nowhere just standing around watching this kid draw. Besides—"

He paused, bent down beside the girl, then with a cry of amazement he snatched the paper up and stared at it.

"See what it is?" he gasped.

Eva shrugged, her blue eyes puzzled. "Looks to me like some kind of pyramid with symbols on it."

"Anything but!" he retorted, and bending down he clutched the child's wrist and jerked him to his feet. "This way!" he snapped, and whirled the surprised youngster out of the building at top speed, Eva following behind with a baffled frown. In five minutes they had gained the room with the central switchboard. Rod stared at the massive panel, then back at the drawing. The girl looked over his shoulder.

"Why, it's a pretty fair representation of the fifth switch!" she cried.

"The symbols in between might pass for combination numbers and— Rod, do you think that—?"

"Listen, kid!" Rod caught the youngster's shoulders earnestly. "Do you know anything about this machine? These switches?"

The child hesitated, then pointed to the fifth switch. Without wasting a moment Rod caught him up in his arms, held him so that his slim fingered hands could touch the profoundly complicated combination lock that held the switch in place.

There was something uncanny about the way those childish hands went in and out of the rings and bars and loops forming the combination matrix—but at last, after five minutes of unerring work there was a sharp click and the lock opened!

"He did it!" Rod gasped blankly. "Well, by all that's incredible! How in the name of wonder—?"

He put the smiling child down and rather hesitantly pushed the switch into place in the lower contact blades—but nothing happened. The machinery in the great room, the forest of tubes, remained motionless.

The girl gave a little shrug. "Obviously one switch alone is no use—all the lot have evidently got to be in circuit before the thing can work. Odd, though, that this kid knew all about that one switch. Unless...." She wheeled round, startled.

"Seven switches—seven children!" she cried hoarsely, eyes wide. "Rod, what fools we've been! It's so obvious. Somehow these children are connected with the board—they're living keys! If this chap knew how to unlock switch Five, it's a cinch the other six in the lab with Ren know the rest between them. Come on, we've got to get them—"

She swung round to head from the building, then stopped in her tracks as Rengard suddenly appeared with the other six children grouped about him. He moved slowly, with obvious effort, clutching the machinery for support as he came forward.

CHAPTER IV
The City Is Unlocked

"Ren!" Eva cried in horror. "Whatever's wrong?"

She stared in alarm, with Rod right beside her. The children caught something of their anxiety and their smiles vanished.

For Rengard was an exceedingly old man! His hair had changed to snow white, was even missing places where the baldness of extreme senility showed through. The formerly strong hands were bony and veined; the face sunken and bloodless. Only a slight semblance of the old fire remained in his vividly dark eyes—the eyes of a young mind housed in a tottering frame.

"Well," he whispered, leaning against a machine, and talking in a voice that was thin and reedy, "I've solved part of the mystery, and at the same time discovered how darned right this kid was when she called Martian water a death liquid. I—I haven't long to live, so listen—carefully!"

Rod and the girl supported him gently as he sighed heavily. Silent, timid now, the children congregated in a little knot and watched with wide eyes.

"The—the Martians died because...because of heavy water,"

Rengard whispered, smiling twistedly with bluish lips.

"Heavy water?" Rod mused, frowning. "Seem to have heard something about that some place—"

"Of course you have. There were—were scientific references to it on Earth a very long time ago, Way back in the early thirties, before the war came...." Rengard took a deep breath. "That water I drank was heavy water. Laboratory tests prove it."

"Well?" breathed Rod tensely.

"I'm—I'm coming to it...," Rengard said heavily, talking again with noticeable effort. "Long ago, the Martians must have been forced underground by expiring atmosphere on the surface. They constructed canals from the polar caps before— before they came below. The canals had water pipes leading down to their new home. For—for ages, the race lived below, out of contact with the surface, until the canals dried up as the pole caps receded. But the water balance in the cavern by that time had been fixed...." Rengard staggered a little, gripped the machine for support before continuing.

"During the ages the atmosphere thinned out, something occurred that the Martians did not suspect. Intense radiations from the sun, unhindered by atmosphere, reacted on—on the canal waters. They produced electrolysis in the Martian water, breaking down oxygen and hydrogen, and leaving a residue, an isotope with more electrons than it should normally have. It happened so gradually that—that the Martians never noticed the difference.

"The ponds and lakes down—down here are heavy water. The Martians, constituted like us to take ordinary water, could— could not cope with heavy water. Instead of them just being stimulated, they were over-stimulated. Over-stimulation leads to a progressive speeding up of the body's molecular activity. They ate more and were given what seemed.... Were given what seemed to be an extremely good state of health, a—a sharpening of mentality amounting to genius.

"As I see it, with this new-found genius they built this amazing city and fixed its machinery, until they suddenly began to discover that it was not anabolism they had got, but extreme ketabolism, the breaking down of bodily structure. The—the same thing that's gotten into me through drinking undiluted heavy water when we first arrived.

"The Martians were burning up, living at a furious rate of energy, skipping whole years of their life span, cramming entire masses of knowledge into a short time, until the body, no longer able to resist this telescoped evolution, broke down and plunged them into old age and—and death. You—you understand?"

"Yes—we understand," Rod whispered. "But, Ren, the forest? That grows round heavy water lakes, but shows no signs of anything unusual."

"Plants are different," Rengard muttered. "Probably their constitution is such that they can break down the isotope into normal water.... Plants are natural chemical factories, remember; can do things a human body cannot. That's the only way I can explain it."

"And these children?" Eva asked. "They're all right."

"Why not?" Rengard whispered. "They know—don't ask me how—that the water's fatal. They only—only use fruit juice, which shows the plants overcome the trouble. I—I haven't solved the mystery of the children, but I'm sure the last Martians suddenly realized, like me, that death was very close and took rapid measures to preserve an achievement they could never possibly use...."

Rengard stopped. His voice had been sinking throughout his last words; now it trailed off altogether. He sighed heavily, slumped from the machine he had been leaning against and collapsed limply on the floor.

In an instant Rod caught him up in his arms, stared down on the waxen, shrunken face. His fingers felt the skinny wrist.

"Dead," he muttered, staring up into Eva's horrified face.

She said nothing; the whole business was too tragically swift for words. The seven children kept silent. It was obvious from their expressions they had no idea what it was all about.

"Nothing we can do except bury him," Rod muttered. "Poor

old Ren! He passed out like a true scientist, anyway...."

Slowly he got to his feet, shook off the lethargy of sorrow. "Better give me a hand, Eva. Afterwards we'll see if the rest of these kids know anything about this switchboard. Then maybe we'll solve the rest of the mystery...."

* * * * * * *

They buried Rengard in the jungle, recited a simple service over his grave with the children around them. Then they returned to the city, had a further meal of fruits, and started anew on their line of discovery.

One by one they tested the children; and one by one it became revealed that each child had a perfect knowledge of one switch. First the boys, then the girls, unfastened the highly intricate combinations as though it were literally child's play. Six of the switches were accordingly closed into contact, but at the unlocking of the seventh one Rod hesitated and glanced uneasily at the girl.

"Ren figured that this entire planet's resources worked by planetary dynamo," he muttered. "What's going to happen if this switchboard starts everything going? We might bring the place down! It's pretty certain the last switch will make the board start working, then things will begin to happen."

He looked uneasily at the titanic circular disk in the midst of its magnets. It seemed in some way to suggest the very matrix of the whole city's resources.

"After all," Eva said slowly, "we can't be much worse off anyway. If we don't throw that switch, we can stick around in this prison of knowledge until we die. Better close it, and trust to luck what happens...."

"O.K." Rod's fingers tightened on the heavy bar. He tensed himself and held his breath as he closed the copper blades. A little shower of sparks spurted from them. Gingerly he stepped back and looked anxiously around.

A low rumbling was creeping out of the heavy silence. The

myriad small machines grouped about the giant metal circle started to hum with sudden power—the ceaseless power of a planet's own electricity generated by its own revolution, passing thereafter throughout the length and breadth of the huge city.

The noise increased, rose to the whining hum of a power-house. Heat began to rise on the already stuffy air. The masses of banked tubes filled with luminous life. The horseshoe magnets glowed with somber redness.

The children gave little cries of fright, clung nervously to the grown-ups. Rod gulped and felt his forehead was wet; Eva shot him an anxious look.

"Wish I knew what was going to happen—what it's all about," he breathed, staring at the filigreed circle in front of him. "Reminds me of a stone starting an avalanche...."

He became silent again, desperately uneasy. The machines had a fixed note now—a singing throb of power that evidenced perfect engineering, of gears smoothed and lubricated to be almost frictionless. Then above the whining came another sound, of heavy clanking, coming nearer.

Rod swung round, started violently. Two robots entered the great place, advancing steadily on their metal feet.

"Hey, wait a minute!" he gasped hoarsely, as they came invincibly forward. "Stop, confound you!"

They stopped dead. Rod stood blinking at them and their lensed eyes stared back, probably photographing every movement he made.

"Say, they—they obeyed!" he stammered, turning. "I just wonder if—"

"I've got an idea!" Eva said suddenly, and swinging round she stared at the great circle of filigree metal, and said sharply, "Take four paces to the rear— March!" Then she turned round again and watched with a triumphant smile as the robots faultlessly obeyed her order and halted

"*Voilà!*" she cried.

"But how—?" Rod gasped in wonder. "What makes 'em tick? How do they do it?"

"Just a hunch, and it worked," she answered lightly. "This city, Rod, is a flawless arrangement of machinery, geared to operate not by ordinary hand action but by thought waves. That isn't so unusual; telepathic experts on Earth can accomplish similar feats in an elementary style.... This central thing here with its meshed face is, I'm convinced, a magnetizer. It receives and holds the tiny electrical impulses of thoughts, just like a phonograph record receives notes. In the same way it amplifies the thoughts and radiates them. One thing is obvious. These robots have telepathic pick-ups responding to thought wave stimulus. The language doesn't matter; a telepathic command is the same in any language."

"If you're right, why did only these two come along? What about the rest of them? Why not the whole army?"

"Probably because they have different duties. These two probably respond as servants—not, for instance, as soldiers, or anything like that. Don't you remember saying you wished you could understand what was going to happen, what it was all about? Well, probably these two can explain, and that's why they came. After all, you gave an unintentional order...."

"Well I'm damned!" Rod looked puzzled for a moment, then gave a discomfited grin. "Darned uncanny, if you ask me. Beats me how anybody could think up a city as perfect as this one."

"Why not? The Martians were probably far ahead of our science in any case, and when they got genius added to it—well! There would hardly be anything beyond them.... Rod, we've got a whole city ready to obey us; we've got to act wisely. Here's to seeing what we can find out...."

The girl turned back to the Magnetizer, said steadily:

"If you two know the secret of this city, know what everything is about, I command that you explain it to us!"

The robots advanced instantly at that, extended pincer hands and grasped her and Rod by the arms. They struggled a little for a moment, then as they realized no harm was intended, they submitted quietly to being led out into the street. In breathless wonder the children came trailing on behind.

"Nice trick you've pulled!" Rod growled. "Lord knows what they'll do to us."

Eva smiled confidently. "They'll only do as they've been told. Machines can't reason. Unless I'm mistaken, we're heading back to the laboratory...."

She was right. Without pause the robots marched them into the place, released them and walked over to one of the massive machines. It was unlocked now; everything was unlocked. The whole Pandora's Box had opened.

With quick movements the robots switched the machine on, stood aside, and became motionless....

CHAPTER V
A Voice from the Past

Rod and Eva waited, hardly knowing what to expect. Then they started forward a little as a concealed loudspeaker inside the machine started to hum powerfully. Followed a clicking, probably a recording tape sliding into place. A deep voice started to speak slowly, in the Martian language. The two waited, tensely listening, stumbling here and there over a word. To the rear the children leaned forward in sheer awe.

"By all the chances of Nature and cosmos," the voice said, "it will probably be you seven children, grown to adult life, who will hear this, my voice, for the first time. Listen with great care! You own a city, the heritage of your creators. You are not natural children; you have no parents. You are synthetic, born of a test tube. When a race is all but dead and must have successors, synthesis is the only course. As I record these words you are still embryos in the test tubes—but you will break free of your glass prisons, will develop, will live....

"Your brains, designed to retain magnetically produced impressions prenatally created, will be your guardians. By common impulse you will break free of your glass prisons, will live for many months on the carbohydrate deposits left around you in the laboratory.

"When that is consumed, your minds will naturally lead you to fruits and their juices. You will live on them, grow strong on their nutriment, will fashion clothes from the leaves of the trees that bear the fruit. Why will you do this? Because it is impressed on your brains as a given factor that you *must* do so. It is a command, an inescapable urge. Because of the bodily construction we have designed for you, you will never touch water. It is rank poison.... Forgive me if I talk to you as yet unborn. I can hardly visualize you as adults, listening to me now.

"You are synthetic successors. Deep too in your brains is imbedded a certain combination code; each one of you, from the moment you grow old enough to use your hands, will have this knowledge perfectly clear—knowledge of the seven combination locks which seal the city.

"When you reach a period when puzzlement causes you to investigate, you will inevitably turn this knowledge to account, will unfasten the city in which you live. And because each of you has this separate knowledge, it will save you warring and fighting among yourselves. Without all seven of you, the city can never be unlocked; instinctively, intuitively, you all know that. But now because you hear my words, you have reached maturity, and unlocked the city. My voice speaks to you though my body has long ago since become dust.

"The city is yours. Build out of it a new heritage. It has everything you can require. Supreme genius built it for you. Train your thought waves on these, the central telepathic brain pan and robots of varying grades; their reception units geared to different telepathic orders will obey implicitly

"Both your sexes have male and female organs; you are not neuter. Marry; beget children—or if you desire, create them synthetically. The two servant robots will show you the formulae for life creation if you wish it. It cannot be done mechanically. It demands your own hands and skill. Attempt it only after long study. Your children, like you, will be non-water drinkers. That is, water will only be taken after natural filterization by plant life.

"We know now that heavy water is the cause of our downfall; your brains will know it, too. For generations vast internal lakes will remain. You will build new canal tracts from the Poles allow the forests to break the water down to normal. If you choose, you can even make the water normal by scientific methods, though it is probable that with your coming the age of water drinkers has passed away. Had we realized in time that we were dying and not gaining eternal life and genius, we would have forced the water to normalcy. The knowledge came too late.

"You need not ever fear invasion. The city is prepared with armaments against any possible interplanetary attack; though we do not for a moment believe you will have that to contend with. Only perhaps the third world will cause you trouble in the future. Be ready for it.

"I, the last of the race, salute the first of the new race.... Salutations!"

The mechanism clicked and became silent. Rod arose from his deep thought and looked at Eva inquiringly, then at the silent children.

"Looks like we stepped in and anticipated things," he said at length. "These kids would have done what we've done in a few more years."

"Does that matter?" the girl shrugged. "We're not going to deprive them of anything—but we're certainly going to make use of what we've found. You realize, of course, that with all this at our command we can do anything? Even return to Earth?"

"And death?" Rod asked slowly. "Oh, no; there are better ways than that. Matter of fact, I'm thinking about Calva Neil and his short wave radio. He's definitely on our side, of course. If we could only get into touch with him...."

"It's an idea!" Eva whispered, her eyes bright. "Ten to one he'll still be experimenting with that short wave radio beam system of his. If we could catch contact with it sometime, and let him know we're still alive...!"

Rod clenched his fists. "Then we could get Holroyd just where we want him," he breathed. "Right here under our fingers is a science mightier than anything be can devise. If we work carefully, we can save the innocent and punish the guilty."

He fell to silence, pondering, thinking of the mighty radio rooms, listening to the dull throb of power from the city's vast engine rooms. Power—power—with which Baxter Holroyd, Dictator of Earth, had yet to reckon.

CHAPTER VI
Preparation for War

With the awareness of the supreme power they possessed, Rod and Eva spent a few further days taking stock of things under their command, particularly resources of attack. They studied too the central telepathic Magnetizer, discovered it was so sensitive that it reacted to thoughts from any quarter of the city, brought the required robots to do any possible service.

In consequence the two Earthlings found themselves installed in the living quarters of one of the great buildings, fan cooled to mitigate the heat of the energy-suns. Fruit food, made into all manner of delectable compounds by unfathomable machinery, was supplied to them at their slightest wish.

They had supreme comfort, and reflected on the wisdom of the Martian scientist that had led him to lock up all this comfort until his synthetic followers were old enough to understand and not abuse its benefits. As it was, now the children did not half understand it all, but for company's sake stayed near the two Earthlings, save when curiosity and remembrance of the recorded speech took them back to the laboratory to study curiously the dusty skeleton that represented the last man of their race. Where the others had gone remained a mystery, unless, as Rod believed, the last scientist had rayed them out of existence to stop any spread of disease from decomposition.

Had they wished, Rod and Eva could have lived divinely in this flawless Utopia, as first lord and lady of a new era, only that their Earthborn heritage allowed them no ease. Persistently, the memory of enslaved Earthlings returned to them. They evolved plans, ordered the servants to direct them to the radio rooms, and once again studied the wilderness of radio machinery, so complicated that it took them weeks of reference to charts and plans before they began to understand what it really signified.

As they had at first suspected, the vast instruments were not only radio devices, able to span to the outermost planet if necessary, but also televisual and telescopic, working on some system of light-wave convergence that was beyond the understanding of anybody save a genius. Not that either of them bothered about the inner workings; they were faced with quite enough difficulty understanding the controls.

But results they got—by degrees. They trained the mirrored picture of Earth in one of the huge telescopic screens, brought it close enough to study its blurless, city-strewn image, the seas thick with maritime commerce, the air filled with speeding shapes. Progress, yes; all of it operating as usual for the good of one man—Baxter Holroyd.

Rod's gray eyes glittered as he surveyed the world. He glanced up at the girl and found her face expressing similar thoughts to his own.

"Revenge, eh?" be murmured, and she nodded stonily.

"Call it justice, Rod. It's more accurate."

He turned aside and studied the chart he had made of the Earth space ship's automatic control device. It gave him the precise wavelength on which to work, identical with the one Calva Neil had used to guide the vessel to Mars.... Satisfied, Rod settled firmly in the chair before the banked switchboard and altered the frequency controls, hurled forth a radio carrier beam across the 40,000,000 mile gulf.

Another screen, immovably connected with the carrier wave, came into action and revealed the light-fast journey across infinity. Earth hurtled upwards out of the abysmal gulf: the carrier wave went clean through it, out beyond into space.... Slowly Rod adjusted the controls, brought the carrier beam under control.

His fingers toyed over the switches he had learned to use. Silently he marveled at the static-free power of the apparatus. He spoke mechanically into the transmitting microphone.

"Calling Calva Neil.... Calling Calva Neil...."

He kept up the call incessantly, the girl taking it over when he got tired. But between them it took two weeks before they got any response. Then it was in Calva Neil's own voice, obviously much puzzled.

"Calva Neil replying. Who's working on this wave system? Is it a cut-in, or what?"

Rod grinned with delight and stared at the screen. The carrier wave had picked up the inflowing light waves from the source of origin, revealed the blond-headed, ruddy-cheeked young scientist seated in his laboratory, his baffled blue eyes searching his apparatus. Around and behind him loomed the essentials of his brilliant system. A brief shifting of the carrier wave brought in the entire laboratory; save for Neil it was empty. Therefore safe to speak.

"This," said Rod slowly, swinging back to the scientist, "is Rodney Calab calling you—from Mars!"

Pause whilst the message crossed the forty million mile gulf, then Neil gave a start of amazement.

"It's—it's impossible!" he gasped. "And yet I...I was testing this carrier wave in readiness for ships to depart from Earth into the void. Ships bound for Venus as soon as they're ready. Somehow you must have gotten onto it as it experimentally reached to Mars...." He paused, rubbed his high forehead. "Guess I'm going nutty," he said curtly. "Whoever you are, you're pulling a damned silly joke, cutting in on my length."

When the message reached Rod he smiled faintly. "If I told you that you were rubbing your forehead with perplexity, what would you say, Calva?" Rod asked calmly, studying the screen.

As the message reached him Neil gave another start.

"Huh?" Neil stared wonderingly in front of him. "You don't mean you can even use spatial television? Over."

"I'm Rod, and this is Mars, and I'm using television," Rod said briefly. "Get that straight, Calva. There isn't any time to waste. You're alone, aren't you? Over."

"Sure. I'm working for Holroyd on this short wave for a space expedition and— But you know that. He may send for me at any moment. Say, I'm darned glad you're alive. How the devil have you managed to do that? Over."

"Forget that for the moment," Rod said. "Just listen...." He went into a careful description of all that had taken place. The distant Neil sat in astounded silence as he listened.

"So now you know," Rod finished grimly. "Holroyd's reign is coming to an end. I want you to take action, take up the plans where I was forced to leave off. You've got to start an uprising, a revolution—anything. Get together all the people who are opposed to Holroyd's rule and collect them so far as possible on the western side of the country. That'll fix Holroyd in the eastern half, and his men will concentrate there too.

"Definitely you'll start a war, but carry on with the assurance that I'll send forces to aid you. I want Holroyd's army drawn into the open so I can eliminate it—and the more you can gather in the west the better. I'll give orders for the west to be left untouched. That clear?"

"Clear enough," Neil nodded; "and I think I can manage it too. The cities to the west aren't as closely guarded by Holroyd's minions as eastern New York. Point is, are you sure of your forces? Remember that Holroyd has heat rays, bacteria bombs, gases, ultra-fast rocket ships—"

Rod grinned mirthlessly. "Leave that to me. I've got stuff right here that'll turn Holroyd inside out. You just do as I say. When you're free to communicate again, do so. You needn't give me any signal when to start; this telescopic apparatus gives me a very good view of all that's going on. Good hunting, old man!"

"O.K. Over and out." Neil's face was set and purposeful. The vision of him faded as Rod broke the carrier wave transmission.

With hardly any intermission, sleeping in turns, Rod and Eva kept a constant watch on the telescopic screen, held Earth steadily in the field of vision in its journey through space— but again several weeks elapsed before they saw any sign of a change, and then it was sudden and violent.

Explosions vomited from various points of the United States, centered particularly in New York. There was evidence too of a convergence of battleships towards the eastern shores. They were thick in the Atlantic. The air too was filled with hurtling, darting shapes.

"War!" observed Rod, lips tightening. "Neil's taken the plunge all right. Dictator armies versus the oppressed, with Holroyd at the head of the former. See those black bombing planes? They're his. The white ones are Neil's own—the ones we were going to use when we were captured. Now we can distinguish between them we can get busy."

He issued a sharp command. "Army, prepare for action!"

It was no meaningless injunction he uttered. Through the intervening time he had learned enough of the vast Martian robot army to realize their artificial brain pickups were geared to all militant orders. Naturally, they could not reason, but they could follow out a whole chain of orders given the initial stimulus. With their actions watched in a televisor screen, they could be controlled to do anything, supreme in the fact that they were deathless, unerring.

Turning a little, Rod switched on the short-length televisor wave, directed it to penetrate to the robot hall two blocks away. Activity was everywhere in the great space. The robots, the command received, were marching. In ten minutes, under further orders, they arrived in the space ship hangar, paused in orderly groups before the fifty vessels. As Rod had reason to know, they were already equipped with all manner of war devices; the armament room's supplies would not need to be touched.

"Enter forty-nine ships!" he ordered; then glanced up at the girl. "The fiftieth one is for us," he explained—and watched the airlocks shut like a row of eyelids.

"Fire your fuel chambers!"

The fuel, which was apparently a rich magnetic oxide, fired not by flame but by a complicated pressure process, hurling terrific recoil power into the gleaming tubes. At Rod's order all tubes flared redly, filled the gigantic place with poisonous blue vapors. Again he snapped an order. The roof slid away under a robot's tug at a lever.

Gently, ordering and countermanding, maneuvering literally with his thoughts, Rod forced the robots to raise their machines in a glittering armada—upwards through the roofless opening, then onwards toward the mighty shaft which gave egress to the surface.

The machines traveled swiftly, held perfectly in the televisor screen. Television followed them as they swept up the long shaft, outwards over the desert, up into the star-ridden void towards the blue star of Earth.

Rod sighed with relief. The most difficult work was over. Forty-nine avengers were on their way.

CHAPTER VII
Holroyd's Defeat

Once the machines were steadily on their way, requiring but little actual guiding in empty space, Rod turned his mind to other things and left Eva in charge.

The weapons owned individually by each ship were not mere ordinary implements of war, but devices infinite and terrific in potency. For one thing, each vessel was supplied with a power pick-up, by which it received power from Mars itself, sent over another radio beam—power born of Mars' magnetic currents, concentrated at the North Pole with terrific intensity from the nickel iron under terrific pressure deep in Mars' core. Power begotten of the planet's dynamo like qualities against the ether.

This power, which gave the city its strength and resources, also possessed an inconceivably strong surplus, which, passed through magnets, transformers, and induction coils could be given to the armada over radio beam and thus utilized. Rod had only the vaguest idea what this power might do. That it fed the vessels' armaments he already knew, but to what extent in action he could only picture.

Satisfied that the power transmitting apparatus was in order, ready to be released by a robot the moment he gave the command, he returned to the radio room and took over the girl's work.

There was one advantage with the Martian vessels—the terrific speed they could attain and the impossibility of the occupants collapsing under the accelerative strain. So it was that the ships streaked across infinity at a speed nearly equaling that of light itself. The passage of forty-five minutes revealed via the televisor that the Earth filled the whole field of view in front of them.

The telescope, on the other hand, revealed a flurry of excited action passing over Holroyd's army, concentrated in and around New York, then stretching half across the less congested regions of the United States to the opposing army of Calva Neil in the west. It was not a flurry that betokened a weakening of morale, but a sudden gathering together of massed forces.

The invaders had evidently been sighted. To question the why or wherefore of their coming was not possible in the urgency. But Holroyd must have wondered at the defiance of his orders when he called on Neil to stop the personal war and instead unite in common attack against the unknown enemy. Neil, knowing full well what he was about, bluntly refused, continued to harass the Dictator's army, his white planes zooming and power diving relentlessly.

But on the ground he withdrew his warfare further westwards out of range of the battle he knew was to come.

Curtly Rod gave the order for power release, issued orders to his now forty million mile distant army.

"Remember to attack only the eastern coast and the black airplanes—no other...."

He waited a few moments. Martian ships and the darting, inquisitive invaders of Holroyd swarmed through the sky. From down below anti-aircraft devices stabbed upward with livid beams of violet. One Martian ship, caught amidships, crumpled instantly.

Rod set his teeth; the power would be there by now, ready for the fleet to utilize.

"Fire!" he commanded, and watched breathlessly with Eva clutching his arm.

The forty-eight machines abruptly glowed deep violet. Energy, released by their power pick-ups, encompassed them in a veritable shell, energy which forced the molecules of the ships' construction into such a tight interlacing, invisible shield that a heat ray was instantly deflected like water against steel.

In that instant Holroyd's fleet realized it was fighting something beyond its powers. The shattering strength of their flame guns, their mightiest shells, made not the least impression.

The Martian machines, incredibly fast, hurtled in and out of the slower Earth masses, flung forth ethereal waves that had the effect of destroying molecular cohesion and forced the vessels to literally fall to bits in mid-air, dropping twisting, turning figures to the raging battle ground below.

Dark red rays, drawing their power from the inexhaustible source on distant Mars, belched abruptly through the Martian vessels' screens, stabbed to Earth. An entire army unit, struggling manfully with anti-aircraft devices in the center of New York, vomited skywards in a sheet of flame in which all trace of matter had utterly gone. Instant conversion into energy was the only explanation, produced by still another ether vibration forcing electron and proton into contact and thereby canceling out atoms into splashes of cosmic rays.

"The tallest building below you—destroy it!" Rod commanded.

He knew that building; his face was rigid with bitter hate as he regarded it. Holroyd's Executive Building, having within it the Hall of Judicature. Also it was the spot from which he would certainly be directing operations.

Rod waited while his message flashed across space, then as it was received, the impregnable Martian fleet swept round to obey. Here and there, essaying a last desperate attempt, the Holroyd machines hurtled up in a solid wall for a final stand. It was final indeed.

A blasting wave of destruction withered against them, sent them hurtling in all directions, smashed them, melted them, blew them into infinite nothingness. Untouched, glowing steadily, the Martian armada sliced through the barrier, swept down in an avenging horde on the tall tower of Holroyd's headquarters.

The tower vanished in a brilliant flash of light as nameless power snicked at it. Then, maneuvering round, twenty of the vessels trained the full force of their devastating powers on the edifice. Bricks, metal, all possible formation, lifted heavenwards out a mile-deep crater! Dismembered bodies, debris, and smoke spouted to the sky. The scurrying people around the building flew backwards under the terrific discharge of superheated gas and compressing atmosphere.

"Continue!" Rod ordered implacably; then turned a little as Eva grasped his arm.

"Rod, isn't it enough?" she asked in a low voice. "After all, you have the mastery now and—"

"There are minions of Holroyd in that army," he retorted. "I'm going right through to the finish!"

He watched in brooding contentment as the armada returned to the attack—but the result now was a foregone conclusion. No ship, no human, could stand against fleshless robots, planetary power, and incredibly destructive devices. On the eastern side of America mile upon mile of battling men were incinerated or buried. Ships ripped to pieces, sank in boiling tumults.

In the air, black ships split in twain or fell, rays swaying crazily as they fell on the maddened hordes beneath. Blackness ate into the ground as it was literally burned into ashes under the feet of the demoralized thousands.

But, still true to orders, the Martians made no effort to attack the western side of the States, whither the survivors of Holroyd's army were painfully struggling, all desire for fight gone.

"It's a massacre!" Eva said suddenly, as the last two black airplanes went down to the ruins below.

"Justice," Rod answered quietly—then he turned sharply as the remote control radio set suddenly livened on its signal tube. Instantly he closed contact.

"Yes?" And he had to wait for the light-fast radio wave to hurtle to Earth and return with the answer. On the screen appeared Neil's grimly triumphant face.

"Call an armistice!" he cried. "We've definitely won. What is left of Holroyd's army is on the run. We're ready for them if they ever get this far, which I doubt. Oh, boy, I don't know what you've got packed into those ships, but it sure is hell! You realize, of course, what you've achieved?" Neil asked, his eyes shining. "Over."

Rod smiled faintly. "O.K. I'll have the ships descend and there wait for further orders. I'm coming back to Earth with Eva at the earliest moment. We'll bring living back to what it should be, where every man can have liberty. I've decided to lock up this city when I leave it. We've had our worth out of it, and it's not our job to interfere with the natural legacy of these Martian children. Nonetheless, I think they'll be useful friends to have. Their city here has such science that it'll be wise for us to cultivate it. And I mean cultivate it," he finished grimly. "Not use it for destructive purposes. Over."

"Naturally, you'll be asked to be the new leader of Earth," Neil said quietly. "Will you accept? Over."

"If I'm asked—yes," Rod assented. "Well, Cal, that's all for now. You've done a swell job. See you on Earth." Rod switched off, turned to the girl, glanced across to where the children were watching with their usual silence. Then he said quietly, "You think it's our duty to lock this city when we leave?"

"Definitely," Eva nodded.

Rod turned aside, pondered for a moment. "Guess the robots and ships don't belong to us," he commented. "They'd better come back here." He broke off, said sharply, "Cease fire! Return immediately!"

"When they're back, we can leave," he smiled. "And shall I be glad. I'm itching to get back to Earth for one very good reason—"

"And that is?"

"So I can have a darned big glass of water!"

Behind them came the sound of childish giggling as their lips met and clung.

ACKNOWLEDGMENTS

These stories were previously published as follows, and are reprinted by permission of the author's estate and his agent, Cosmos Literary Agency:

"Valley of Pretenders" was first published in *Science Fiction* #1, March 1939. Copyright © 1939, 1941 by John Russell Fearn; copyright © 2013 by Philip Harbottle.

"Outlaw of Saturn" was first published in *Science Fiction* #1, March 1939. Copyright © 1939, 1954 by John Russell Fearn; copyright © 2013 by Philip Harbottle.

"Moon Heaven" was first published in *Science Fiction*, June 1939. Copyright © 1939 by John Russell Fearn; copyright © 2013 by Philip Harbottle.

"Frigid Moon" was first published in *Future Fiction*, November 1939. Copyright © 1939 by John Russell Fearn; copyright © 2013 by Philip Harbottle.

"Lunar Consession" was first published in *Science Fiction*, September 1941. Copyright © 1941 by John Russell Fearn; copyright © 2005, 2013 by Philip Harbottle.

"Locked City" was first published in Amazing Stories, October 1938. Copyright © 1938 by John Russell Fearn; copyright © 2010, 2013 by Philip Harbottle.

ABOUT THE AUTHOR

British writer JOHN RUSSELL FEARN was born near Manchester, England, in 1908. As a child he devoured the science fiction of Wells and Verne, and was a voracious reader of the Boys' Story Papers. He was also fascinated by the cinema, and first broke into print in 1931 with a series of articles in *Film Weekly*.

He then quickly sold his first novel, *The Intelligence Gigantic*, to the American magazine, *Amazing Stories*. Over the next fifteen years, writing under several pseudonyms, Fearn became one of the most prolific contributors to all of the leading US science fiction pulps, including such legendary publications as *Astounding Stories*, *Startling Stories*, *Thrilling Wonder Stories*, and *Weird Tales*.

During the late 1940s he diversified into writing novels for the UK market, and also created his famous superwoman character, The Golden Amazon, for the prestigious Canadian magazine, the Toronto *Star Weekly*. In the early 1950s in the UK, his fifty-two novels as "Vargo Statten" were bestsellers, most notably his novelization of the film, *Creature from the Black Lagoon*.

Apart from science fiction, he had equal success with westerns, romances, and detective fiction, writing an amazing total of 180 novels—most of them in a period of just ten years—before his early death in 1960. His work has been translated into nine languages, and continues to be reprinted and read worldwide.

www.ingramcontent.com/pod-product-compliance
Lightning Source LLC
Chambersburg PA
CBHW021243260626
47155CB00004BA/1284